What readers are saying

LETHAL PROPERTY

and

The Val & Kit Mystery Series

FIVE STARS! "My girls are back in action! It's a hilarious ride when Val is implicated in a series of murders. We get a lot of the hotness that is Dennis Culotta this time around . . . Also, we get a good dose of Tom. But the best part of *Lethal Property*? Val and Kit. Besties with attitude and killer comedy. The banter and down-to-earth humor between these two is pure enjoyment on the page. Five bright and shiny stars for this writing duo!"

FIVE STARS! "Rosalind and Patricia have done it again and written a great sequel in The Val & Kit Mystery Series . . . full of intrigue and great wit and a different mystery each time. . . . *Lethal Property* is a great read, and I did not want to put the book down. I do hope that someone in the TV world reads these, as they'd make a great TV series. . . . I cannot wait for the next. Rosalind and Patricia, keep writing these great reads. Most worthy of FIVE STARS."

FIVE STARS! " . . . Val and Kit—forever friends. Smart, witty, determined, vulnerable, unintentional detectives. As has been the case with each book written by Rosalind Burgess and Patricia Obermeier Neuman, once I started reading, I really didn't want to stop. It was very much like catching up with old friends. Perhaps you know the feeling . . . Regardless of how long the separation, being together again just feels right."

FIVE STARS! "Reading *Lethal Property* was like catching up with old friends, and a few new characters, but another fun ride! I love these characters and I adore these writers. Would recommend to anyone who appreciates a good story and a sharp wit. Well done, ladies; you did it again!"

FIVE STARS! "OK . . . so I thought I knew whodunit early in the book, then after changing my mind at least 8-10 times, I was still wrong. (I want to say so much more, but I really don't want to give anything away.) Just one of the many, many things I love about the Val & Kit books. I love the characters/suspects, I love the believable dialogue between characters and also Valley Girl's inner dialogue (when thinking about Tina . . . hehe). I can't wait for the next one."

FIVE STARS! "When meeting an old friend for coffee and a chat, do you think to yourself 'Wow, I really miss them. Why do we wait so long to catch up?' That is exactly how I feel every time I read a Val & Kit Mystery. Like I just sat down for a hilarious chat over coffee and cake followed by wine and chocolate. These girls are a hilarious mix of Laurel and Hardy with a dash of Evanovich sprinkled with Cagney & Lacey. Comedy, love and mystery: a brilliant combination."

FIVE STARS! "Val and Kit are a couple of sometimes-serious, wise-cracking hometown gals. . . . funny, well-done, mysterious, and often comical."

FIVE STARS! " . . . Val and Kit . . . the combo is dynamic. What one doesn't research, the other imagines . . . they could have been the love children of Erin Brockovich and Columbo! . . . they mix their fun-loving, diverse personalities with by-the-seat-of-your-pants investigations."

Lethal Property

A Val & Kit Mystery

Rosalind Burgess
and
Patricia Obermeier Neuman

Cover by

Michael Gerbino

Laura Eshelman Neuman

Blake Oliver Publishing
BlakeOliverPublishing@gmail.com
This is a work of fiction.

Acknowledgments

We are once again indebted to those who have read the early versions of our work—you know, the readers who point out where we have an extra word or a missing word, a lamb chop that becomes a pork chop two pages later, or a joke only Val and Kit and Roz and Patty could understand. You are invaluable to us, Michael Gerbino, Kerri Neuman Hunt, Jack Neuman, John Neuman, Betty Obermeier, Clayton "Pete" Obermeier, Sarah Paschall, and Melissa Neuman Tracy, and we thank you.

Lethal Property
A Val & Kit Mystery

The Val & Kit Mystery Series

CHAPTER ONE

I hate being the first one in the office. It forces me to hang around waiting for Billie to arrive and work her magic with the cappuccino machine. But she is the only one in our office of four people who can produce the delicious coffee capped with creamy, white froth. Prepared to wait, I set my purse down and switched on my computer just as my phone pinged, announcing two new texts.

First one was from Billie. *Hang tough, Val. On my way. Be there in five. Traffic snarly.*

Second one was from Perry. My fellow Realtor and nephew of Tom Haskins, the owner of Haskins Realty, where we attempt to sell houses every day. *Running late. Sorreeeeee. Be there in a jiff. Don't touch anything on my desk. Puhleeeeze. Love ya.* This was followed by three smiley faces.

I immediately crossed the four feet of space separating our desks for a look-see. Apart from an oversize coffee cup bearing a picture of the sultry Jessica Rabbit, I saw nothing out of the ordinary. I picked up a framed photograph of Perry and Tom. Perry looked handsome and absurdly young, for a thirty-year-old. He had one arm around his uncle's shoulders and was grinning like a model for a teeth-whitening product; Tom was scowling. Nothing new there.

"Hey."

"Billie! Good morning." The cavalry had arrived.

Billie Ludlow was barely five feet tall, with silky chestnut hair cut to just below her baby face and a smile that sometimes took my breath away. A twentysomething, she was the office know-it-all (but in a good way).

"Won't be a second, Val." She rushed past me to the back of the small office and the tiny kitchen.

"Good girl," I said, opening the middle drawer of Perry's desk. Impressed by the neatness of the contents, I quickly closed it. "Wonder Boy is running late. By the way, he told me not to touch anything on his desk. What's that about?"

"Oh, you know how our Perry loves drama."

"You don't think he meant this, do you?" I took a sheet of paper from his otherwise-empty in-box.

"What have you found?" Billie raised her voice above the hissing sound of steaming milk.

"Has Perry joined a choral group?" I called back, studying the flyer that touted the superior voices of the Hinsdale Male Chorus sponsored by McVaughn Chevrolet.

"Sounds about right," I heard Billie say. "Gee, his uncle will be proud."

Feeling wicked, I could hardly wait for Tom Haskins to learn of his young nephew's latest undertaking. I put the flyer back in the box and turned toward Billie just as my phone rang. "Haskins Realty, Valerie Pankowski speaking. How may I help you?"

The caller was a man interested in viewing a house he had seen on our website: 3396 Lavender Lane. Four bedrooms, two and a half baths, spacious backyard, and on the market for just under two months.

"May I have your name?" I asked, pen ready.

"Gardner. Jim Gardner."

"I know that house well, Mr. Gardner; it's really lovely." That wasn't untrue. Apart from its fragrant address, the house was in perfect condition for an older home and located in a quiet, upscale neighborhood. "What would be a good time for you?"

"How about five? Is that too late? I'll be tied up most of the day."

"Yes, five would probably work. I'll check with the owner."

"Could I meet you at your office and we drive together? I'm not familiar with this part of Chicago. Or any part of it, really. I'm transferring here, and I'm in town for just two days."

"Sure. Obviously, you've seen the house online; it's a nice size, more than three thousand square feet."

"Yes, perfect. I have a wife and three children back in Utah."

"Your wife sent you ahead to scout for a home, is that it?"

"Exactly. I've seen a few already. But I think I'm going to really like this one. So, I guess I'll see you at five?"

"I'll be here."

***

Perry arrived at the office thirty minutes after Billie and I had enjoyed our first cappuccino. He came in with his usual fluster, cheeks red, as if he'd run from a parking lot half a mile away rather than the spot a few feet from the front door where he always parks his Corvette.

"Greetings, Val. Hola, Billie. Is Uncle Tom here yet?"

I strained my neck to look over Perry's shoulder through the glass front of the office and saw the three cars parked there. "Let's see. Did you notice his Mercedes?" I asked.

Perry actually turned and checked it out, as if he really might have missed his uncle's mammoth automobile, roughly the size of an ocean liner.

"No. I don't see it."

"So, my guess is that he isn't here, unless he hitched a ride from downtown."

"Good," he agreed with my assessment. Then he plunked down in his chair. Perry is gorgeous. Like a red setter is gorgeous. But if you want your dog to fetch the stick, and then balance it on his nose, you're better off with a Labrador.

"So," he said, taking a six-inch mirror from his desk drawer and grabbing a quick peek at himself. "This is good. I don't want him to think I was late. Has he called? Is he coming in today? You haven't been poking around my desk, have you, Val?"

"Absolutely not. I'm insulted you would even ask me that. And by the way, you do know that male choruses are fronts for money laundering, don't you?"

***

It was nearly twelve thirty when I looked at my watch. I'd had a busy morning. Two new clients had called, and I'd set up showings with both of them. Lower interest rates had turned the market a little to one side, the good side, and although it wasn't completely back to where it had been, business was much better.

From my cell phone, I dialed Kit James, my best friend for more than forty years. Kit is what they call a homemaker, and what I call damn lucky. I'd had the same homemaker title myself once, when David and I were married. But after our only child, Emily, had entered high school, I'd asked my lifelong friend Tom Haskins if I could work for him part-time. It seemed like a fun distraction.

Then after David and I divorced, and I left the Big House and moved to a tiny apartment, finances dictated my job could no longer be just a distraction. It had to become my livelihood.

"Whatcha doing?" I asked Kit.

"I'm looking at my neighbor's house across the street. She had it painted this morning."

"So, you are literally watching paint dry?"

"Val, the color is all wrong. Why didn't she check with me first?"

"Huh? Why should she check with—"

"It's a hideous, barfy, sea-foam bluey-green. Remember you used to have a car that color?"

"I was nineteen, for Pete's sake. How do you even remember—never mind. Wanna meet for lunch?" I asked, steering the subject away from my first car, which, I realized upon reflection, had been a little barfy.

"I have a lot to do today—"

"C'mon, take a break. What's so important? I have a Perry story."

"I do have that date with Yuri, my Israeli lover. But I could squeeze you in before."

"Does he have a friend for me?" I slipped my purse strap over my shoulder and headed toward the door.

"How do you feel about eye patches?"

Kit has been married to Larry for about thirty years. A good guy. She has impeccable taste in everything, including husbands.

"I can live with an eye patch," I said. "Let's meet at Berto's Deli. It's close. Don't want to wear you out for Yuri."

I heard Kit sigh. "As if I have the energy for a lover. Okay. But first I gotta drop Larry's pants off at the tailor. See you in twenty minutes."

Who was she kidding? She had enough energy for ten Yuris.

***

5

"Where's that listing sheet I stole from Parson's Realty?" It was Tom Haskins yelling from his desk. His private office was the only room in our little facility that had an actual door. "I gave it to Perry."

"Never saw it," I yelled back.

"And just where the hell *is* Perry?" Now Tom was standing in his doorway. He was a large man, attractive if you liked rugby players with bald heads. He removed the unlit cigar from his mouth and pointed it my way. "That list has a lot of information not on the Web yet. I went to considerable lengths to get it. Perry was supposed to study it and get it right back to me. And where the hell is he, anyway?"

"Don't know, Boss. Look on his desk. Check the in-box. I see something there; maybe that's your precious list."

"What're you up to today?" he asked.

"Today? It's nearly four thirty," I reminded him. "I was here early, but I do have a guy coming in a half hour to see the Lavender Lane place."

"Good. Good deal. That place is a peach." I wondered how he knew that, since he rarely checked out the listings personally. "There's a pond two streets over. Ducks and stuff. Make sure you drive the guy by it." Okay, so maybe he did check out some things. "I need that list, Val."

"Look in Perry's in-box," I said again, eyeing the lone flyer, urging him to take a peek.

"What does he need an in-box for? Do you have one?"

I tapped my temple with my index finger. "Mine's in here," I said.

"You got that list in there?"

"No, you gave it to Perry. Remember?"

Tom, who now had two hands on the edge of my desk and was leaning forward, turned slightly toward Perry's desk.

"I don't see it."

"Are you blind? There's something in there."

"Just one sheet of paper."

"Well, maybe that's it. At least check it out."

"Nah. That's not it."

"You can tell without looking at it?"

"Yes, I can."

My desire for Tom to learn about the Hinsdale Male Chorus sponsored by McVaughn Chevrolet was overwhelming. "Okay," I said, rising, "*I'll* see what Perry's got there." But Tom put a hand on my shoulder.

"Val, I think we both know that's not a real-estate list."

"Then what—"

"Some damn boys' choir. You know it, I know it, and pretty soon every poor bastard in Hinsdale is gonna know it. But hey, nice try."

He walked away chuckling to himself, drawing on the unlit cigar.

"Okay," I said, following him and stopping to lean against his door frame, arms crossed. "Was there ever even a list?"

"Ha! If there was, d'you think I'd give it to Perry?"

I could hear his chuckling grow even louder as I closed his door and returned to my desk.

***

By five forty-five I was alone in the office. Billie and Tom had both left, and Perry had never returned from wherever it was he'd been all afternoon. I picked up my cell to call Daphne Travister, the owner of the Lavender Lane house, and cancel the appointment. It was bad manners to call her so late, but I'd been sure Jim Gardner would show. When my cell rang before I could dial, I answered with relief.

"Ms. Pankowski, Jim Gardner here. Sorry to call so late, but I was in meetings and couldn't get away. Is it too late to see the house?"

"I don't think that will be a problem. Let me check with the owner and find out. Stay where you are, and I'll call you back in two minutes."

***

The neighborhood looked as inviting as always, with its towering trees and well-manicured lawns. I went a little out of my way to drive past the pond Tom had mentioned. It was very pretty, and there were indeed a handful of ducks floating peacefully on the still water.

Daphne Travister had told me on the phone that she didn't mind our coming late, but she wasn't prepared to leave the house again. No problem, I assured her. Sometimes it was even a plus to have the home owner around during a showing.

"Come in, Val," she greeted us at the door. She was in her early sixties. A tall, slim woman, recently retired and planning to downscale to an apartment for seniors. Her short gray hair looked freshly permed, and she wore no makeup.

"Daphne Travister, please meet Jim Gardner; he's—"

"Embarrassed to be so late. Thank you for letting us come."

"Not a problem. Please, take as much time as you need. I'll be in my bedroom if you have any questions. Although I think Val knows as much about this house as I do." She smiled and patted my arm as she said it.

We watched her disappear down the hall and then heard the door close, along with sounds from a television.

"Okay, Mr. Gardner—"

"Jim, please."

"Okay, Jim. Shall we start in the kitchen? It was remodeled four years ago. All appliances will stay. Granite countertops—"

"Does Daphne live alone?"

"Hmm." Instead of responding, I studied my clipboard with the specs of the house. I never answered personal questions about my clients. "The schools are excellent. That much I do know."

"You have children, Val?"

"I have a married daughter who lives in California. She's in her twenties. But many of my clients have children in school here. How old are your kids, Jim?"

"School-age." He had wandered over to look at the backyard through the large windows in the eating area of the kitchen. "This is lovely," he said.

"Yes, it's very nice," I agreed.

"Why, thank you."

We both turned to see Daphne in the kitchen entrance. "I'm so sorry to be in your way. I just need to get my medication; I should have taken it at six. It's in this cupboard." She opened the door and took down a pill container.

"Nothing serious, I hope," Jim said, closing the door after her.

"No. Just an antibiotic for a chest infection."

"Can I ask you a question?" Jim smiled, leaning back on the counter, his hands in his pockets.

"Of course; anything you like."

"Your yard is magnificent. I'm gonna go out in a minute and take a better look. Do you have a service to take care of it?"

Daphne looked pleased with the compliment. "Good heavens, no. I do it myself."

"That's hard to believe; it's a big job."

"I know. But I don't mind. My husband did it before he died; we both enjoyed gardening. It's my exercise."

"You're doing a great job. Val was just telling me about the schools. I have three children. Little monsters, but we love them. How about your children? Did they go to school here?"

"I don't have any children, Mr. Gardner."

"Jim, please."

"Okay, Jim. My husband and I weren't blessed that way."

"They can be a trial, that's for sure."

"But still a blessing."

"Of course. So, you're planning to move to one of those places for seniors?"

I wondered where Jim had picked up that information, and then my eye fell on a leaflet on the counter advertising Morning Sun Community, a luxury residence for seniors.

As I looked at it, Jim Gardner picked it up. "This looks very nice," he said.

"Yes, I'm lucky they had an opening."

"So you're retired?"

"Yes. Happily so."

"Good for you. Tell me about your neighbors here. Nice?"

"Yes. I don't know any of them really well. Most of them are a lot younger than me, and some are new to the neighborhood."

"I think we should let Daphne get back to her TV show," I said. "Come, Jim; let's go outside and see the yard."

"Yes. Good idea."

Once outside, I watched him carefully walk the perimeter of the fence. "The only access to the yard is through the garage or kitchen door," he said, more to himself than to me.

"Looks like it," I said.

He was done in a few minutes, and we returned to the kitchen. I led him through the remaining rooms, and he asked very few questions; but I noted that he carefully studied the living space, opening the doors to each room and closet.

"Okay," he said when the walk-through was complete ten minutes later, "this is very nice. Shall we say good-bye to Mrs. Travister?"

"Daphne, we're leaving," I called down the hall. She opened the bedroom door and stepped out.

"It was nice to meet you, Jim. I hope you'll consider this house. My husband and I were very happy here for many years."

"I can tell," Jim said. "And I'm gonna call my wife as soon as I get back to my hotel."

Daphne gave me a twinkly smile and walked us to the door.

"Make sure you lock up after us," Jim said. Then he gave the dead bolt a quick twist.

***

I drove Jim back to my office, intent on discussing some financial information. But he said he didn't have time to talk money; he had plans for dinner and would contact me soon. I couldn't gauge whether or not he liked the house; he was hard to read. Before driving away, however, he did give me a business card with home, cell, and office numbers in Salt Lake City. He also said he would give me a call.

But he never did.

***

Two days later I heard on the evening news, which I had switched on for background noise, that a woman was found dead in her Downers Grove home. Described as elderly and living alone, she was recently retired with no next of kin. A friend had stopped at her house to go on their daily mall walk and discovered the body. The deceased's name was Daphne Travister. When I heard it, I said a silent thanks to TiVo and rewound it, paying closer attention to the details.

That's when I heard the newscaster say the police suspected foul play.

CHAPTER TWO

The cold chill I'd felt when I first heard the news about Daphne Travister stayed with me all evening, like a wet garment I couldn't shake off. I was filled with sadness that Daphne was not going to enjoy the retirement she'd planned.

Sometime during my restless night of little sleep I decided I should call the police. It was the right thing to do for Daphne. Plus, a good reason to see Detective Dennis Culotta of the Downers Grove Police Department. It had been far too long.

With that in mind, I took longer than usual choosing what to wear to work the next morning. I wanted an eye-catching outfit, since I felt certain I'd be seeing my favorite detective.

What I didn't know is that *I* wouldn't be making the first move.

I settled on a yellow linen skirt that showed off my tan legs, and a short bright-orange jacket with yellow piping. The hot July day called for sandals, so I slipped into a flat pair made with strips of orange and yellow leather. (I was glad I'd finally used my Mother's Day gift card for a pedicure, about ten days ago.) Coincidentally, I had some clunky costume jewelry in the same color scheme, but opted instead to wear only my pearl earrings. I smoothed a touch of Moroccan oil over my blond hair one last time to ward off the humidity that threatened to turn it into a ball of fuzz, and then I headed to my car in the parking lot behind my building.

And there he was.

It was like old times, seeing him leaning against his unmarked car. Only this time he had a phone to his ear and barely nodded as I approached. I felt an excitement that increased with each step I took.

I also felt trickles of perspiration that I knew had nothing to do with the fact that it was already seventy-seven degrees at only nine o'clock in the morning. Trying to decide what to do, I willed him to stay on his phone call while I figured it out.

Ordinarily, I would advise myself to barely nod right back and to get in my car and drive off. But that would assume he was not there to see me and instead had needed to make a call and so had pulled off the main road and parked behind a random apartment building. Coincidentally, mine!

Luckily, my feet came to the conclusion that since I'd already been planning to tell him about Daphne Travister, I should just do so now.

When I found myself standing less than a foot away from him (while he still talked on the phone), I looked down at my halfway-decent toes and silently congratulated them. Feeling hotter by the moment, hotter than the Chicago weather warranted, I stood before him while he continued his call. I placed my right hand over my heart, as if I were about to sing the national anthem. But really, it was to stop any visible signs of fluttering caused by this tall, handsome man.

"Yeah . . . yeah," I heard him say into his phone. Then he looked directly at me and winked. Never was there such a wink.

I winked back. But instead of the cool gesture he'd tossed my way, too much mascara forced me to whip my sunglasses out of my purse and hide my now-watering eye. I told myself it wasn't really *him* that did this to me; it was just that combination of his thatch of prematurely white hair and piercing azure eyes. You'd have to be clinically dead not to lose control of your makeup at the sight of those.

" . . . , Valerie?"

I realized that at some point he had quit talking on his cell and had apparently addressed me while I was silently addressing myself. *Damn.* I hated the effect he had on me. Why had I even *considered* contacting him? Well, no matter. He was here, in my parking lot, so there wasn't much I could do about it now. Except respond to him. "What? What are you doing here, Dennis?"

"Good morning to you too. Again. And I repeat: how are you, Valerie? So busy you have to dispense with the niceties?" His words could have sounded harsh, but they didn't. Not with his baby blues twinkling instead of piercing.

"Sorry. I have a lot on my mind. I thought you were still talking on the phone."

"You did?" He patted his back pocket, proof that his phone was no longer anywhere near his face and I might need a guide dog to go along with my sunglasses. "And just what is it that's on that overactive imagination—I mean mind—of yours?"

Something about the way he said it made me think he knew what I had to say. But how could he know I'd met the woman he was no doubt investigating? Could he maybe be here just to *see* me? That wouldn't be impossible. There was no denying we'd once had quite the chemistry—sort of.

"Is this an official call?" I asked, cutting to the chase. I could hardly wait to tell Kit about our conversation, and it had only just begun (I hoped). She'd be proud of my sounding forthright in spite of the tentative teenage-girl feelings consuming my insides.

"Why would you think it's official?" he asked.

"Why else would you be here?"

Of course I wanted to hear him say it *was* just to see me. That he thought it was about time we had dinner again. That maybe we had something worth pursuing, maybe we could build on that spark that we both had so obviously felt at one time . . .

Instead, he held out his arms to give me a hug. It was so spontaneous, I didn't have time to hug him back before it was over. My arms remained limp at my side, as if I were paralyzed. "So," he said, releasing me and taking a step back, "as a matter of fact, it is official. Want to go back up to your apartment?"

"I'm on my way to work," I said, in a tone meant to imply *as you should be able to tell, even if you weren't a detective.*

"Maybe you'd rather go to the station."

"The station? That sounds serious."

"It's where I work."

It wasn't the first time he'd made such a threat, I remembered, thinking of the murder of another woman and how that case had introduced us to each other. I sighed and turned around. "Okay. My apartment."

As I heard his footsteps following behind me, I was gripped with a familiar feeling. And not a good one. Like I had some 'splaining to do.

I remained silent as I unlocked my apartment door, removed my sunglasses, and then proceeded to my coffeemaker, which I filled with water and loaded with freshly ground Starbucks coffee. I didn't ask if he wanted any, but I handed him an empty cup since he was now standing right next to me. I waved my own empty cup in the air, almost grazing his nose, as I decided to one-up him—again. "Actually, I was on my way to see you, Detective."

"Then why did you say you were on your way to work? And *Detective?* Really?"

"Yes, *Detective*. What do you want me to call you? Denny? Didn't you say this was official?"

"How about we call a truce and start over?"

"Good idea. Dennis, I was coming to tell you I knew that woman who was found dead in the house on Lavender Lane. The TV said you guys suspected foul play. I mean, I didn't really know her. She was a client, and I was trying to sell her house. But I'd just been with her, probably not long before she died, and I thought I should tell you—"

"You think you were the last person to see her alive?" Thankfully, for both of us, he'd put an end to my babble.

"Good heavens, how would I know that? I don't even know when she was . . . when she was . . ."

"Strangled."

"Oh no. That's so terrible. She was such a nice lady."

"She died sometime between late Tuesday evening and early Wednesday morning. Yesterday."

"Tuesday evening. Okay, so I saw her on Monday night. On Tuesday I had dinner with Kit and Larry." I heard myself sigh with relief, as if I'd just produced a solid alibi. Which was ridiculous, of course; why would I even need one?

"How are they?" he held out his empty cup, and I filled it with coffee.

"Fine. Good. We are all good."

"Your coffee has improved." He took a sip as he wandered into my tiny living room. "Is this new?" He was staring at a framed poster of a red London bus that I'd bought on a whim and hung on the bare wall.

"Not really," I said. It had been a while since Culotta had been in my apartment.

"I like it. It's cheerful. Were you alone?"

"Oh no. My daughter picked it, really. She loves London, even though she's never been there—"

"I meant when you last saw Daphne Travister."

"Oh. No. I had a client with me. He was here from Utah looking at houses. He's moving his family here."

"Is he still in Chicago?"

"No, my understanding was that he was headed straight back to Utah."

"Utah," he said. "Never been there."

I took a seat on the couch, which he was slowly circling. "I think it's nice." I watched his back while complimenting Utah, a place I'd never been to, either.

He turned suddenly, finishing his coffee in two gulps. "It's good to see you again, Valerie."

Something inside my tummy did a little cartwheel. "You too."

And then he walked the four or five steps necessary to reach my kitchen, and I heard him place his coffee cup in the sink.

"Why did you really come here this morning?" I rose from my seat. He met me at the kitchen entrance. He was scrutinizing my face, and I was so intent on studying *his* face that I only vaguely realized he'd reached into his jacket pocket and pulled something out—until he waved it right in front of my nose.

"I came across this at the crime scene—"

"What in the—" And then I saw what it was.

My business card.

***

"What did he think about that Jim Gardner?" Kit asked. "And all the personal questions he asked? What did he think of that?"

I'd driven right to her house as soon as Dennis Culotta left my apartment. And now she stood across from me at her kitchen counter, holding the coffee cup her son had sent her last Mother's Day. It had a picture emblazoned on it of him when he was about five years old, holding a soccer ball in one arm, the other arm wrapped around a much-younger Kit, who had squatted down to his height. I knew she cherished that cup.

I dreaded answering her questions, although I didn't know why. "Well, that's just it. I told him I was with Jim Gardner, but I didn't share my opinion of him."

"Why not? Don't you think you and Jim might have been the last two people to have seen . . . what's-her-name?"

"Daphne, Kit. It's Daphne. Show some respect."

"Excuuuuse me. Like you always remember every name you want to say."

We both knew that was far from true. "This is different, Kit. She just . . . passed away. You shouldn't call her *what's-her-name*."

"First of all, she didn't 'pass away.'" She'd set her coffee cup down just so she could put air quotes around the words, one of her favorite things to do. "She was *murdered*."

"How do you know that?"

Kit gave a heavy sigh and picked up her cup and took a long sip. Then she set it down again and came around the counter and gave me a hug. "Val, we know she was murdered—"

"Possibly murdered . . ."

"Okay. So she leaned over to tie her tennis shoes and somehow strangled herself with the laces?"

"How do you know about the tennis shoes?" I asked.

"I read it in the paper. It said she and her friend walked in the mall most days. Her friend had come to pick her up, and when Daphne didn't answer the door, she used the key she'd been given and let herself in."

"Oh, okay; Dennis confirmed she'd been strangled."

"Oh, what a great detective he is. But we both know you should have told Detective Dishy about all those questions Jim Gardner asked Deidre."

"Daphne."

"Okay, Daphne. Why are you holding out?"

"How come you remember Jim Gardner's name, but not hers?"

She didn't answer, but instead gave me another squeeze and then went back to her side of the counter, patting her auburn hair in place, as if fearing she'd mussed it up when she hugged me.

Kit was like that. Precise; orderly; and impeccably dressed, made-up, and coiffed at all times. But paradoxically, she liked to push envelopes, break rules, talk brashly, and shock people—even me. As she was doing now, staring at me, her raised eyebrows indicating I shouldn't have withheld anything from the law.

"What?" I showed my alarm. "First of all, it was just my personal opinion; I don't know that it was relevant. And I'm quite sure it is not. But second, if it *were*, well, you know that's exactly what *you* would have done, keep some information to yourself, at least for a while. You'd never relinquish control, especially to Dennis Your Nemesis."

I giggled at the name that had just popped into my head. But it was fitting. Kit hadn't appreciated Dennis Culotta suspecting her and/or Larry of murdering Susan Reed during our last encounter with him.

"Maybe. But I don't believe that's what you're thinking, Valley Girl." Her brown eyes held a glint of amusement. "I think you want an excuse to call him." She raised her voice a notch and pretended to be me, an imaginary phone held to her ear. "Dennis, there's a two-for-one special at the Pie and Die on Thursday; oh, and by the way, there's one teensy thing I forgot to mention—"

"Really, Kit; that's ridiculous." I grabbed my tan leather Banana Republic handbag from the floor by my feet and hefted it over my shoulder. It was big enough to hold everything I owned—and it almost did. "You know how he is, and I didn't want to send him off in a direction that would lead nowhere. Plus, some people might think all those questions Jim Gardner asked Daphne were legit."

"But you didn't."

"Sheesh, I wish I hadn't even mentioned it to you. I'm done talking about this. I gotta get to work."

"Oh, sorry, honey. I was just teasin'. Got time for a breakfast taco?"

That's one of the many things I love about Kit: her good cooking. "With chorizo sausage?" I asked.

"Naturally."

I set my bag back down on the floor with a thud, belatedly hoping I hadn't broken my brand-new smartphone, the one that was supposed to take pictures that would be good enough to use for my realty purposes. I also hoped I hadn't squashed the sandwich I'd made for my lunch that day. I had newly resolved to shed a few pounds—which had nothing to do with the thought that Dennis might be back in my life—and I knew that eliminating heavy lunches was probably all I had to do to accomplish that. But Kit made the best breakfast tacos this side of Mexico City, and surely one wouldn't hurt.

CHAPTER THREE

I stared at the white embossed business card that I'd fished out of my Franklin Planner. I still continued to use my paper planner because I didn't think my smartphone was, well, smart enough to organize my life all by itself.

James (Jim) Gardner
Director, Sales and Marketing
Tennent, Fisher and Company
Salt Lake City, Utah

Jim Gardner and I hadn't discussed what Tennent, Fisher and Company produced back in Utah. And now I was consumed with the uneasiness I'd felt while touring Daphne's house with him.

"What do you have there?" Perry asked, as he removed two iPod buds from his ears. He looked dashing in his crisp white shirt and red bow tie, his blond hair slicked back and perfectly in place. Rather like a twenties matinee idol.

"Oh, nothing. This guy, Jim Gardner. He was the one I showed the Travister house to." I waved the card at him.

"OMG," Perry replied. "Seriously, Val, OMG. Can you believe that? A client you've been working with for almost two months, murdered?"

"I know. It's horrible."

"So what happens now? With the house, I mean."

I smiled at Perry's question, noting that the apple didn't fall far from the tree. It was the very same question his dear uncle Tom was sure to ask me.

"I assume it will go to her next of kin. I don't know. The police are still working the case."

"How do you know that?"

"I don't; I'm just assuming. What are you listening to?"

He held the iPod up for me to see a smiling Placido Domingo. "He's considered the world's finest tenor," Perry said, as if he were a great authority on the subject. Then he turned the iPod around to look at it closely. He appeared awestruck as he smiled at the picture of the album cover, like a Little Leaguer looking at a Mickey Mantle baseball card.

"I didn't know you liked classical music." Just two days ago he'd been gushing over Taylor Swift, proclaiming her the greatest singer on the planet.

"It's to die for. And Señor Domingo is recommended listening for some of us."

"That's what I understand." I tapped my keyboard with Jim Gardner's business card.

"No, Val, I don't think you *do* understand. Guess who I mean when I say *some of us*."

"Er . . . off the top of my head . . . you?"

"Oh, Val." He rose and took a few steps toward my desk, perching on the corner. "I really shouldn't be telling you this—"

"Then keep it to yourself—"

"—but I'm auditioning for the Hinsdale Male Chorus. Superbig secret. Don't tell Uncle Tom. I want to surprise him."

"Good for you," I said, sounding about as surprised as Uncle Tom would.

"Anyone around here selling houses?" We both looked toward the front door. Tom Haskins had arrived.

"Uncle Tom." Perry jumped off my desk, like a gymnast doing a perfect dismount. "Val and I were just discussing the house on Lavender Lane."

"Move on." Tom strode through the narrow pathway between my desk and Perry's. "Val, in my office. Now."

"So," he said, as soon as he had removed his jacket and carefully hung it on a hanger on his oak coatrack. "What do you know about this Travister woman?"

"Not much. Just that she was very nice, and I feel awful."

"*You* feel awful. Why?"

"Hmm, let's see. How about the fact that she was strangled, and someone left her body in her recliner?"

"Here's the thing. Don't go flashing it around town that you were involved—"

"Wait just a minute; how was I involved?"

"You were there at her house, right before she died. I don't want any bad publicity over this. Keep the business out of it, okay?"

"So, in my upcoming interview on *20/20* I shouldn't mention Haskins Realty. Is that what you're saying?"

"Got it in one, Pankowski."

"I must say, I'm surprised. I thought selling houses belonging to dead people was one of your specialties."

"Not when an employee of mine was at the scene of the crime." He paused to take a cigar out of an aluminum tube and proceeded to light it. Smoking regulations apparently did not apply to him. "Let's put the whole thing behind us. It's terrible, but it's none of our business."

"Gee, Boss, that big ol' heart of yours is gonna get you in trouble."

"Just go back to work, okay? Sell some houses, and I'll be a happy camper."

***

We're sorry; the number you have reached is no longer in service. I listened to the recording three times when I dialed Jim Gardner's office number, direct number, and cell phone. Next, I googled Tennent, Fisher and Company, and big surprise. No such entity to be found.

It was Thursday evening, and I was in my pajamas, curled up in one corner of my couch. I wasn't sure what my next move was, but I felt a growing anger toward Mr. Jim Gardner. When I heard the opening music from *Law & Order: Special Victims Unit* playing on my TV, I reached the remote to turn it off. TiVo was set to record it for me.

After some thought, I went into the kitchen and poured myself a glass of pinot grigio from an open bottle in the fridge and then settled back on the couch, my phone at the ready. I scrolled down my list of contacts until Culotta appeared. Taking a big gulp of wine, I tapped my screen to place the call.

***

"Why didn't you mention this before?" he asked. He claimed he was still in his office at the station, and I had no reason not to believe him.

"Because I'm only giving you my opinion—"

"Run it by me again."

I sighed deeply. Was he even listening to me? "Okay. Jim Gardner is the man I showed Daphne's house to. And I was a little uncomfortable—"

"Tell me again: why?"

"If you'll stop interrupting me, I will. He asked too many personal questions, certainly nothing a prospective buyer would ask, and . . . I dunno . . . I got the feeling that he was staking out the house rather than being interested in buying it."

"And now you're saying the numbers on his business card are all bogus."

"Exactly. And the company he supposedly works for doesn't appear to exist."

Culotta was silent for a few seconds, and I pictured him leaning back in his chair, his tie loosened at the collar, and lazily chewing the end of a pencil the way he did when he was thinking. "So," he finally said. "What does it all mean?"

"I don't know. You're the detective. I'm just giving you my impressions."

"You know, maybe he just didn't want you to call him. Some people don't like being bugged by Realtors."

"And some people are grateful for our services. Look, I'm just telling you what I think. Take it or leave it. I don't care." I said it, but I didn't really mean it.

"Woulda been nice if you'd told me this stuff earlier."

"Really? What actual difference does it make?"

"Withholding information is a crime, Valerie. It's called obstruction of justice."

"Are you freakin' kidding me?"

"Yes, I am. You know I am."

I felt relieved, even as I cursed myself for being so gullible. Dennis Culotta was good at citing various crimes I might have committed. "Look," I said. "I just wasn't sure if I should mention it. But since I found out his card is a fake, I thought you should know. Just trying to be a good citizen."

"Yeah. I'll pass that along to the mayor. Did you see what kind of car he was driving?"

"I'm not sure. I assumed it was a rental."

"So you didn't get a license plate number?"

"Er, *no.*"

"Okay, here's what I want you to do. Come down to the station tomorrow; we'll hook you up with a sketch artist."

"I suppose I could do that," I said, vainly thinking about what I'd wear and wishing I hadn't eaten the chorizo taco. Damn Kit and her fantastic cooking.

"Good. Then I'll see you tomorrow, okay?"

"You got it."

"And Valerie, make sure you lock up." He ended the call before I could protest. Was he kidding again?

With my second glass of pinot, I took a stroll into my bedroom to look through the closet for something to wear tomorrow. What *did* one wear to visit a sketch artist?

And then something occurred to me.

Was I really able to give a decent description of Jim Gardner? He was tall, I remembered that. But kind of bland. Kit would have asked me to pick an actor to play him in a movie. That was one of her favorite tricks for describing people. She always picked Catherine Zeta-Jones to play her, and for me she suggested one of those kids on *The Brady Bunch*. She never said which one.

But for Jim Gardner, no actor came to mind.

CHAPTER FOUR

By the way, Val, you were wrong," Perry said, when I'd barely made it through the doorway. "Good morning, Perry. What a day brightener you are."

He sat at his desk wearing black linen pants with sharp creases, a pale yellow shirt, and a smug smile. "Thanks," he said, as if my compliment had been sincere. Perry has, along with countless other traits both endearing and annoying, the naiveté of a twelve-year-old boy. And, as always, he was waiting for me to drag out of him whatever nugget of information he thought he had. But I was in no mood to drag.

So I set my purse under my desk, turned my computer on, and made my way to the cappuccino machine. "Where are Billie and Tom?" I called to Perry over my shoulder.

I heard him sigh. "I have no idea where Uncle Tom is. Billie had to hand deliver some contract for him. Urgent."

I chuckled as I returned to my desk and sat down. "Yes. I'm sure it was urgent." *Otherwise he would have had* you *deliver it,* I thought.

"So, as I was saying, you were wrong," he tried again.

Of course I was curious about the "mistake" I'd apparently made. But it was much more fun to make him tell me, which I knew he would do long before I'd finished my cup of coffee.

Turns out I hadn't even taken a second sip.

"Male choruses *aren't* fronts for money laundering. You just made that up, didn't you?"

I sputtered, and some drops of coffee flew out of my mouth. I wiped them off my computer keys and turned to look at Perry. I felt embarrassed for him as I wondered who he'd asked about it.

"Well, first of all, I was kidding, Perry. But second, how can you be so sure? You don't admit something like that."

"Because I asked my director—"

"Billie back yet?" Tom's deep voice interrupted our conversation, and I felt sure his next question would be an attempt to find out just what our ridiculous exchange was about.

So I headed him in a different direction. Or tried to. "No, Boss. Not yet. But I drove by a new listing on the way to work that—"

"Yeah, and when was that? Two minutes ago?" He held out his arm until his watch escaped from under his jacket and shirtsleeve. He peered at it, but I didn't tell him he was pretty close to right.

"The Fiedler house," I said. "Or mansion, more accurately. Garlock's selling it. Wonder why they chose him. I heard he's about to go under—"

Tom just stood there and stared at me, looking annoyed, as if I'd been responsible for the Fiedlers choosing Ray Garlock to sell their 1920s eight-thousand-square-foot home. "You might think he's about to go under, Val. *I* think he's probably our biggest competition."

"Does that mean *we're* about to go under?" Perry asked. He looked worried, no doubt afraid he might have to give up his highlights and manicures.

Tom scowled at him, and as if his uncle had flipped a switch instead of grimacing, Perry twirled around on his chair and began tapping on his keyboard.

"Val, I need you to go with me to meet a potential client this afternoon. Three o'clock." Tom strode into his office without waiting for a response.

"No can do, Boss," I called in his direction, since he'd left his door open. "I already have a three o'clock appointment."

"Cancel it," he called back, as loudly as if I were out in the parking lot instead of just a few feet from his door.

"No can do. I—"

"Get in here." Tom wasn't a guy to be afraid of. More a guy who needed my coddling. Still . . .

I rose from my chair, aware of Perry's eyes—and no doubt his ears—on me as I stepped into Tom's office, closing the door behind me. I started to sit in his visitor's chair, but the look on his face told me not to get comfortable. So instead, I stood in front of him, tapping my fingers on the edge of his desk.

He looked up at me as if awaiting an explanation, but I decided to let him go first.

I smiled. I knew Tom's impatience wouldn't keep me waiting long.

"You know I wouldn't ask you to reschedule unless it was vital that you come with me," he said.

My smile broadened. "Yes, you would. You'd ask me just to keep yourself from getting bored."

He snorted. "Get over yourself, Pankowski. And what have you got to do that's so important?"

"As a matter of fact, I have an appointment with the police, with a—"

He turned off his smile instantly. "Val, I told you not to involve us in that—"

"I didn't involve us in anything. Detective Culotta came to me. He wants me to meet with their sketch artist so they can—"

"Damn him. Okay, fine." He waved me out of his office, making it clear that my meeting with a sketch artist was anything but fine. But then he called after me, "What the hell were you and Perry talking about when I came in?"

I pretended not to hear him.

***

If Detective Dennis Culotta was dishy, his sketch artist was delicious. A cool blonde who looked like she should be sketching haute couture, not potential murderers.

But man, was she good.

I made sure I arrived early, so I'd have time to chat with my favorite detective if there was an opportunity. And there was. I wondered if he'd made sure that would happen, or if it was just a fluke.

I was introducing myself to an officer at the front desk who looked far too young to serve and protect. I was still growing used to that phenomenon where it seemed everyone *was* younger than me: my doctor, my dentist—even the new superintendent of schools who'd just bought a house from me looked closer to Emily's age than mine.

"That's okay, Cody," I heard a familiar voice interrupt the young officer's response. "I'll take Ms. Pankowski back."

Even though I'd been on alert for signs of Detective Culotta, I hadn't realized he'd approached and now stood just behind me. I turned, and as always, he took my breath away. Not noticeably, I hoped. "Oh, hi," I said.

"Afternoon, Valerie. Follow me."

Okay. It was apparently going to be all business. I did as instructed, but soon realized it wasn't exactly *all* business. Walking behind Dennis, I couldn't help but notice once again how tall he was. How muscular his broad shoulders appeared beneath his white shirt. And the way his collar was flipped up a little at the back of his neck, as if he'd put his tie on in a hurry. I resisted the urge to reach up and fix it.

He entered a tiny office that was lit up more by the beautiful young woman sitting at a computer than by the bright artificial lighting. I noticed she had a sketchbook and jam-packed pencil holder on her desk and wondered which method she'd be using to draw a picture of Jim Gardner.

"Hey, Tina, meet Valerie Pankowski," Dennis said. Was he practically cooing, or was the green-eyed monster in me distorting what I'd just heard?

"Hey, yourself, Dennis. Valerie, nice to meet you; I'm Tina Reilly," she said, looking at him, not me. The flash of her smile, with those sparkling white teeth, increased the brightness of the room tenfold. She rose from her chair, and I was struck by how tall she was, much closer to Culotta's height than mine.

Her hair was the golden shade that comes with a glossy shine built in. She wore it in a bob that ended at her chin, the kind of cut she probably washed every day and then waited a few minutes for it to fall into perfect position. Okay, enough about her hair. Her dark-brown eyes gleamed as she continued to look at Culotta and then, almost reluctantly, at me.

He looked at his watch and then smiled at Tina. "Right on the dot. Three o'clock."

"Hello, I'm Valerie Pankowski," I unnecessarily repeated my name.

He turned to me with raised eyebrows, and then he took a step behind me, heading toward the door. "I'll leave you with Tina, then. *Valerie.* Let her do her thing. She's good."

I had no doubt.

We both sat down, and I was a little overwhelmed by her perfume. I would have preferred something cheap that anyone could buy at the drugstore, but clearly it was an expensive fragrance.

"So, shall we begin?" she asked.

"That's why I'm here," I said, trying to guess her age. Early thirties at the most.

"Okay," she said, and dammit, even though I didn't want to like her, I could find nothing objectionable. Except perhaps the way she'd given Culotta a little smile and watched him leave the room. A private something-or-other between them that I didn't like.

"I'll start with a rough sketch," she said, "and then we'll plug it into the computer." She took a pencil from the holder on her desk. "Let's begin with the shape of his face. Can you describe it?"

"It was round, and long, with a square chin. I think."

"Okay," Tina said, drawing a perfect oval on a blank piece of paper. "Can you be a bit more specific?"

"Isn't that specific enough?"

"We need to settle on one. Round, long, square chin— they all sort of contradict each other." She smiled.

I reached across the desk and turned the paper around, taking another pencil from her holder. I drew what I thought might be his face shape, but even I could see I'd drawn the beginnings of Mr. Potato Head.

She took the paper back, erased the chin a bit, redrew the overly large forehead, and drew two grape-shaped eyes. "How's this to start?"

"It's a start, I guess."

Next, she turned to the computer and began moving the mouse around. "So, how do you know Detective Culotta?" she asked.

"We're old friends." It wasn't really a lie, although he might have disputed the friends part. "We go back a long way," I added, immediately wishing I hadn't said that.

She took her eyes from the screen for a second and smiled at me, indicating she was far too young to go back a long way with anyone. "He's a great detective," she said. "We're lucky to have him."

"Hmm." I was about to add that he was no Sherlock Holmes, but stopped myself for fear I might have to explain who Sherlock was. "How long have you worked here?" I asked her instead.

"Oh, this is part-time for me. I'm an artist. Mostly commercial stuff."

I nodded, not sure what commercial really meant. Was she designing Corn Flakes boxes, or murals for The Field Museum?

"How am I doing?" she asked after a few minutes. "Why don't you come sit on this side of the desk?"

I rose and went around to her side. A man's face filled the screen. "I think you've made him too handsome. He was much more ordinary-looking."

"Okay," she said pleasantly, moving her mouse rapidly, changing the eyes and eyebrows. "What about his nose?"

"Long."

"Like this?"

"Too long."

She moved her mouse again. "Like this? Fatter? Thinner?"

"Thinner. No, maybe fatter."

"Like this?"

"That's more like it." I had to admit I was impressed by her dexterity with the mouse, and before long, with just a few more adjustments, she had a drawing that looked like Jim Gardner. Or at least what I remembered of him.

***

When I got back to the office, Perry handed me three pink slips of paper. All reported phone calls from Detective Dennis Culotta. I reached into my purse for my cell, which I'd silenced before going into Tina Reilly's office. Sure enough, it showed *four* missed calls from him.

Debating whether to return his calls, I set my purse down under my desk just as the office phone rang.

"Your turn," Perry said. "I've been answering it all day."

"I didn't leave until after two," I reminded him, and then picked up the phone on my desk. "Haskins Realty, Val—"

"Where the hell did you go?" I heard Culotta demand.

"Obviously, to my office. That's where you just called, isn't it?"

"You know what I mean."

"No, as a matter of fact, I don't." I leaned back in my chair, feeling happy that he sounded disturbed. I slipped off my uncomfortable red heels, the ones I had worn just for him. What a waste of foot-damaging glamour. Not to mention that my red silk dress would now have to be dry-cleaned, and I doubted he had even noticed how slimming it was.

"I wanted to talk to you, and I didn't realize you were done with Tina—"

"Oh, I'm done with Tina, all right."

"What's that supposed to mean? She's really good at her job—"

"Yes, I'm sure she is."

"I need to talk to you. Can you come back?"

"No, I certainly cannot. I've already missed enough work—"

"I'm coming to your office, then."

I glanced over at Perry, who was filing his fingernails. "No. Never mind. I'm leaving now, anyway. I'll stop by your office on my way home."

He stayed quiet for a few seconds past my comfort level, so I spoke again. "Would you rather wait until tomorrow?" I asked. "Or meet at my apartment?" *Damn! Where had* that *come from?*

"I can't really do either," he said. "I'm just going to tell you now, and I don't want you to breathe a word to *anyone*. Or . . ." Again, he grew quiet.

"Or what? Are you threatening me? This sounds like police harassment, Detective Culotta." I grinned. It felt good to throw a bogus offense his way for once.

"There is nothing funny about this, believe me. And I'm not threatening you. I'm warning you. For your own good."

"Go on." I sat up straight and glanced at Perry again. Still filing his nails. Still, no doubt, listening to every word I said.

"Your business cards, Valerie."

What the . . . "Yeah? What about them?"

"It seems another one has turned up. In a different house, in a different neighborhood."

"So? I leave a business card in every house I show. So what? And why—"

"It seems the owner of that house also ended up strangled."

CHAPTER FIVE

"Culotta told me not to breathe a word to anyone," I reiterated as soon as Kit opened her front door. She handed me a beautiful Mexican margarita glass with crushed ice floating on the top and salt encrusting the blue rim. I noticed she had her iPad tucked firmly under one arm.

"And you shouldn't," she agreed, implying she wasn't just *anyone*. "Let's go out on the patio. Larry won't be home for a while. Come. I've found stuff."

I followed her through the spacious kitchen, out the French doors, and onto the stone patio. Her backyard was lovely, landscaped to perfection. A home magazine's dream. I took a seat at the glass table, under a maroon-striped umbrella. Kit's margarita sat alone on the table.

"Okay." She sat down by her drink and opened her iPad. "Culotta said it was in Aurora, right? But he didn't give you the woman's name? Am I correct in assuming it was a woman?"

"Yes, Aurora. And yes, it was a woman. But he didn't give me any details—well, apart from the obvious."

"Serial killer?" She asked it as casually as if she were looking for blue shoes to match her dress, scrolling and pinching the screen of her device.

"Oh, don't even say that, Kitty Kat. I meant he told me about my business card. *Serial killer* sounds terrifying." A recurring panic, one I thought I'd gotten under control on my drive to Kit's, engulfed me again. But she seemed oblivious to my possible connection to a madman running around town handing out my business cards.

"Here, this must be it," Kit said. She turned the iPad around for me to read the headline from the screen: AURORA WOMAN FOUND DEAD IN HOME. Then, in the brief article: *The police identified the victim as Juanita Juarez, 29. They are ruling it a homicide.*

"But we don't know for sure they are connected, right?"

"Oh, we do. Keep looking." Kit's manicured nail indicated some text a few lines down. *Aurora police are investigating a possible link to the recent murder in Downers Grove.*

"It doesn't give the address."

"Oh, that was easy. I just looked her up on the Internet. Juanita was the home owner, and I think she lived alone. And look, do you see the For Sale sign in this picture here?" Once again her finger moved the page down.

"But how did my business card end up in her house?" I was actually hopeful that the resourceful Kit would have an explanation.

But as good as she was, she wasn't that good. "You've never been there?" she asked, dashing my hope that she might have found the murderer through Wikipedia.

"No. I've never been there." I picked up the heavy glass and took a sip. "This is really good, by the way. But no, I never work in Aurora," I said of the suburb about thirty minutes west of Downers Grove. "Can't even remember the last time I was there."

"Juanita Juarez could have picked up your card anywhere, ya know. Or someone might have given it to her. How often do you hand them out?"

"All the time, but mostly to potential customers."

"That's all?"

"I don't park at a tollbooth and toss them into passing cars, if that's what you mean."

"Parties? Luncheons? You go to a lot of those."

"Hardly. You go to more of those than I do."

"But I don't go promoting Haskins Realty. Here, look closely." She tapped on the screen once more. "Can you read the sign in the yard? Do you know this realty company?"

I looked. "Yes, and I have a good buddy there who actually owes me a little favor."

"Did you girls start without me?" We both looked up to see Larry James, Kit's husband, standing at the French doors. Larry is tall and a little overweight, with a pleasant face and shaved head. A mature version of the friend I so adored in high school. He stashed his briefcase on an empty chair and fell heavily into the one next to it. "How are you, Val? Kit tells me you're quite famous these days—"

"Kit," I said, looking at her, "what have you told—"

"Phew." Kit waved a dismissive hand in the air, not looking up from her iPad. "Larry is like me. He's no one. Don't get yourself all tied up in a knot, Valley Girl." Then, still not looking at me, she rose and retreated to the kitchen, presumably to fetch her husband a drink.

"While she's gone," Larry said, leaning toward me, "promise me you two won't get all mixed up in—"

"Mixed up in what?" Kit asked. Clearly, she was the fastest margarita pourer in the world.

"In anything." Larry leaned back in his chair. "If Val's card was also found at this second murder scene, it's serious business. I'm just saying, let the police handle it."

"Of course it might be serious as far as our Valerie is concerned." Kit patted the top of her husband's shaved head. "But we'll stay out of it and let the boys in blue do their job. We'll say no more."

Larry smiled weakly, taking the drink his wife handed him. But it was obvious he didn't believe her declaration. "Promise?" he tried.

"Promise. By the way, do you have any clients in Aurora?"

Larry sighed. "I have several. Why?"

"Do you know a Juanita Juarez?"

He put his drink down on the table. "As a matter of fact, I do. And don't you dare tell me she's—"

"The victim. Sorry, second victim. Yes, what do you know about her?"

"Ah crap." Larry ran a hand over his face, looking genuinely distraught. "She's a lovely lady. Owns a flower shop in Aurora. I've been doing her taxes for a few years."

"Married?"

"No."

"When did you last see her?" Kit sounded more like Culotta than Culotta.

"In May. She came by the office. Had a couple of annuities she needed help with. Nothing major. Damn, I'm really sorry to hear this. She was sweet."

"Where's this flower shop?"

Larry picked up his glass and sipped some more. "If I *don't* tell you, will you have to kill me, anyway?"

"Oh, keep your precious secrets, Larry." Kit had returned to her iPad and was busy typing. "Here it is. Juanita's Flowers. Ogden Avenue. Lucky for you, Larry, you get to live."

"Kit," he said, serious now, "don't even think about going there. I mean it."

"Of course not, darling. Why would we do that?" She didn't look at her husband, but I noticed the little smile that had formed on her lips. I could see she'd pulled up MapQuest and was busy typing. And I also wasn't oblivious to the word *we*.

After an excellent dinner of shrimp étouffée that Kit had somehow whipped up while Larry and I were still on the patio talking about everything *but* Juanita Juarez, I left. I had the Saturday shift in the office the next day, and I needed to get some rest.

On my short drive home, with my thoughts on Jim Gardner, I suddenly remembered something. When I'd followed him out to Daphne's backyard, I'd been startled by a strip of black hair that sat among his otherwise sandy-blond hair just above the nape of his neck. Was it natural, I wondered now, or had he just had a very bad dye job? I'd been startled by it again when I was walking behind him in Daphne's living room and got a better look at the anomaly. At one point he'd actually put his hand to the back of his head; was he trying to cover it up, knowing I was getting a good look at it?

I dialed Culotta, eager to share this with him and hoping the good news might inspire him to invite me to dinner, followed by a weekend in Acapulco. But I was directed straight to his voice mail. I didn't leave a message. Then, just as I turned my phone off, it rang, and Perry's handsome face appeared.

"Hi," I said. "Everything okay?"

"Yes, yes. Just wanted to give you a heads-up. You're in the office tomorrow, right?"

"Hmm," I replied. It was a bone of contention between us that I seemed to pull the Saturday shift twice as often as he did. Even though it was usually a busy day in the office, Tom believed we should have at least *some* Saturdays off. What a guy.

That seemed to be answer enough for Perry. "If you get any personal calls for me, would you just take a message?" he asked.

I nearly pushed the brake pedal to the floor, but I refused to try to worm it out of him. Instead, I said, "Of course. Don't I always?" It was an exaggeration; I couldn't remember the last personal call I'd received for him. And it occurred to me that I wasn't even aware of any friends he had.

"Good," he said. "Just wanted to be sure."

"Sure that I'd take a message? What did you think I'd do?"

"Val, I'm just asking a simple favor here."

"Okay. Got it," I said, assuming my best robotic voice. "Take message for Perry. Write it down on paper. Call Perry and relay message."

The line was silent for a few seconds, and I knew Perry wouldn't be able to stand it much longer.

"Like I said," he continued, "I may get a call. If I do, could you let me know immediately?"

"Understood. Let Perry know immediately." When I didn't ask who this mysterious caller might be, poor Perry was forced to elucidate.

"I gave a friend my cell phone number, of course, but sometimes I don't hear it ring, if I'm with a client. So my friend might call the office."

"Comprendo," Spanish Robot replied. The possibility that Perry might be with a client, however, especially when he had a day off, was about as likely as him being a contender in a cage fight.

"That's good," he said, and then, when he finally figured out I wasn't going to ask for more details, he spilled it. "So . . . if a call comes from a T. L., you'll take a message? And then call me immediately?" It was like taking candy from a baby Perry.

"T. L. call. I write down. I call Perry. Wait a minute—" I returned to normal human speech. "Who's T. L.? Man or woman?"

"Terry Lee," he replied triumphantly. Then he hung up. Damn him. He'd made me the worm. And he hadn't really answered the question.

***

Saturday actually turned out to be rather slow. I figured everyone was at a pool or lake. Two calls to set up viewings for Sunday, a crank caller asking if I was wearing red panties, and Tom calling to make sure I was really there. I used the free time to call my mother in Door County, Wisconsin, and my daughter in Los Angeles.

At one o'clock, just as I was halfway through the egg salad sandwich I'd picked up at Fong's Delicatessen on my way in, the door opened and Culotta was standing there. My first thought was that it's not possible to chew daintily on anything containing egg salad when you've got a six-foot hunk standing in front of you.

I overly wiped my mouth with the flimsy deli napkin, which proved all but useless for the job. "Hi," I said, running a hand over my lips for any stray egg salad. "Take a seat. How did I rate a personal visit?"

He was wearing a gray suit made of a light linen fabric that was a little wrinkled, and his tie was loosened at the collar. "Just wanted to be sure you hadn't left the country." He slid into the visitor's chair across from my desk.

"Then you're lucky you caught me. I was planning to catch a flight to Argentina as soon as I finished my lunch."

"So you heard what happened in Buenos Aires?"

"What?" I asked, alarmed. "What happened in—"

"Only kidding," he said. "But this isn't funny, Valerie."

"Then stop with the jokes, which aren't even amusing, by the way."

"I've spoken to the Aurora police, and I'm trying to keep you out of this. But it's not easy. They'll want to talk to you."

I felt a little happy that he was defending me, in some weird way, against the Aurora authorities, until I realized I didn't need defending. "They surely don't think I have anything to do with this."

"Whadda they know? They have a dead woman, and there seems to be some connection to you. You sure you don't know this woman?"

"No, I've never met Juanita Juarez—"

"Wait. How'd you know her name?"

"It was in the paper, dummy."

"Friggin' press. Not supposed to publish her name till all the next of kin are notified."

"I don't believe she had any."

"And how do *you* know that?"

Yikes. I knew I really should plead the Fifth or whatever it was you pleaded when you would be wise to shut the hell up. "Larry James knew her; she was a client of his and—"

"Didn't I tell you not to breathe a word?"

"Yes, but Kit read it on the Internet—"

"Oh, great. Now you've got her poking around."

"Dennis, it's public knowledge; you can't keep people from reading newspapers and checking the Internet."

"Did they mention your business card?"

"Geez, do you ever pick up a paper?"

"I make the news; I don't have to read about it."

I'd forgotten his arrogance, and I was reminded of just how irritating his bravado could be.

"Just answer the question," he pressed. "Did it?"

"No."

"That's good, because it doesn't look good where it was found."

Now he was scaring me, and a trip to Buenos Aires was starting to sound like a good idea.

"Where?" I tried to compose myself, not really wanting to know the answer. "On her kitchen table? Tell me it was on her kitchen table." That would be normal. Maybe a Realtor to whom I'd given my card had mistakenly put it there.

"Wish I could, Valerie."

"I'm waiting," I finally said into the silence.

"She was holding it in her hand. Not exactly holding—she was dead, after all—but it was propped between her thumb and her index finger." To demonstrate, he ripped a yellow Post-it from a stack on my desk and placed it between his fingers. He waved it like a tiny flag. Then he loosened his tie a little more and reached across to the open bag of Lay's Potato Chips on my desk and took one.

Suddenly I wasn't hungry for my chips. Or my sandwich. Six bucks for lunch, and now I felt like throwing it up.

CHAPTER SIX

I watched in silence as he finished chewing. Then he spoke. "Valerie, it's very important that you don't tell anyone about your business card at the scene. We're keeping it out of the papers."

I nodded in compliance, but of course it was too late. And now I couldn't wait to tell Kit *where* my business card had been found.

My deeper fear, however, was it showing up at all in a house I'd never been in, one that was owned by someone I'd never heard of.

"Are you listening to me?" he asked.

I nodded my head, both in answer and also to try to force myself to pay attention. My thoughts wanted to run wild.

"You need to. I'm telling you, something like that, if it isn't leaked, could help us put someone away. And I don't think you want that someone to be you, so you need to cooperate."

"Why in the world would I have to worry about that? Why would *I* ever be a suspect? It's me they seem to be targeting—"

"Valerie, there's a connection. That's reason enough for you to be a person of interest. Or a person in danger. Either way, we need your cooperation. Got it?"

"Got it."

"Speaking of cards, we also need Jim Gardner's business card. Here's the thing, Valerie. Tina says you're holding back."

"Tina?" I was outraged. Tina with the golden hair and computer magic who conjured up a dead-on image of Jim Gardner? "What the heck does she *mean*, I'm holding back?"

"She thought you weren't being honest with her. In this business, you get a sense for that." He stood up and tightened the knot of his tie, as if ready to go someplace important. "She wasn't sure if you were leaving something out or if you were making up what you told her. Your Jim Gardner *is* a really ordinary-looking dude."

"And that's *my* fault?"

"It is if you're not telling the truth."

"Well, Tina can just shove—" I stopped my Kit-talk before I said something unladylike. Even though my stomach was roiling with negativity bordering on hatred toward Culotta and his not-so-veiled accusations right now, I still didn't want to tarnish my image or standing with him in civil, as opposed to police, issues.

What I really wanted was for this morbid case to be solved and for us to see if we really might be able to have a relationship that didn't involve murder.

And I didn't think I was just imagining that he might like that too.

"I'm just warning you, some of the officers on the case think you might have fabricated Jim Gardner, or at least the way he looks. Your card appearing at the second murder scene has them convinced something is off, that you might be holding out on us."

Now I stood up, furious. "Well, you can just tell them they have it all wrong. It's not my fault Jim Gardner's looks are so . . . plain. It's not my fault he's ordinary."

"But Valerie, you said yourself, he doesn't even seem to exist. He wasn't at any of the numbers you tried. Now let me have his business card."

Reluctantly, I opened my desk drawer and retrieved the card, holding it in my hand and staring at it, as if it might reveal something I hadn't thought of. But Culotta reached across and grabbed it from me.

"Who's heading the investigation?" I asked.

"I am, of course." He suddenly appeared a little taller. "But if my team has questions, I have questions. We need answers." Then he sat back down and bent over, as if studying his shoes. He heaved a sigh and then looked up at me. "Valerie, it's obvious you're involved somehow, but I don't think for a minute you've done anything wrong."

"Well, thank you *so* much for believing in my innocence."

"Ha! I wouldn't ever describe you as innocent." He laughed a little too sardonically, and I chose to take that as a Culotta-style compliment. "But you're gonna have to help me help you."

I nodded. I could do that.

He nodded back and then stood up. He turned to leave, but stopped at the door and looked back at me. "So you're sure the sketch looks like this Jim Gardner?"

I sighed. "Yes, I'm sure. Just like him. I know he didn't have a parrot on his shoulder or peg leg."

"Good. So we can rule out any pirates or Johnny Depp." He paused. "Watch yourself, Valerie. And if there's anything you might have forgotten to mention—"

"There is one thing," I blurted.

"Go on."

"Well, I told Tina that he had sandy-colored hair—"

"And?" His tone of voice was cool, and he turned fully toward me again. "What are you saying? He doesn't?"

"Yes, he does, but he also had a strip of black hair at the back of his head." I moved my hand to my own head, to demonstrate where it was located. "Very unusual; I've seen it only once before. My cousin in Des Moines had one that was—"

"You mean like a skunk?"

"No, not a skunk. It was about an inch long, at the back of his head."

"And you didn't mention this to Tina?"

"I forgot about it at the time. She was concentrating on his face. It didn't occur to me until later, and I didn't think it was important."

He fell back into the chair. "You didn't think it was important? That's hard for me to believe."

"Well, then don't believe it. And by the way, I did try to call you but got your voice mail."

"The whole point of a sketch artist is that you tell her everything. You'll have to go back to Tina and do it again."

"Okay, I will, and I'm sorry. Are you happy now?"

"I'll be happy when we find Mr. Gardner. If he exists."

Before I could protest, Culotta rose swiftly and reached the front door, stopping briefly to turn toward me once more. "And as I already cautioned you, don't leave the country," he said, and then a lazy smile crossed his face. But he was out the door before the copy of *Chicago: A Place to Live and Grow* that I threw his way could reach him. Instead, it hit the closed door and bounced to the floor. "You throw like a girl," I saw him mouth from the safety of the other side of the window. Then he raised his hand to his ear in a gesture indicating he would call me.

Or was I supposed to call him? Ugh!

When I was sure Dennis Culotta wasn't coming back, I reached for the phone to call Kit. Of course I had to tell her. Right now Kit was the only person in Downers Grove I fully trusted.

But before I could place the call, Perry entered the office. "Any messages for me?"

"No, Perry, no messages. If you're so certain you're going to get a call here, why didn't you just work today? In fact, you can take my place right now—"

"Nope. I just stopped by for a coupon. I need to order some flowers, and I have a coupon for twenty percent off at a florist someone highly recommended."

"It's not in Aurora, I hope," I mumbled, more to myself than to him.

"Aurora? Why would I use a florist in Aurora? No, it's in Downers Grove, not far from here." He reached into his desk drawer and apparently located the coupon, because he headed toward the door.

"Who are the flowers for, anyway?" I asked, not really caring to hear the answer.

"If you insist on knowing—"

"Hold on; I don't insist on knowing anything." I raised my hand to stop him, but didn't add that the only thing I really wanted to know right now was why my business card kept showing up at murder scenes.

"Okay, if you must know, they're for a friend. But not anyone you know. So don't go prying it out of me."

"Believe me, there will be no prying."

He stopped at the front door, smiling and waving the coupon like it was a lottery ticket with all the winning numbers.

"I'm seeing someone, Val."

I looked up, surprised. "Really? Well, good for you."

"It *is* good for me." His smile broadened. "And don't bother asking who."

"Who?" I asked anyway.

"We've been seeing each other for months." He stepped back into the office.

"Who is it?" I asked again.

"Someone I met. You know how it is."

I wish I could say I did. "I hope it's someone nice."

"Of course. And don't bother asking where we met."

"Okay. Where did you meet?"

He came closer to my desk and leaned in toward me. "You'll never guess."

"So just tell me."

"Val, must you know everything?"

"No." In fact, I didn't give a flip where he and his friend had met. I had much bigger fish to fry.

"If you must know, it was at the fish market," he said.

Whoops. Had I mentioned fish out loud? I smiled. "Sounds romantic," I said dismissively. I wasn't even aware we had a fish market in the area. Then I had to add, "Wait! *You* were buying fish?"

"Fish sticks."

That was more like it. "Well, enjoy," I ended our conversation.

And then he was gone, and all I cared about was calling Kit. When I told her about my business card in Juanita's hand, she was silent.

Kit was never silent.

"Well, what do you think?" I asked.

"What I think, honey, is that this is not good. You need to be very, very careful, and we need to get to the bottom of this. Are you there alone?"

"Yeah, Perry just left."

"Then close up that office and get over here."

"I can't leave for at least another hour. Tom would—"

"Val, call him if you have to, or else I will. You cannot be there alone with all this going on."

"Dennis Culotta didn't seem concerned that I was here alone."

"Ha! *Dennis Culotta*. So he's not as bright as you think he is. I'm telling you, Val, I've got a bad feeling. I'm calling Tom right now."

That, I knew, would be a dangerous situation. I don't know which one of them disliked the other more, and I always ended up feeling in the middle of any dissension or barbed exchanges between them. "I'll call him," I said. "Then I'm coming over."

"Good girl. I'll make some fresh margaritas."

Tom answered on the first ring, as if expecting trouble and ready to meet it with his usual bluster. "Whaddya need?" he greeted me.

"I need to leave now. I'm closing up early." I knew better than to *ask*. Tom liked done deals, not uncertainties.

"Uh, that's a question, right?"

Well, he also liked to be asked permission. "It's important, Tom; I—"

"Of course it's important. I know you wouldn't ask otherwise. Go ahead. Lock up. Is there anything I can do?"

That was Tom. That's how quickly his gruff *whaddya need* turned into an *anything I can do* for a friend.

***

I declined the margarita Kit offered and suggested she do the same. "We have to think straight, Kit. I'm really getting worried."

"I'll think *better* with this." She filled her glass to the salty brim. "But I can assure you, you can't be half as worried as I am. When you first told me, I wondered if someone was trying to *frame* you. But then I realized no one would place your business card in that poor woman's hand and expect the police to think *you* did it." She took a long sip but managed to do so daintily; no need to wipe her mouth with the cocktail napkin she was busy shredding with her free hand.

Wow, I thought, *she really is worried*.

But I was kind of happy. After Culotta's near accusation that I was involved, I was still smarting. But I wondered now why he hadn't realized that if I was the murderer, I'd hardly leave my own card at the scene. Or had he realized that? My recollections of conversations with that guy were often fuzzy.

"Is someone, like, what? Giving you a warning? Threatening you? But who?"

I knew Kit's questions were rhetorical. We both knew she was privy to my every thought, relationship, and acquaintance. If I had any idea who might have it in for me, or why, Kit would already be aware of it.

Suddenly she set her glass down on the countertop—hard enough for some of her drink to slosh over. She grabbed what remained of her napkin and wiped up the spill. Then her eyes met mine as she said, "I have an idea."

CHAPTER SEVEN

Kit's idea was to take a little trip to Aurora. She was chewing on a chunk of ice as she laid her plan on me.

"What will that accomplish?" I asked.

"Don't know yet. We have to find out Juanita's connection to you, though. We can check out her house and the shop she owned. We might even come across some of her relatives." Suddenly she raised both hands in the air in excitement, suggesting we were off to a carnival instead of to check out the home of a dead woman. "Who knows!"

"*I* know you guys are not planning to go anywhere within a five-mile radius of Aurora." It was Larry, standing at the entrance to the kitchen.

"When did you get home?" Kit jumped down from her stool. "Hungry? I'm preparing lamb chops for dinner."

"I mean it. Don't you even think about going there."

"With garlic mashed potatoes and Le Sueur peas."

"Did you hear me?"

"You want a margarita while you wait?"

He stared at his wife, then briefly at me, and finally shook his head. "Okay. I'm reporting you two to the police." He turned and walked out of the kitchen and headed across the hall to his den.

Kit remained behind the massive granite counter. "He won't do it," she stage-whispered across to me.

"Doing it!" Larry yelled.

"He's bluffing."

"Not bluffing!" Larry countered.

"Oh, for crying out loud." Kit lifted a dish towel from the oven handle and whacked the edge of the counter. Then she walked out of the kitchen.

I remained on my stool, watching her back as she leaned against the den's door frame.

"Larry James. You put that phone down immediately," she said.

"I will. If you promise, on our son's life, not to go digging around in Aurora."

"Why would you even say a thing like that?"

"Because I know you, and when you get together with Val, you just can't seem to help yourselves—"

"I meant the part about Sam. Why would you bring our son into this?"

"To make you realize how serious it is."

I craned my neck and watched as she walked farther into the room and went up to Larry. He was sitting in a leather desk chair and immediately swiveled away from his wife.

"Larry," she said, putting her arms around him and resting her head on his back. "If it's so important to you, then of course we won't go. We'll just let the police handle it. I'm sure the man who killed those two women will be caught in . . . what? A couple of months? Six months to a year, tops. And even though the killer seems to have implicated our Valerie in his dangerous game, I'm sure she'll be perfectly safe until he's caught."

"Val can stay with us if she's afraid," he said, not turning toward his wife, the phone still in his hand.

When I heard this, I jumped off my own stool and rushed to the den door. "I'm not staying anywhere but my own home." It sounded a little rude, so I added, "But thank you, Larry; that's so sweet of you."

"Oh, I'm sure you'll be fine, Val," Kit said. "Apartments are rarely the scene of a crime; they're known for their safety, and just because the killer probably knows your address and definitely what you look like, and a newborn baby could get past your so-called security system—"

"Stop." Larry swung his chair to face us, causing Kit to jump back. "I can't believe the ego of you two. Not so much you, Val, but definitely this one." His index finger indicated his wife. "What can you possibly do that the police can't, except get in their way and put yourselves in danger? I'm telling you—"

"You're right, you're right. We won't go anywhere. Happy, Larry?"

"Are you making applesauce?"

"Of course, my love."

"Then I guess I'm happy."

***

We said no more about Aurora, and after our scrumptious lamb chop dinner, Kit walked me to my car parked in their driveway.

"You working tomorrow?" she asked.

"Yes. Till about four."

"Perfect. I'll pick you up at your place."

I knew, of course, that there was no way Larry could shut down Kit's plan. But I was a little hurt by his lack of confidence in us.

In that way that close friends can almost read each other's minds, Kit put her arms around me and gave me a hug. "Don't pay any attention to him. He's just worried about our safety. And ya know, I'd be upset if he wasn't worried."

"Exactly what *do* you have in mind?"

"Just a look around, to check things out, nothing more."

"So we're still going?"

"Why not?"

I turned to open my car door, and when I looked back, I saw Kit reach deftly under her yellow peasant blouse into the back of her waistband and whip out a gun. A Glock 9mm. I wasn't a gun expert, by any means, but I knew that's what Kit and Larry owned.

"What the hell are you doing?" I asked, as Kit pulled one strap of my bag off my shoulder to create a wider opening and dropped the gun in.

"The safety catch is on. But it's loaded. All you have to do is release the safety, point, and pull the trigger."

"Kit, I don't want a gun—"

"Just forget you have it. And by that I mean don't *ever* forget you have it."

I opened my bag and tried to retrieve the firearm, but Kit's hand was quickly on my own, stopping me.

"If you don't take it, then I will insist you stay here until this business is over."

I sighed. "I'm not staying here."

"Fine; then I'll come stay with you."

We both knew she'd won the argument. Kit and I living together in my tiny apartment would most certainly bring about murder number three. I closed my purse, yielding to her wishes.

"Thank you," I said. Knowing there was a gun in my purse didn't make me feel any safer, but I was grateful for my pal's concern.

"Gotta go." She turned. "Larry will start the dishes if I don't, and then I'll wish I hadn't given you the gun. Bye." I watched her walk up the sidewalk to her front door.

"Love you," I said quietly to myself, not really intending for her to hear.

But she stopped at the front door and turned. "Love you too."

***

At five o'clock Sunday I peered through the peephole of my front door. Kit was standing there, arms crossed over her chest, wearing skinny jeans and a rusty-brown linen blouse.

"Kit," I said, opening the door and giving her a hug. "How did you get in the building? And what did you tell Larry?"

"It's way too easy to get in your building. You're not safe here. And I told Larry to have a good golf game. That was hours ago. He'll be gone forever. The nineteenth hole, ya know."

"Let me just put some shoes on, and I'll be right with you."

I disappeared into my bedroom and returned, shoes in hand, to find Kit sitting on one end of my couch.

"I was wondering," I said, taking the other end and leaning over to put my tennis shoes on, "how do we do this?"

"We take I-88—"

"I was thinking more of what we do when we get there, not *how* we get there."

She looked at me with genuine surprise. A real you-should-know-better look.

"Okay." I rose, feeling almost winded from the exertion of tying my shoes. The second lamb chop last night had not been a good idea. For all her fabulous cooking, Kit remained the same size she had been in high school. Of course she ate like a baby bird, so no wonder she retained her slim body.

"Ready?"

I grabbed my keys from the kitchen counter and slipped my purse straps over my shoulder. "Yes, I guess I'm ready."

"Are you packing?" she asked.

"Packing? What do you mean?"

"The gun, for crying out loud. You do have it somewhere in that sack you lug around, don't you?"

I tapped my purse. "Yep. But honestly I don't really think—"

"Good. Just don't leave home without it, as they say."

I felt uneasy. Since she'd insisted I take it, I decided my ritual would be to remove it from my purse whenever I got home and carefully place it in the drawer in my bedside table. I knew I'd actually feel a little safer once it was tucked away in its temporary home every night, and out of sight.

And then I would return it to my purse every morning, as I had today, to the inside pocket, where I kept my wallet and reading glasses. It was scary, even though it was safely stored—as safely as a lethal firearm can be stored—and I'd rechecked the safety lock a million times already (but still wasn't certain I'd remember how to release it if necessary).

"Let's go," I said, anxious to end the discussion.

Once in Kit's BMW, we headed toward I-88 and Aurora. "Did you hear from Culotta today?" she asked.

"No. And I thought I would. I wonder if he found any prints on Jim Gardner's business card."

"He got that little idea from CSI Thursday night, ya know."

"Or maybe CSI got it from the Downers Grove police."

"Right, because we know how cutting-edge they are."

"Here's 59," I said, changing the subject to the next step in our route. I'd expected, hoped, to hear from Culotta, and his silence was irritating. There was some nutcase on the loose doing a very poor job of drumming up business for me, and the least Culotta could have done was check in to see that I made it through the night.

"Okay, watch for Ogden Avenue." She no sooner said it than we both saw the street sign, and within minutes we reached our final destination.

***

Juanita's Flowers was a nondescript structure trapped between Cyral's, a slightly shabby restaurant that claimed the world's best gyros, and an even shabbier discount auto shop offering oil changes for under twenty bucks. We pulled onto the cracked and worn concrete that served as a parking lot for Juanita's, and Kit stopped the car. The sign on the door said Closed, which didn't come as a big surprise. Cyral's had one car parked in front of it.

"Guess there's only one place open right now." Kit stood by the trunk of her car and checked out Juanita's neighbors.

"Well, I'm not sure what you have in mind. Are we—I mean you—planning to go and actually speak to—"

"Yeah, let's check Cyral's out. Looks like they have only one customer, so someone might be in the mood to talk."

We entered the dark establishment and were immediately hit by the smell of something fishy. The place was basically a long corridor, with tables attached to the wall on the right and a bar stretching all the way to the back of the restaurant on the left.

The only person I could see was a youngish man leaning on the serving side of the bar, a newspaper spread open in front of him. The bell that sounded as the door opened alerted him to our presence, and he looked up. Then he smiled, a brilliant smile that showed perfect white teeth setting off a handsome Mediterranean face.

"Ladies." He folded the newspaper and grabbed a couple of menus covered in greasy plastic. "Let me show you to a table."

His appearance—sleek black hair, crisp white shirt, and formfitting black pants—would not have been out of place in a taverna in the heart of Athens. And when he spoke, his words were tinged with a charming accent, which I assumed was Greek. Coming from behind the bar, he gallantly extended his arm, indicating we should follow him.

"Actually, we're not here to eat," Kit said. *No kidding!* Kit would have to be kidnapped at knifepoint by a bunch of Greek sailors and force-fed to eat anything here. I, on the other hand, was getting used to the fishy smell. Plus, the photograph of presumably the world's best gyro, blown up to the size of a small Honda and hanging behind the bar, was making me hungry.

"This way," the handsome Greek guy said. "We have a special today. Just for beautiful ladies."

"Sweet," Kit said, not moving farther into the establishment. "However, we're not in the mood to eat right now. Actually, we wanted to go to the shop next door, Juanita's, but it's closed. Naturally."

Immediately, the Greek put his hand to his heart, and his knees bent a little. "Oh, tragic, tragic, tragic. You were a friend of Juanita's?"

"No," I said, ready to explain. Explain *what?*

"Yes," Kit trumped me. "She was close to my husband and me. My husband was her accountant."

"The scum who did this to beautiful Juanita should be hung from his—"

"The police have no leads," Kit interrupted the beginning of his rant. "Did you know her well?"

"Please." He stretched out his arm again. "Let me give you a coffee on the house. Greek coffee. Best in the world. Ladies, please sit."

We took seats nearest the door, and our new friend left us for a few minutes and then returned with two demitasse cups, each one covered with a layer of foam on the top.

"I am Giorgos," he introduced himself, as he placed the coffee in front of us. At first I thought he'd said gorgeous, which wouldn't have been a lie. "It's George in English," he explained.

"Lovely to meet you, Giorgos. I'm Kit; this is Val. Tell us about Juanita."

"She was my dear friend. I loved her very much. Every morning we have our coffee together. We joke. We tell stories." His black eyes sparkled as he spoke, and even though I never knew Juanita, I was glad she'd had such a guy in her life.

"So," Kit said, picking up the tiny coffee cup. I felt nervous as she placed it close to her lips, and then she took a sip. A broad smile covered her face. "Giorgos, this is excellent. Do you use a briki?"

He laughed. "Of course. I am Greek. It's the only way to make coffee."

"I understand Juanita was selling her house," I interrupted, before Giorgos gave Kit a tour of the kitchen.

"That's true."

"Where was she planning to move?"

"Not far." Then he held up his index finger to show something had just occurred to him. He ran to the end of the long restaurant and removed something from the wall. Then he returned with a framed photograph of him and a lovely young Hispanic woman. They had their arms around each other and were laughing at something off camera.

"Here we are last Christmas at a party."

"She was very lovely," I said, as a creepy image of my card placed between her fingers filled my head.

"Yes," he said. "Lovely."

"And why was she planning to move?"

"She was getting married." The smile disappeared as quickly as it had arrived.

"You didn't like her choice?" Kit said.

"I never met him. Maybe Juanita thought he'd be jealous, no?" His eyes danced now.

"Where did they meet?"

"He came into her shop, and . . . you can see how beautiful she was. She was twenty-nine. She wanted a home, children. You know how it is."

We both nodded, finishing the delectable brew.

"So how come you didn't snatch her up yourself, Giorgos?" Kit asked.

He looked sad again. "Me? Dear lady, I have a wife already. And three children, with another to come into the world soon. My wife is Greek, like me. Her parents, my parents, they made a plan a long time ago for us."

Kit now looked as sad as he did. "Arranged?"

"I prefer to call it duty. But Juanita," he said, taking up the photograph and smiling at it. "She was very special. I miss her so much."

We all heard the clang of the rusty bell above the door, and Giorgos rose. "If you will excuse me. A customer."

"Of course. And thank you so much for this delicious coffee," Kit said. "One last thing. Do you happen to know if she had anyone in particular who wanted to buy her house?"

"Hmm, far as I know, only one person interested. Like I told the police, someone came to look at it the night she . . . passed from this world up to heaven." As he spoke, he fingered the heavy gold crucifix around his neck and held it up to his mouth to kiss.

"Did she say who this man was?"

"Oh no, dear Kit. It wasn't a man. It was a woman."

CHAPTER EIGHT

Not caring if it was a man, woman, or French poodle, Kit was determined to track down the interested party. As soon as we were back in her car, she said, "Okay, Ms. Realtor, how do we go about finding out who wanted Juanita's house?"

"Take me to my office," I said. My mind started spinning for the best way to give Kit what she wanted to know.

Thanks to the Internet and multiple listing, it didn't take me too long, in spite of Kit hampering my progress. I had to keep one eye on her because she busied herself snooping around the office while I tapped away at my computer and then made a couple of phone calls.

"Stay away from Perry's desk," I whispered harshly at one point, holding my hand over the phone receiver so the fellow Realtor I was speaking with couldn't hear.

"What's he doing with a flyer about a men's chorus? Can he even sing?" She cackled.

I waved frantically with my free arm, motioning her to get entirely away from Perry's desk.

She ignored my signal. "Look at this." She held up Perry's word-of-the-day calendar, on which he'd written in bold black letters **HMC AUDITION TUESDAY!!!!** This was followed by several of his trademark smiley faces.

"Put it back," I mouthed.

This time she did as I asked, but moved straight over to Tom's office door, where she tried to turn the doorknob; but just as I rose from my seat to stop her, we both realized he'd locked it. Smart man.

Finally, I had the name I wanted. "Shirley Herzog."

"Huh?" Kit asked. She was now at Billie's desk, looking at a picture of Billie holding her cat, a stray she'd taken in and named after her favorite rock group, Aerosmith. Kit set the photo back on the desk. "You mean you found out already? That's who was interested in Juanita's house?"

"You got it." I felt proud. I could tell Kit was impressed, and she didn't impress easily.

"You got an address or phone number?"

"Well, not yet. And besides, *you* could get that."

"Of course I could, but you're the one with the computer right now."

"I know, I know." I turned back and typed in *anywho.com*. But the truth was, it didn't always bring me results, and I wasn't sure what I'd try next. Kit really was better at this sort of thing. But before I had to admit that, AnyWho came through for me. "I think I've located our mark, I mean suspect, I mean person of interest."

Kit giggled at seeing me so flustered. "Guess you don't need a *Law & Order* fix anytime soon." She patted the top of my head as she leaned over my shoulder to see what I'd found. "Hmm . . . she lives here in Downers Grove. Why would she want to move to Aurora?"

"My Realtor buddy said Shirley wants something cheaper—seems she's divorced and even though she got the house, she can't afford the upkeep. I can relate."

"I still say you shouldn't have let David keep the Big House. After all he put you through—"

"Not now, Kit. Besides, we've discussed that ad nauseam, and I've never regretted my decision." And that was the truth. I loved my cozy little apartment and the fact that I had some discretionary income left over after paying my rent each month. Taxes on the house David and I had raised Emily in cost more than two years of my current rent. Plus, I couldn't clean it in an hour like I could my apartment. And the Big House was *not* cozy. It hadn't felt cozy to me since I'd learned of David's first affair.

"Then let's roll." She scribbled Shirley Herzog's address on a Post-it note she grabbed from my desk, and I couldn't help but remember that Dennis Culotta had been the last person to take one of the yellow squares of paper. I wondered if *he'd* already discovered Shirley Herzog.

***

I thought eight thirty was too late to call on someone, but it *was* still light out. So I bit my tongue as we drove to a McMansion in one of the quaint older neighborhoods of Downers Grove.

A short, dark-haired woman opened the door. Shirley Herzog, I presumed. She looked to be somewhere in her late forties and was wearing an oversize white T-shirt with a pink symbol that proved she supported the fight against breast cancer. Her toned legs were visible below a pair of baggy black shorts, and a quick glance told me she did some sort of workout. Her hair was pulled back into a ponytail, with some wiry gray strands slipping out at her temples. She had a strong face, and although free of any makeup, it showed she'd probably been pretty when she was younger.

"Ms. Herzog, I'm Kit James, and this is Valerie Pankowski. We hate to bother you, but . . . I'm sure you heard about Juanita Juarez, who was a close friend of ours and—"

She raised one hand to stop Kit's rhetoric, and if she'd had a whistle in her mouth, she would have blown it.

To say Shirley Herzog was huffy with us would be a bit of an understatement. It seemed Culotta *had* already gotten to her, and she didn't appreciate being grilled by anyone else. Her exact words. "I don't need to be grilled by you, too, and besides, all I wanted to do was buy Juanita's house. But I'm sorry about what happened. She was a nice young lady."

"So when did you learn her name?" Kit asked, ignoring Shirley's bark that I felt might not be worse than her bite. She had an angry demeanor that looked rather permanent.

"What do you mean?"

"I mean, prospective buyers don't usually know a seller's name if they're working with a Realtor. Do they, Val?"

"Um, no," I answered my friend, but Shirley's attitude almost made me forget anything I'd ever known about real estate and its rules and customs.

"The cop who was just here told me, if you must know." She folded her arms across her chest, and I figured this was a stance she used often.

"Look," Kit said, her own belligerence replaced by a mellow tone I usually heard only when she was trying to wheedle something out of Larry. "We're really sorry to inconvenience you, but we're here for an entirely different reason."

"That so?"

"Yes, you see Val is a Realtor, and she's worried about her own safety." She looked at me as she motioned in my direction, and I looked back, hoping to convey that Shirley was probably the biggest threat to my safety.

But then Shirley softened just a tad. "Why don't you gals come in," she ordered, rather than invited. She stepped aside so we could, and we followed her to a mammoth living room. The ceilings were high, and the all-white color scheme combined with the room's large dimensions to make it seem even bigger than it was. Shirley Herzog's short frame seemed lost in such a huge dwelling. She directed us to a white leather couch, and Kit and I each took an end. Only a vestige of the threatening Shirley remained as she sat across a wide glass-and-chrome table from us on a matching leather recliner. "What are you worried about . . ."

"Val," Kit reminded her of my name. "Valerie Pankowski. I'm Kit James."

"I know." The old Shirley had returned, and I glowered at Kit. Soft Shirley looked at me. "What are you worried about, Val?"

I wasn't about to share the connection between my business card and dead people. So instead, I told a partial truth. "We Realtors put ourselves at risk, you know, meeting strangers in strange homes. So of course I have a vested interest in discovering whether Juanita Juarez's murder had anything to do with the fact that her house was for sale."

"Have you spoken to the Realtor who had her listing?" Shirley sounded a little irritated, as if to point out we should hassle *that* person before we ever bothered *her*.

It was hardly an attorney/client relationship, but I was afraid if I told her that's how we got her name, it might get my Realtor friend Mark Bartlett in trouble. He had Juanita's listing, and he unintentionally gave me Shirley's name as we discussed it on the phone. I doubted he even realized he said it. "I suppose I should . . . ," I said.

"That would seem to be a better place to start than with me." She placed her hands on her knees and then stood up, as if she'd done her part. End of discussion.

We followed her to the front door—what else could we do?

And then Kit apparently thought of something else. "Say, Shirley, er, Ms. Herzog—"

"Shirley's fine." The words were neutral, but it was obvious to me and, I felt sure, to Kit that Shirley Herzog had a softer tone of voice she used with me and a harsher one with Kit. "What is it?" she asked, when Kit still didn't finish her sentence.

"I was just wondering. Did you happen to meet Ms. Juarez's fiancé?"

"Huh. That would be a most unlikely occurrence. One hardly ever meets even the home owner, let alone a fiancé or anyone else connected to the home owner." It seemed to me Shirley Herzog knew an awful lot about the realty world. But before I could ask her if she'd ever been a Realtor, she continued. "As a matter of fact, though, I did. Juanita returned home when I was having my third viewing of the house, and he was with her." And then she added a shocker. "The police should have asked me that. You're good." She gave a grudging nod in Kit's direction. Then she looked at me. "I think your friend knows how to take good care of you."

Now, *that* was a real understatement.

"What did he look like?" Kit asked.

"Oh, nothing out of the ordinary. White skin. Brown hair. I don't see what she saw in him, as a matter of fact. She was beautiful, dark and exotic, and so bubbly. He was just . . . he just *was*."

By now we were out the door, and we thanked her profusely. For what, I wasn't sure.

But by the next morning I was.

***

I arrived a little late at the office Monday morning. I felt grateful when I saw that I'd beaten Tom in, although Billie and Perry were already there.

"Morning, guys," I said to both of them as I entered the office. And then I saw a woman stand up from one of the chairs that surrounded a small, magazine-laden coffee table. Shirley Herzog. "Why, hello," I said.

"Ms. Pankowski." She nodded. "I just realized I had something you might be interested in."

Perry's head practically fell off his neck as he strained to hear everything Shirley and I said. I quickly put an end to that. I grabbed a sheaf of papers from my desk and thrust them at him. "Perry, Tom wants these delivered to First National. Now." Perry had no choice but to take them and disappear. Billie was intuitive enough to excuse herself to make fresh coffee, even though Shirley had declined an offer for a cup.

Once Shirley was seated in the visitor's chair in front of my desk, we got down to business. "What is it you have?" I asked her.

She pulled a small envelope out of her handbag but spoke before revealing what was in it. "I remembered that day Juanita and her fiancé returned while I was still there. I was taking pictures inside and out—you know, to help me when I got home and was making my final decision. And the two of them ended up accidentally being in one of the outdoor photos."

"You're kidding."

"Why would I kid about something like that?" She sat up straighter and leaned forward a little aggressively in the chair.

"No, no, I was just—"

"Here." She removed a photo from the envelope and pushed it across my desk toward me. "I enlarged and cropped it, to show them better."

Juanita looked beautiful in a flowery summer dress. Her fiancé wore jeans and a snug T-shirt. His baseball cap pulled low on his forehead obscured his face, but his height and build were a match for Jim Gardner.

CHAPTER NINE

"Val, a word. Now." It was Tom, who arrived about ten minutes after Shirley Herzog left. "My office."

From her desk, Billie gave me a raised-eyebrows look. I returned it and followed Tom.

I watched him carefully remove his suit jacket and hang it on the coatrack. He was wearing red suspenders over a crisp blue-and-white-striped shirt.

"Juanita Juarez," he said, taking a seat and placing his elbows on his desk, pressing the tips of his fingers together.

"She's the other—"

"Yes, I know who the hell she is. Was. My question to you is, did you know her? Did you have any business with her? Why was your card found at her home—"

"How do you know that—"

"I know stuff, Val," he interrupted my interruption. I knew Tom was well acquainted with Dennis Culotta, and they occasionally played poker together. But after the stern warning Culotta had given me about not sharing this information, I was surprised at Tom's revelation. But I knew I shouldn't be. He really did know stuff.

"Well?" he asked, tapping his fingertips together.

"No, I didn't know Juanita. Never heard of her, or that her house was for sale. I'm as shocked as you are."

"Who said I was shocked?"

"Well, you appear to be—"

"My only concern is that the business be kept out of any murder investigation."

"Really?"

"Yes, really. What the hell else do you think I care about?"

I didn't state the obvious, that he might have a little concern for me too. Instead, I waited for him to continue.

"Okay, Pankowski. I care about you too."

***

Back at my desk, I saw Billie shoot me another look.

"Everything okay?" she asked.

"Yes. It's just that he's so worried about this . . . situation. These two murders." I hesitated, deciding not to mention my business card. But if Tom thought *he* knew stuff, he was a novice compared to Billie. Still, I wasn't going to bring it up.

She rose from her desk, walking past Tom's closed door, and came over to me. "You just need to be very careful, that's all. Always let me, or someone, know where you're going. Try not to be showing houses after dark. That sort of thing."

"Why?" I looked innocently up at her pretty face. "Do you think there's a connection to Haskins Realty?"

She sat down in my visitor's chair, facing me now. "It's just a little scary, that's all."

"I don't get it, Bill, two murders in houses listed with different Realtors. What's the connection?" I watched her pick up one of my business cards from the stack I kept in a holder on my desk. She studied it for a few seconds before she spoke.

"I know a connection, Val." She glanced toward Perry's desk. "The Juarez house in Aurora. The owner approached us first."

"What?" I sat up straighter. "Tom didn't mention—"

"He doesn't know. Perry took the call. He actually told Ms. Juarez she'd be better off finding a Realtor in Aurora. He just blew her off. In fact, he recommended Bartlett."

"But why would she call here, when she lives in Aurora?"

"She apparently had heard good things."

"About Haskins?" I found that hard to believe.

"Not so much Haskins. More specifically, you."

"And Perry never mentioned it. Why wouldn't he tell me?"

"Probably jealousy. If Juanita called here praising you, he wouldn't want any more competition. As it is, he's hanging on by a thread here. His sales are way down, even though the market has really picked up."

"But I still don't get it. I've never sold a house in Aurora. And I've never met or heard of Juanita Juarez."

"She obviously heard of you."

"Oh, for Pete's sake. Tom would kill Perry if he knew." Tom's basic theory of home selling was to not turn anything down. One of his favorite mantras was, *if it's standing, we can sell it.*

"I know. We were the only two here when the call came in, and believe me, I jumped all over his case. But you do see now, don't you, that there is a connection?"

***

I hadn't spoken to Culotta since Saturday, and just as I was trying to decide whether or not to call him with the Perry information, my phone rang, displaying his number.

"Wanna get a cup of coffee?" he asked, before I'd had a chance to say hello.

"Yes," I said firmly. "I need to talk to you."

"Meet me at Starbucks on Main, twenty minutes."

"Make it thirty," I said, and hung up. I debated whether to go home and change. I was wearing my least favorite outfit, which Kit had once described as a sack over another sack. The baggy top concealed the elastic waistband and billowed over the flowing skirt. Then I realized that was ridiculous. What did I care what Culotta thought?

***

He was already seated at a round table for two at the back of the coffee shop. In front of him was a cup holding plain black coffee and another with caffè mocha. My favorite.

"You remembered," I said, impressed and wishing I had changed clothes.

"I consulted my notes." He smiled at me. "You look nice. Have a seat."

He was wearing an ultra-white starched shirt, open at the neck—no tie—and tucked into pressed khaki pants. I wasn't sure, but it seemed his sense of style may have stepped up a notch since we first met. I also noticed he was wearing his hair a little shorter, and it looked good. Oh hell, let's face it; he'd look good wearing a hockey mask and a clown's wig.

"So." I pulled the double sack down as I took a seat across from him. "What's on your mind? Got any leads?"

"You tell me." He sat forward, his elbows on the table, both hands cradling his coffee cup.

"Me? You're the detective, not—"

"What were you and your pal doing at Shirley Herzog's house yesterday?"

I picked up my cup and took a long sip, wondering how to explain. I took another sip.

"Well?" he pushed.

"Did I break any laws?"

"Obstructing justice."

"You've already used that," I said, relieved.

"Okay, how about interfering in a homicide investigation?"

"That sounds a little better." I tried to smile, but saw that he was not finding anything amusing about this. "How did you know we were there, anyway?"

"Easy. I tailed you."

"Isn't that stalking?"

He sat up straight and gave his hearty laugh. "That's a good one. So, what did you learn?"

"Nothing you don't already know, since you were there before us."

He leaned back. "Not me," he said. "The Aurora guys talked to her, for sure. But not me."

"Oh. Well, she said she'd taken a picture of Juanita's fiancé—"

"Let me see it."

"Why do you think I have it on me?"

"I know you, Valerie. Let me see it. Please."

I fished through my purse and produced Shirley's cropped picture. "It could be Jim Gardner," I said, handing it to him.

He studied it for a few seconds and then slipped it into his little notebook. "Could be a lot of people, but I better keep it, if you don't mind." It wasn't a question. "Anything else you've dug up?" He looked at his watch as he asked it, and I had a sinking feeling he was almost halfway out the door.

"Well, yes, as a matter of fact."

"Go on."

I told him about Juanita Juarez calling Haskins Realty to sell her home, and how Perry had recommended she go elsewhere.

"Perry's Tom's nephew, right?"

"Right. He's somewhat of an idiot, but you know, he's *our* idiot. He doesn't mean any harm."

"And I'm guessing he wouldn't hurt a fly?"

"He'd be terrified of a fly."

I watched him scrunch up his face; then he put both hands flat on the table and hoisted himself up. "Let's make this the last of your forays into detective work. Okay?"

I nodded.

"Okay?" he repeated. Then he put a hand on my shoulder and squeezed gently. "I wanna catch the guy who did this, and soon."

"Guy? Are you sure it's a guy?"

"Nope. Just generalizing." He squeezed again. In the few seconds his hand was on my shoulder, it was more effective than any hundred-dollar massage. No, it was nothing like a massage I'd pay a hundred bucks for. It was downright titillating. "Valerie, there's something I need . . ."

"Go on."

He smiled his tough-guy smile. "It's nothing. Stay safe. I'll be in touch."

I sat alone in the coffee shop for several minutes after he left, trying to gauge how I felt. It was the same feeling you get as a kid at Christmas after you've opened all your presents and you just want to keep going.

So now what? What did I want? I felt sure he was about to ask me out, but for some reason he'd stopped himself. Was it because I was a victim in his case, or worse, a suspect?

I finally left, feeling deflated.

I didn't drive back to the office, but instead headed straight to an appointment I'd set up. A third appointment with prospective buyers who, I felt sure, were going to make a decision in Haskins Realty's favor. On the way, I called Kit and filled her in on Shirley Herzog's visit, Billie's revelation about Perry, and finally, my meeting with Culotta.

"I just don't know what to do about him," I said, finishing my long recap of the day so far. "I mean, I *think* there's something there, between us. I'm sure he was about to ask me out, but he stopped himself."

"Yikes. You've got far more important things to worry about than waiting for your boyfriend to ask you for a date. There's a killer out there, and he or she has some sort of vendetta against you."

"Vendetta? Really? We're not in Sicily," I said, but her words had brought me back to the present and out of my daydreams about Dennis Culotta.

"Come over after work and show me the picture."

"I gave it to Culotta, and I'll be too tired to get together tonight. But let's have lunch tomorrow."

***

By ten o'clock that night I was in bed, flipping through the TV channels to find something to watch. The phone beside my bed rang, and I answered, snuggling down beneath my comforter. Although the weather outside was warm, I had my air conditioner set to icy cold.

"Val." It was Tom.

"Hey, Boss." Late-night calls from him were not unusual, especially if we hadn't spoken much during the day. "What's happening?"

"I just had a long talk with Hal Bartlett." I knew Hal was the father of Mark Bartlett, my buddy over at Bartlett Real Estate who'd given me Shirley Herzog's name. Tom and the elder Bartlett were old friends. I waited for him to continue, not sure what he knew about Perry refusing Juanita's listing.

"Seems my genius nephew talked the latest dead girl out of listing with us. He sent her over to Bartlett."

I remained mute. I didn't want to get Perry in trouble, although he deserved it, and I didn't want Billie to be in hot water, either.

"I'm sure Perry had his reasons," I finally said, when it was clear Tom was waiting for my response.

"Yeah; normally, I'd kick his ass. But it seems he might have inadvertently done the right thing for once. Not for Juanita, of course, but for you. The further away you are from this business, the better."

"But my card—"

"I know; that part scares the shit out of me. But don't worry, Kiddo. We've got Downers Grove's finest working the case."

At the mention of Culotta, I had an adrenaline rush. "Have you discussed this with Dennis?" I asked, trying to sound calm.

"Of course. What did you think? I'd let my best Realtor get mixed up in this mess and not put in my two cents' worth?"

"Well, he's a good detective. I just hope he's quick, before anyone else gets . . . murd . . . hurt."

"Yeah. Let's hope Culotta isn't too distracted to do his job."

The adrenaline rush turned into a sprint. "Distracted? What does he have to distract him?"

"That good-looking blond working down at the station. Tina Something."

"Reilly. Tina Reilly. Why would she distract him?"

"Pankowski, have you seen her?"

"Yes, I've seen her. She's an artist."

"Yeah, I hear she's been giving our old pal Culotta some private showings."

"Really?" I tried to sound as nonchalant as if I'd heard Culotta was seen with his maiden aunt discussing crochet patterns.

"I saw the two of them at Romano's a few nights ago. They looked cozy. If you know what I mean."

It dawned on me that maybe *that* was what Culotta had been about to tell me: that he was dating Tina, not that he wanted a date with *me*. "Good for him," I managed to say.

But really, really bad for me.

CHAPTER TEN

You know," Tom said, "I always thought Culotta had a thing for *you*. Guess I was wrong."

"Me?" I said. "Hardly. We're just friends. That's all."

"Friends?"

"Acquaintances, actually. Nothing more."

"I'm glad to hear it. He's no good for you."

"Oh, for heaven's sake. I have no interest in Culotta. And I still don't understand why a girlfriend would be a distraction to a detective."

"Again, Pankowski, have you *seen* her?"

"For Pete's sake. She's attractive, but she's hardly the most beautiful woman in the world." Determined to get a grip, I swung my legs over the bed and stood up. I grabbed my robe from the foot of the bed and put the phone between my chin and shoulder so I could slip into the warm terry cloth.

" . . . you there, Pankowski?"

I wondered what I'd missed. Probably not much. Then again, he'd already managed to shock me once in our short conversation. "Yeah, I'm here, just dropped the phone. What did you say?"

"I said I gotta go. Gotta get to sleep so I can be sharp for work tomorrow. You might wanna follow my lead."

"Hey, you called me. I was already in bed." I didn't add that I knew I wouldn't be sleeping tonight now.

And I probably wouldn't be very sharp at work tomorrow.

***

I arrived at the office early. I hadn't been able to do more than drift in and out of a restless sleep all night, and I couldn't wait to occupy my mind with something besides Dennis Culotta. I knew my best chance for that was to bury myself in real estate. Figuratively speaking, of course.

I realized right away that wasn't going to work, however. I did not manage to get to the office before anyone else. Tom and Billie were both already there, already sipping Billie's hot cappuccino. And they were joined by the man who'd kept me awake all night.

"Dennis!" I practically yelled before I could stop myself.

He stood up from the chair next to Billie's desk, as if he were a gentleman instead of a son of a bitch. "Good morning, Valerie. Glad you're here. We've been discussing the case—"

"Cases," I corrected him, satisfied when he raised his eyebrows in grim agreement. I wanted to make it clear that the matter at hand was the two murdered women and absolutely not the one he was seen cozying up to at Romano's.

"Yes, unfortunately, cases. You are quite right." His eyes moved boldly up and down, checking me out in an obviously personal, not professional, way.

I'd given no thought whatsoever to what I was putting on that morning and had to actually glance down to check it out.

Crap! I'd grabbed a pair of pants that hadn't fit me right since my latest five-pound addition. I'd kept them in my closet, so certain that summer would bring the usual melting off of a few pounds. Wrong. And unfortunately, I'd paired my pants selection with a top that barely covered the waistband, so I knew I was hiding nothing.

"You wanted to discuss the cases?" My tone got a little snotty as I tried to yank his attention from my burgeoning waist.

He sat back down and motioned for me to do the same in my own chair.

Not willing to let him direct me to do *anything*, I went instead and stood next to Tom at the other end of Billie's desk.

Culotta nodded, now that he had everyone's eyes on him. "We're starting from the beginning," he said. "Billie told me you got Daphne's listing because she called looking for a Realtor. And you and Perry take turns when a seller doesn't specify a preference?"

I nodded.

"And it was your turn?"

Was he dense? "Yes," I said, making it sound like *duh.* "Perry had taken the previous caller, so the next one was mine. That's generally how taking turns works."

He looked down at his notes, as if he had to consult something, but I could see him bite his bottom lip. Probably holding back what he really wanted to say. "So the first time you met her was when she came here to, what, sign some paperwork?"

Was he trying to trap me? Surely, Billie had already told him. Billie didn't forget anything, even if it had been a couple of months since Daphne had listed with me. "No, I went to her house. I could hardly get all the information I'd need without going there."

Dennis frowned at me and then looked down at his notebook again. "Billie, Tom, did you ever have occasion to meet Daphne?"

Tom, unusual for him, had remained silent so far, leaning against the edge of Billie's desk, his arms folded across his chest. He continued his silence as Billie answered Culotta.

"No," she said. "I never met Daphne. Only spoke to her a few times when she called looking for Val. I just took messages."

Culotta nodded as if Billie had said something crucial. "Tom?" He turned his attention to his poker buddy. "Did *you* ever meet Daphne Travister?"

"No. Did I, Billie?" Tom uses Billie like most people use their address books and calendars—paper *and* digital.

"Not that I know of," she answered.

Culotta rose then and shook Tom's hand. "Thanks for your time. You too, Billie." He turned and shook her hand. Then he looked at me. "Valerie, do you want to grab a cup of coffee?"

"Sorry, no time." I strode over to my desk and turned on my computer. I could feel his presence behind me as I sat in my chair. I was aware of Tom closing his office door behind him and Billie retreating to the kitchen. When Culotta didn't move, I swiveled around, and my knees brushed against his legs. "I beg your pardon," I said. "Do you need something?"

He grinned. "Yeah, I need to know who strangled Daphne and Juanita."

"And you need my help?"

He looked perplexed, and I wondered if Tom had his facts straight. "Valerie, I just need to be sure you've told me everything—"

"You know I—"

"What I should have said is, if you remember anything, anything at all, please call me."

"Duh. Don't I always?"

His phone rang from his inside pocket; he answered it gruffly, and then he ran out the door. Was it Tina calling to tell him she'd broken a pencil and needed someone big and strong to work the pencil sharpener? And could I get any lamer?

***

"What's up, Val?" Kit slid into the chair across from me at Rathbun's, where we had agreed to meet for lunch. Before I could answer, the waiter appeared and took Kit's order for a glass of pinot grigio. She nodded at my Diet Coke with its slice of lemon. "You got rum in there, I hope. You sounded like you could use it."

"Nah. I gotta work today, not to mention drive. With clients, no less."

"I wish you had that picture of Juanita Juarez's fiancé. Too bad you gave it to your boyfriend. But you think it looks like your Jim Gardener, huh?"

I smiled. "Gardner. Two syllables. And yeah, I wish Culotta hadn't taken it. What a jerk."

"Which one, Gard-ner, or Coo-lot-a."

"Culotta, of course."

"Wow. You sound pretty harsh. Don't you think it might make sense for him to have it? I mean, sure, I was curious, but—"

"You don't understand. That's not why he's a jerk."

"Enlighten me."

"Remember Tina? The blond sketch girl, person, whatever the hell she is. Apparently, she and Culotta are an item."

Kit took a sip of her drink and stared at me.

"So?" she said, when I didn't continue.

"Did you hear me? I said he's seeing Tina."

"I heard you. Why are you so surprised?"

"Why?" I repeated. "First, because he never told me about her—"

"Who did?"

"Tom. He let it slip."

"Ha!" She actually laughed a little. "And you believe him?"

"Well, of course. Why would Tom lie?"

"Because he's Tom? But forget him; why are you so pissed off? You had your chance. And you haven't seen Culotta—in that way—in . . . a while. It's not beyond reason that he would get snapped up. Personally, I don't get it. He's hardly boyfriend material—"

"Wait. Culotta is great boyfriend material." Even as I said it, the word *boyfriend* sounded ridiculous. "He's loyal, he's smart, he can be funny—"

"So can a golden retriever." I didn't respond, but watched Kit raise her eyebrows over the rim of her glass. She was looking at me now like a teacher whose pupil had just figured out a calculus problem all on her own.

"So you're saying I shouldn't feel led on?" I finally asked. "I'm telling you, he was flirting with me, and all the time he was having cozy dinners with Tina."

"Look, the guy who came to clean my windows last week was flirting with me, too, but I'd hardly call him boyfriend material, either. Let's face it; even though he looked a bit like Matt Damon, I wasn't waiting for him to propose that we run away together."

"Oh, come on, this is totally different," I said. "And please stop saying the word *boyfriend*. We're too old for boyfriends."

"Okay, *lover* then."

"That's even worse, not to mention totally inaccurate. And anyway, it's still different."

"Not really. You suspected some attraction between you and Culotta; but honey, he's just doing his job."

"There's a big difference between a guy who's trying to solve a couple of murders that I am involved with on a daily basis and a guy who makes your windows all sparkly once a year."

"Easy for you to say. Do you have any idea how much bird poop we get on our windows?"

Exasperated, I put my lips around the straw in my Diet Coke and sucked up half the liquid. She didn't get it. "So I shouldn't be mad?"

"Of course not. You didn't make your move when you had the chance. And this Tina beat you to it. You should just let it go."

"But why should I have to make the first move?"

"It's a moot point. Someone else did, and that's that. Move on, Valley Girl."

"But—"

"So he led you on a little. Hey, he's not the first jerk to do that."

"But you should *see* this Tina."

***

Kit and I had barely gone our separate ways when she called me. "Your dear Detective Dennis Culotta might be a jerk, but he's a busy one, I'll tell ya. Hard to believe he has time to date Miss America, let alone try to get another girlfriend on the side."

I bit my tongue. I did not like being referred to as *a girlfriend on the side*. "What are you talking about, Kit? And be careful. You shouldn't have had that last drink."

"I didn't finish it. I didn't even start it. You might have noticed if you hadn't been so busy analyzing Culotta's love life."

"Well, what about him? What makes you think he's so busy?"

"Because I just heard on the radio that another body has been found."

CHAPTER ELEVEN

As soon as I reached my office, just a few minutes after ending my call with Kit, I rushed to my computer to look up the local-news website. I found the story under the heading *Breaking News*.

Christine Fullerton, age twenty-seven, was found strangled to death in her backyard. She was married, no children. The picture of Christine showed a pretty, young woman with strawberry-blond hair, perfect white teeth, and deep dimples. The article said she'd been a cheerleader for the Oak Ridge East High School Fighting Wolverines.

"Oh crap," I said, reading the article for the second time.

"What? What is it?" Perry, looking striking in a mustard vest and black bow tie, leaned over my desk.

"See for yourself." I sat back in my chair.

"OMG," he said. "You don't think—"

"I don't know what to think."

"You should call your dashing detective and find out."

"Brilliant idea, Perry." I dug my cell phone out of my purse. Expecting my call to go to his voice mail, I was surprised when Culotta answered on the first ring.

"Hey," he said.

"Hey. I just read about Christine Fullerton."

"Yeah. I was gonna call you. I'm just finishing up here."

"Well, tell me, is it connected? Was there—"

"Look, you need to come in. We need a statement."

"Can't you just tell me—"

"No, not over the phone. You have to come in. We need an official statement from you."

"Wait just a minute. Does this mean you found my business card—"

"Just get over here. Now."

"Tell me when it happened."

"Sometime between ten last night and one this morning. Won't know for sure till the M.E. finishes."

"The Internet said she was strangled."

"Just come in."

"Was her house for sale?"

"Get over here."

"Just tell me *something*. Please."

"I will. As soon as you get here."

My hand was shaking as I shut off my phone and put it back in my purse.

"Well?" Perry said.

"He wants me to go to the station. I have to make a statement."

"Oh no. You?" Perry twiddled with the bow tie at his throat. "They don't think *you* had anything to do with this, do they?"

I resisted the urge to pull the elastic band that I was sure his bow tie was attached to. "Of course not," I said, my voice rising, but not in any way sure that was true.

"Let's face it, Val. This doesn't look good for you—"

"Oh, Perry, just shut up, will you? I need to think." Now I was shouting.

"What's going on here?" It was Tom, bursting out of his office. "What's all the racket? Perry, what have you done?"

"Not me, Uncle Tom. The police want to question Val." Perry almost smiled. "There's been another murder. She has to go down to the station and make a statement. She's probably their chief suspect."

"Oh, thank you so much for that little insight." I opened my desk drawer, for no reason, and then slammed it shut.

"Val, you should get an attorney." Perry folded his arms across his mustard vest.

"She doesn't need a damn attorney," Tom said. "Perry, get back to your desk and do some work. Val, let's go."

"Tom, there's no need for you to go too."

"Hell yes, I'm going. I'll drive."

I grabbed my purse. I didn't say I was grateful to Tom, but I was. As we reached the front door, he turned and called to Billie.

"Get Marcus Willoughby on the phone. See if he's in town. Tell him I may need him later."

I wasn't sure if Tom wanting to speak to his attorney was good news or bad.

***

"Twice in one day," Culotta said, coming out of his office with a hand extended toward Tom. "Valerie, come in here." He pointed to a room with a sign on the door. Interview Room 1. The police station was small, and I'd never seen any evidence of Interview Room 2, or 3, but I followed Culotta, and Tom followed me. More important, I didn't see Tina Reilly anywhere around.

"Er, Tom, I need to speak to Valerie alone. You can wait here." Culotta stopped in the doorway.

"The hell I can." Tom stepped past him and took a seat at the wooden table.

I heard Culotta sigh, and then he came into the room and closed the door. "Okay. This is informal, so I guess your ... what? ... boss? ... can be here. I need a statement from you, Valerie. Very simple."

"Wait," Tom interrupted him. "First, tell us what happened. Then we'll determine if Val is gonna give you a statement. Without an attorney present, that is."

Culotta, who was now sitting on the other side of the table, leaned back in his chair. He picked up a pencil and used it to tap the palm of his right hand. "Okay," he said, after considering Tom's orders for a few seconds. On the desk in front of him was a manila folder, and he leaned forward as he opened it. Then he began to read. "Christine Fullerton. Age twenty-seven. Married to Wendell Fullerton. He's thirty-two. Has a dental practice in Naperville. He was at an awards dinner at his country club. Got home around one. Found his wife in the backyard. No one else home. He called it in ..." Culotta flipped to a second page in the folder. " ... at one twenty-three."

"Why'd he wait twenty-three minutes to call it in?" Tom asked.

"Er ..." Culotta ran a finger down the page. " ... let's see. Okay, he got home at one, poured himself a drink. Assumed his wife was in bed. Didn't check on her till one fifteen. Discovered she wasn't in the bedroom. Did a search. Went out to the backyard and found her body on a chair by the picnic table—"

"Wait," Tom said. "Why'd he go out in the backyard? Wouldn't he just assume she wasn't home?"

"Nope. Says here the patio light was on, which was unusual, and from the kitchen window he could see her sitting there."

"Strangled?" Tom asked.

"Yep." Culotta flipped the file shut and leaned back in his chair again. "And it looked like her body was moved there after she was killed." He tapped the manila folder with the pencil.

"Okay, Dennis," Tom said, "we're all dying to know. Did you find anything else at the scene?"

"Matter of fact, we did." He frowned.

My hand went to my throat. "Oh no," I said. "My business card?"

"Afraid so, Valerie."

***

We remained in Interview Room 1 for the next forty minutes. I learned the Fullerton house had been on the market for ten days, listed with Millennium Realtors. The Fullertons, who had been married for five years, were looking to upgrade to a larger home and start a family. Christine Fullerton was an elementary-school teacher, and according to her neighbors, everyone loved her.

Although I'd never met, or in fact heard of, Christine Fullerton, my business card was found lying face up on the glass picnic table in front of her. I shivered at the gruesome photograph that Culotta pushed toward us. Taken at the scene, it showed Christine looking nothing like the photo I'd seen of her on the local-news website.

Her head was drooping forward, her chin almost touching her chest. Her blond hair had been separated at the back of her neck and fell over her shoulders. It might have looked like she'd simply fallen asleep, except for the dark-red line around her throat forming a bloody necklace.

After answering a few perfunctory questions from Culotta, with nodded approval from Tom, I did sign a brief statement. The main issue seemed to be my whereabouts at the possible time of death.

Tom was quick to assure Culotta that I was safely tucked up in my own bed. He cited his telephone call to me at ten o'clock as evidence.

Culotta listened carefully, still tapping the folder with the pencil, but even I knew he considered my so-called alibi flimsy. Tom and I had spoken for about thirty minutes, and

Burgess and Neuman

I knew Dennis was probably picturing me driving over to the Fullerton house and strangling Christine. My panic at the image evaporated, however, when Tom pointed out that obviously I wouldn't leave my own business card if I'd committed the horrible crime.

"Not to mention Val has the strength of a flea," he said, looking at Christine's bruised neck. "She can barely squeeze ketchup out of a bottle, much less the life out of someone's throat."

***

"I know the Fullertons," Kit said. "Larry's played golf with him. He's a dentist, right?"

I nodded and grabbed the glass of pinot she held out. "Poor guy," I said, after I took a big gulp. "Apparently, he was at some dinner at his country club in Naperville Monday night, and when he got home, he found his wife dead. Culotta said he and Christine were planning to start a family."

"Not that night, I hope."

"Oh, Kit, you're horrible."

"Sorry," she mumbled, not looking at all sorry.

"Don't you feel really bad for him?"

"Of course." Kit sat down on the other end of the couch, curling her legs under her. "Unless, of course, he killed her."

"Why would you say that?" I tried to keep the alarm out of my voice.

"He's really handsome, Val. And he's rich. Maybe he wanted the wifey out of the way."

"Handsome and rich. Well, Kit, seems you've cracked the case. So, you're thinking he murdered Daphne and Juanita to throw us off the track when his real intention was to get rid of his own wife?"

"I don't know. I'm just thinking out loud. This whole thing has me totally . . . I'm just so worried about you."

90

I watched her take a sip of wine and run her hand through her hair, which fell immediately back into place, the way any ridiculously expensive haircut should. She and Tina Reilly had that in common. If I ran a hand through my hair, it would most certainly not return to where it was supposed to be, and I'd look like a blond Carrot Top.

"How well do you know him, anyway?" I asked. "He's not your dentist, is he?"

"No. I told you, he's really handsome. I don't want a looker digging around in my molars. But we've been to a few dinners and stuff at the club. He's very outgoing; she's kinda mousy. *Was* kinda mousy."

"She looked stunning in the picture on the Internet," I said, but all I could recall was the less-than-stunning crime-scene photo Culotta had shown us.

"Val, you think everyone looks stunning. I'm guessing that picture was taken several years ago. We all looked stunning then."

After finishing my wine and assuring Kit I wasn't afraid to be alone, I returned to my apartment, totally exhausted.

***

It was almost ten o'clock, and I marveled at how much had happened in twenty-four hours. I removed the little makeup that still remained on my face before slipping into my pajamas and climbing into bed.

Then I hit the button on my blinking phone base. I had two messages.

The first was from Tom. *Val, just calling to check on you, and yes, you can expect a call every night until this maniac is found. So get used to it. Call me.* Well, he called me most nights, anyway; still, I was touched.

The second message was from Culotta. *Valerie. We need to talk. Call me. Please.*

While I was deciding whether I wanted to speak to either one of them again tonight, the phone rang. I picked it up without checking to identify the caller, and I was shocked to hear Perry's voice.

"Val. You'll never, never guess what." He sounded extremely excited, even for him.

"Perry, I'm really exhausted. I had a very long and scary day—"

"*I got in!* You're talking to the newest member of the Hinsdale Male Chorus sponsored by McVaughn Chevrolet."

"Perry, I was at a police station all afternoon being questioned about a murder I'm innocently mixed up in. I don't give a flip if you made it into the Mormon Tabernacle Choir."

"Is that sour grapes I hear?"

"Oh, for Pete's sake. I hope you choke on your scales."

"Scales?" I heard him say as I hung up.

CHAPTER TWELVE

In less than sixty seconds I had Perry back on the phone. I felt bad that I was letting my troubles, however horrific, blind me to his joy. After all, even if he'd steered a potential listing away from me, Perry probably didn't have much else going on in his life—or many other people to share good news with. Then again, there was that new friend he'd sent flowers to.

He answered on the first ring. "I accept your apology, Val," he said, which of course wiped out my feelings of guilt.

"I wasn't calling to apologize. I just wanted to congratulate you."

"I know; it's incredible, right? I can hardly believe I got in. That's really somethin', isn't it?"

"I had no idea you could sing."

I heard what sounded like Perry moving to a different spot and putting his hand over the receiver of his phone to muffle the sound. "Between you and me, I'm not that good. But I have a great ally."

"So tell me about your new friend," I asked, certain this must be the ally he referred to.

"Friend?"

"Look, never mind. You don't have to tell me. I've got to get some sleep. Congratulations again, and I'll see you when—"

"No, Val, wait. I'll tell you. Obviously, you won't get any sleep until I do."

I marveled at Perry's sense of drama. Not to mention the fact that he didn't even ask me how my day at the station had gone.

"They were for T. L. Terry Lee. You remember, the one whose phone call—"

"Well, what did T. L. do to deserve flowers?"

"It's our three-month anniversary. Plus, she has faith in me, Val. You might not believe this, but not a lot of people do."

"You've been seeing this T. L. for three months?"

"Yes. Three divine months."

"Then I'm very happy for you."

"She moved here from up north."

"So their loss is our gain?"

"Speaking of T. L., she wants to meet you, Val."

"Me? Why?"

"Because I've told her so much about you. She knows how close we are."

I might have disputed that, but it had been a long day, and I really was tired. "Then I'd love to meet her. Let's do lunch sometime. And Perry, I'm glad you found yourself a Terry Lee," I said, and wished him good-night.

Then I did call Tom, because I knew he would keep calling until I reassured him I was home safe and sound.

"It's about time," he said, before I'd even heard a ring.

"Sorree! I just got home."

"From where? I thought you were going home right from the station."

"Why did you think that? I never said—"

"It doesn't matter. I'm just glad you're there now. Got your door locked?"

"Yes, Daddy."

"Bolted?"

"Yes," I lied. I still hadn't gotten around to getting a dead bolt. And the truth was, Tom *had* been my protector since my marriage to David had ended, long before our divorce. My father was dead, and my only brother, Buddy, one of Tom's best high school friends, lived in Washington, DC.

"Answer me. Are you?" I heard Tom ask.

"Am I what?"

"Pankowski, listen to me. Are you going to be careful, no opening doors to anyone, no going out after dark, no—"

"I'm in for the night, and I'm going to be careful. I'm also going to look very haggard tomorrow if you don't let me get my beauty sleep."

"Oh, you always look beautiful."

I do believe I blushed. I'm not sure Tom had ever paid me such a big compliment, and he said it with utter sincerity—also unusual for him. I realized he really *was* worried about me.

"Good-night, Tom."

"Good-night."

"Wait—one more thing. I just spoke to Perry—"

"Yes, I understand I'm the proud uncle of the newest member of the Hinsdale Boy Band."

"So you knew already?"

"Knew? Who do you think made it happen? I called Ray McVaughn, who sponsors the damn thing. He owes me a few favors."

I wasn't surprised. Apparently, Tom has people all over the city who owe him favors. "So Perry can actually sing?"

"Who knows? Who cares? It's a chorus, Val. One bad apple ain't gonna make any difference one way or the other."

"And do you know this T. L. person? Terry Lee? Perry's new friend?"

"Never heard of him—"

"Turns out it's a her."

"Even better."

After hanging up, I felt a bit shaken from our conversation, realizing I really might be in jeopardy. I leaned back on my pillows for a few minutes to collect myself. And then I remembered Culotta had a girlfriend. I wanted to punch him, but instead, I punched in his phone number. *Well, at least Tom thinks I'm beautiful,* I reminded myself.

"Valerie?" Culotta said.

"I'm returning your call; you said we need to talk." I was immediately on the defensive, especially since his voice mail had sounded so urgent.

"Right."

I could almost hear him flipping the pages of his damn notebook to remind himself of the reason. "Look," I continued, "it's late; I've had a long day. Is there something about the investigation you need to tell me?"

"I just want to hear again how often you give out those cards of yours."

"I think we've covered that. I give them out all the time. Why? Have you discovered something?"

"Just that the card at Christine Fullerton's had no fingerprints, except hers, of course. And yours."

"Not such a leap is it? The murderer wore gloves." I let that thought run through my head.

"But here's the thing," he went on. "We've got to find the link; why pick on Christine Fullerton? We know the other two murdered women both had a connection to you."

"I've told you, I never met her. Never heard of her."

"Yep. That's what you said about Juanita Juarez, too, but we know she did try to get Haskins Realty to sell her house in the beginning."

"But I didn't know that—"

"So you keep saying."

I hated the way he said that. "Why would I lie?" I asked lamely. Like if he really thought I was a serial killer, did it necessarily follow I was a liar as well? "I don't like the way this is going," I said finally. But that sounded twice as lame. *A serial killer who didn't like the way things were going?*

"Sorry to upset your delicate balance. But do me a favor; just try to remember if you've ever had anything to do with Christine Fullerton."

I sighed. "I've already told you—"

"Yeah, I know. But remember how the strip of black hair, or whatever the hell it was, on the back of Jim Gardner's head suddenly occurred to you? And don't forget, I want you to come in for another sketch. Tina thinks you were withholding—"

"Speaking of Tina . . ."

"What about her?"

"Well, it's nothing, but Tom said he saw you two at Romano's." *Crap. Why did I say that?*

"Yeah, he probably did. What about it?"

Yikes. I wanted to pull my tongue out of my head. This was high school nonsense, but I was somehow unable to stop. "So, are you two dating?"

"As in having dinner at a restaurant?"

"Oh, forget it. I'll make an appointment and go see her."

"You sound mad. Are you mad?"

"Not even slightly. She seemed like a nice girl."

"I'm glad you approve."

My brain leaped forward to Culotta and Tina getting married. They'd look good at a wedding together, as long as he planned to hand her over to a groom from the same generation as hers.

"Well, good luck," I finally managed to say. "She's certainly very beautiful."

He hesitated for just a second. "So are you," he said, very quietly and very quickly, and then he hung up.

CHAPTER THIRTEEN

And just what the hell was I supposed to do with *that?*

I decided Kit had been right, as usual. Why had I let myself believe there was the possibility of something with Culotta? After all, I'd had several cozy dinners with him myself, although they seemed like an eternity ago. If I really had felt something, why hadn't I acted on it?

Then I shuddered at the thought of *that* and how humiliating it would have been to actually make a move on Dennis when he had the hots for the beautiful Tina. I'd do just as Kit had suggested, and move on.

But upon reflection, I realized it wasn't such a bad day, after all. I'd been called beautiful twice.

***

"Okay, here's what I found out." It was Kit, calling at seven the next morning. I'd just finished brushing my teeth and was now giving the bathroom mirror a swipe to remove the stray toothpaste my Sonicare had flung its way. I was pretty certain Tina could manage an electric toothbrush without having to call in a cleaning service.

"Tell me," I said, heading toward my miniscule kitchen for some coffee and dismissing all thoughts of Tina.

"Wendell Fullerton. His alibi doesn't work. He said he was at the golf dinner in Naperville, right? But I called Deanna; she's the wife of one of Larry's buddies, Charlie Somebody. She goes to all those damn things."

"You are so amazing."

"I know. I got to chatting with Deanna about poor Wendell and how terrible it must have been for him to be at a dinner and then go home and find his poor wife, blah, blah, blah, and she said *no way*. He wasn't even at the dinner. She knows this for certain because he was supposed to get an award for some damn golf thing, like those idiots deserve awards for hitting a ball. But when his name was called, he wasn't there."

"We should tell the police."

"We should go speak to Wendell."

"Well, the police will most certainly check out his alibi. Isn't the husband the first one they look at—"

"And they'll screw it up for sure. Let's just have a little chat with Wendell, and then if there's anything pertinent, we'll let the cops know."

I sighed. The police would surely be way ahead of us, but this was how Kit rolled, and since I couldn't let her do this sort of thing alone, I had to roll right along with her. "Okay, what's your plan?"

"Let me think about that. I'll call you as soon as I have one."

***

When I got to the office forty-five minutes later, I parked between Perry's Corvette and an old Buick I'd never

99

seen before. As I entered the building, I could see the back of a person sitting in Perry's visitor's chair. An unusual sight.

Even more unusual was Perry himself, sitting with his elbows on the desk, his clasped hands resting under his chin, listening intently to his visitor like a priest hearing a confession. When he saw me, however, he jumped up, a look of sheer delight filling his face. "Val, Val, look who's here." He walked over and grabbed my arm and then led me back to the woman sitting at his desk. "T. L., here she is. This is Valerie Pankowski."

The woman didn't rise, but she did at least turn in my direction. The first thing I noticed was her hair. A bad dark-brown dye job, too severe for her pale skin. It was styled in a bouffant with flipped-up ends, the kind Annette Funicello had made so fashionable a million years ago. The resemblance to Annette stopped there.

When T. L. stood up, I was impressed at how tall she was. Her face was rather angular, her makeup was a little too intense, and her pink lipstick strained to upstage her thin lips.

"This is Terry Lee. Or T. L., as she's known to her friends." He looked about as delighted as I'd ever seen him, while T. L. gave me the once-over and I tried to guess her age. Early forties, at least. Maybe even late forties.

"So nice to meet you." I extended a hand to shake.

"So you're the famous Val." She took my hand in her own and offered a firm shake in return. But her smile was weak, and I noticed the pink lipstick wasn't doing her yellowing teeth any favors.

"I'd hardly say famous." I moved toward my desk and put my purse underneath it.

"Val's being modest, for once." Perry smiled. "She's helping the police with their inquiries. Oh, don't worry, she's not a suspect, are you, Val?" He flapped his right hand at the wrist; apparently, this confirmed I wasn't a murderer.

Normally, I'd have lambasted him for such a ridiculous question, but I had a sense he was trying hard to look good in front of his girlfriend, so I let it go. I was about to say I hoped not, but T. L. said it for me.

"I doubt that very much," she said, taking her seat again. She was wearing a cheap-looking beige linen suit, and I noticed the skirt was already creased across her thighs. Her old-fashioned blouse had a large, floppy bow at the throat.

"T. L.'s a librarian," Perry said, as proudly as if he'd just announced she was captain of the next space shuttle.

"I understand you moved here from up north," I said. "Do you live in Downers Grove now?"

"Yes." Her voice was kind of nasally, and when I switched my glance to Perry, I could see the gushing he was trying hard to contain.

"I'm so glad you got in early for once, Val," he said. "The library doesn't open until nine, so T. L. stopped by to meet you."

Phew. He was really pushing it. "Me too," I said, turning my attention briefly to my computer and switching it on. "But you'll have to excuse me; I've got a lot of work to get to."

"I know; let's have lunch," Perry said excitedly.

"Yes, soon," I said, although I wasn't sharing Perry's enthusiasm for the Downers Grove librarian. "I'll check my calendar."

"Great." Perry lightly clapped his hands.

Then T. L. stood and wrapped the long strap of her purse over her thin shoulder and attempted to smooth her creased skirt. I noticed she was wearing rubber-soled lace-up shoes, the kind nurses wear. Maybe a good choice for a library, to keep noise at a minimum. "I should be going, Perry," she said. "See you tonight." It was more of a command than an invitation.

"*Absolutely*." He took her elbow. "Can't wait," I heard him say, as the door swung closed behind them. Then he walked her to her car.

Within a few seconds Billie approached with a steaming cup of coffee for me. "Wow, what a dud," she said.

"Perry seems to adore her." I took the cup gratefully. "How old do you think she is?"

"Older than him by at least a decade, for sure. And not exactly the world's greatest conversationalist. I have a feeling she really came here to get a look at you. Before you arrived, Perry was talking you up a storm, like you two were joined at the hip. Notice she left as soon as you arrived."

"Hmm. I'm surprised he used me to impress her."

"Oh, don't worry. I don't think she was a bit impressed." Billie winked.

Through the front windows I could see Tom exiting his Mercedes. He parked as far from the Buick as possible and walked quickly into the building, giving a brief wave to Perry and his new pal.

"Geez," he said, inside the safety of our little office. "Who's the frump?"

***

"Larry has absolutely forbidden me to speak to, approach, or go anywhere within twenty miles of Wendell Fullerton," Kit said.

I'd had a spectacular afternoon at the closing of a seven-figure house I'd been working on for less than a month. It felt almost good enough to make me forget about the murders, at least long enough to stop by Kit and Larry's on my way home for a celebratory glass of champagne. At Kit's insistence. I watched her pour the sparkling Cristal into two elegant flutes. "So, when do we go see him?" I took one of the flutes and gently touched it against the one Kit now held.

"Congratulations on the sale," she said. "And I'm serious, he has banned me."

"Yes, you said that. But when do we go?"

"We don't. Larry is being all caveman. It's not so much about Wendell, but more about Larry's standing at that damn country club. He's afraid I'll embarrass him."

"Well—"

"Don't you dare agree."

"Well, perhaps Larry *is* right. We should let the police deal with it. They'll question Wendell and discover he wasn't at the dinner that night. They know things we don't."

"Ah yes, but they don't know Deanna Thingamajig."

The bubbles from the Cristal tickled my nose a little as I laughed. "Sounds like you don't know her too well, either."

"I know her well enough. But I can never remember her last name. Funkelstein, Flugelhoff . . . something like that. And here's the very best part: while I was preparing to remove Larry's fingernails with my tweezers, he let it slip that Deanna was bugging Charlie to move. So, I'm thinking if they don't already have a Realtor, it's time they get one."

She clinked her glass against mine again. "Who needs Wendell Fullerton, anyway?"

***

Later, when I was home in bed, I got my phone call from Tom. It was brief. *How are ya? Lock up good! And great job on the sale.*

Just before I was ready to turn off the light on my bedside table, the phone rang again.

Perry.

"So Val, what did you think of T. L.?" He sounded excited.

"She seems very nice," I lied. "But . . . what do you two have in common?"

"Oh, didn't I tell you?"

"No."

"I thought I did."

"You didn't."

"Are you certain? Because I'm sure I told you."

It was like talking to Emily when she was fourteen and I was trying to coax some teenage gossip out of her without letting on I was really interested.

"For Pete's sake, tell me now." Of course, that was totally the wrong approach with Perry. But I was tired and didn't have time for his games.

"She's the choir director of HMC."

"HMC?" I repeated. "Oh, Hinsdale Men's Chorus."

"Male Chorus, Val. Not Men. Male."

I couldn't be bothered to argue the distinction. "So," I said instead, "you have a woman directing all those men. Sorry, males."

"I know. Isn't she a hoot?"

Hoot was hardly how I would describe T. L. She seemed more suited to running a men's prison than a male chorus.

"I'll let you in on a little secret," Perry continued.

"Okay. But make it quick. My show is about to come on, and I don't have time for twenty questions."

"She's the reason I got into HMC. There were better candidates, but she's taken such a shine to me. I'm very lucky."

"Hmm," I said. I was burning to tell him that his uncle was the real reason he got in. But I literally bit my bottom lip to stop myself. "Well, good for you. I gotta go."

"Okay. And Val, congrats on the sale today. T. L. was very impressed when I told her about it."

***

Deanna Finkelmeyer agreed to meet us for lunch the following day. Kit set it up for noon at Sullivan's Steakhouse, a good restaurant in picturesque Naperville. Kit and I both arrived about the same time and took our places at a table for four at the back of the dimly lit restaurant.

"What's she like, anyway?" I asked, unfolding a linen napkin and placing it on my lap.

"Oh, she's awful. Really bitchy, really showy. I like her."

"Yes, you would."

Deanna Finkelmeyer kept us waiting for twenty-two minutes and finally arrived in a flurry, holding two shopping bags in each hand. She dropped them on the empty chair at our table and then leaned across to kiss Kit on the cheek and shake my hand.

"So nice to meet you, Val."

She was well into her fifties, but trying to look decades younger. Her ample bosom was squeezed into a stretchy black top, and layers of gold chains around her neck almost disappeared into her cleavage. She wore leopard-skin pants, also too tight, and her blue toenails peeked out of gold mules. She sat down across from me, next to Kit, who looked elegant in a navy cropped jacket over a simple white blouse. They could have been candidates on a makeover show, Deanna the *before* and Kit the winning *after*.

She got right down to business, telling me she had her home listed and was not happy with her realty company, Harris-Wiggins. I was surprised, since they were definitely among the top ones in the area, with signs everywhere. She assured me, however, that she was ready to switch agents, and she'd love me to take a look at the place.

"Val just closed a million-dollar deal," Kit said.

Deanna's blue eyes widened, and she ran a hand through her dark-blond hair (unfortunately, she had the same problem as me—her hair didn't quite fall back into place, and I resisted the urge to lean across the table and pat it down for her).

We chatted aimlessly through our lunch (shrimp salad for Kit, small tenderloins for Deanna and me), and as we were waiting for the check, Kit finally broached the subject of Wendell Fullerton.

"It's a nightmare," Deanna said, several heavy, gold bracelets jangling on her wrist as she waved her hand in front of her face, as if she were having either a hot flash or a heart attack.

"I know," Kit agreed. "You knew Christine well, didn't you?"

Deanna nodded. "Yes, we were really close."

I pictured Christine as she had appeared in the article on the Internet, and merely going by age and appearance, she and the flashy Deanna seemed an odd couple.

"You really liked her?" Kit asked.

"Oh, I loved Chris. It's Wendell I can't take."

"I heard somewhere they were planning to start a family," Kit said.

Again Deanna waved her hand, and the bracelets jangled some more. "Yeah, well, that would have made a change for him. He's much better at breaking up families than starting them."

"You don't mean—"

"I mean he's a hound dog."

Her reference made me think of Elvis Presley in a gold jacket, with his famous hip and leg gyrations.

"That bad?" Kit asked.

"Oh yes, that man was all over town, let me tell you." But she didn't. Instead, when the check was placed at our table, she snatched it out of the black leather folder it came in. "This is on me. Val, it was so nice to meet you. I want you to come to my house just as soon as you can. I need a sale, and quick. We have a house in Colorado, and we're thinking of spending more time there."

"Haskins Realty will do its best," I assured her.

"Haskins Realty," she purred. "I know Tom Haskins." She extracted an American Express Gold Card from her Louis Vuitton wallet.

"Oh?" I said tentatively. When people mentioned they knew Tom, I was never sure if that was good or bad.

"I just adore Tom. Tell him Deanna said hi. He'll know." She gave a saucy wink as a waiter silently glided by and removed the folder with the Amex card.

"I will." I laughed, a little relieved. "Give me your number, and I'll call you this afternoon with a time."

"Great," Deanna said, reciting her number. "And Val, do you have a card or something I can have?"

I glanced briefly at Kit before digging into my own purse and removing a business card. I almost didn't want to pass it on; it felt as heavy in my hand as Kit's Glock, but before I could think about it any longer, Deanna took it from me and held it up to her face.

"This is gonna bring me some good luck; I just know it." She dropped it into her purse. "Oh, and tell Tom to stop by too. I'd like to see him again."

CHAPTER FOURTEEN

It was about time one of my business cards brought someone luck, instead of death. At least that's how I now viewed them.

And then, it seemed, I had a bit of luck myself. But it had more to do with *Jim Gardner's* business card.

As I made my way to my car after lunch with Kit and Deanna, I took my phone off *silent* and also noticed I had two missed calls, both from Culotta. Without thinking, I started to call him back, but then I did stop to think, given his parting comment the other night. I liked how we'd left off, so decided to wait.

Then I checked my text messages. An inane one from Perry about not being able to wait until he and T. L. could have lunch with me. He ended his text with an *OMG, this is so exciting.*

The other message was from Culotta and was anything *but* inane. *Hit pay dirt with Jim Gardner's card. Found him. Call me.*

For some reason, that made me feel like the killer had been caught, and I was out of danger. Immense relief coursed through me.

I whipped around to catch Kit before she could drive out of the parking lot, but it was too late. So I climbed into my own car, started it and then the air conditioning, and called her.

"Whassup, Valley Girl? Miss me already? What did you think of Deanna?"

"Always. And Deanna seemed nice. But Kit, they got him."

"Who got who?"

"Whom."

"Really? You're correcting grammar? Now?"

"Sorry," I said quickly, feeling mean. It had been an automatic response that I'd often thrown at Emily when she was growing up and her grammar slipped (my habit stemmed from my own mother, who considered correcting grammar one of her hobbies). Besides, Kit was the last person who needed her English usage corrected. "Jim Gardner! Culotta said he got him!"

"And just when did you talk to Culotta? I just left you—"

"He texted me. I just saw it. Do you know what that means?"

"Not sure—"

"It means I'm going to live. It means I don't need your gun. No one is going to kill me."

"Hold on there, Bette Davis. So you're saying Gardner was the murderer? And how did they catch him?"

Her questions made me realize I'd read entirely too much into Culotta's brief text. But I wasn't ready to resume my worry mode. "Well, I don't have all the details yet. I have to call Dennis first. But I'll let you know."

As good as his text had sounded, however, I felt reluctant to call him. Not only for the same personal reasons I'd already had, but now because I was afraid he might tell me they'd found Gardner but not necessarily the murderer. I didn't want to lose my euphoria.

So I pulled out of the parking lot and headed to the office.

**

I shouldn't have been surprised to see Dennis Culotta's car parked right in front of the office door. But I was. At least judging from the slight tremor in my hands.

I pulled into the first spot I came to, rather than the empty one next to his. In case he was sitting in his car, I wanted at least a few moments to compose myself. Plus, I didn't want to have to open the door of my SUV and make an awkward exit that he might see. When *would* car manufacturers—or tight-skirt designers—figure out a solution? It would be nice to climb out of a vehicle without looking like I was about to give birth to triplets.

By the time I clumsily disembarked—with no one watching, thank you very much—and headed up the sidewalk toward the office, I saw him already walking my way.

"It's too hot to talk out here," he said. "Wanna go in your office, or grab lunch somewhere?"

"I've had lunch. I want to know about Jim Gardner." *Please tell me he's behind bars*, I willed him to say.

But Culotta had yet to do what I willed, and now was no exception. "I said it's too hot to talk here. Your office, then? Since *you* aren't hungry. Never mind that I'm starving." He gave his irresistible grin, the one that started in his blue eyes and encompassed the lips most women would kill to kiss.

"Fine. Let's get you something to eat." *And the good news faster*, I thought. "I'll follow you."

"You can ride—"

But I'd already turned and was heading toward my vehicle.

I felt annoyed when he turned into Fuddruckers. For two reasons. It was one of my favorite eating places (I'd first been introduced when visiting my cousin years earlier in Houston), and I wasn't hungry. What a waste.

But also, it didn't seem the quickest or quietest route to sitting across the table from Dennis and looking into, er, listening to him explain about Jim Gardner's business card and whereabouts.

Nevertheless, I met him at the front door and made my way to an empty table while he went through the line building his burger. And, it turned out, procuring a large order of fries and a huge chocolate shake. He also had a large Diet Coke for me. So he remembered my favorite fountain drink. Big deal.

I was determined not to beg for information, but this guy was about as bad as Perry, albeit in a more manly way. So I watched as he placed a napkin over his lap; grabbed his burger, with its onions and tomatoes slipping out all around the edges; and pulled it toward his mouth.

Then I couldn't stand it any longer. "Would you please tell me about James Gardner and his business card?"

He bit into his burger and took his time chewing and swallowing. Then he set it down and sighed. "I didn't mean to get your hopes up. We haven't actually located James Gardner in the flesh."

I groaned. So why was I watching him devour a burger? And wishing I'd put some fresh lipstick on in my car when I had the chance?

"Do you think he's the perp?" I asked, biting my bottom lip and loving being in the law loop. Or any loop that contained Dennis Culotta.

"I think there's a good chance he's the serial killer, yes." He nodded slowly and took a huge bite of his burger. A tiny crumb appeared on his cheek, but before I could reach across and flick it away, he ran a napkin across his face.

"You think he's our guy?" It was important to me for Culotta to confirm this.

"He's a person of interest." He picked up a French fry and chewed on one end.

"But you haven't caught him yet?" I couldn't hide my dismay.

"First of all, James Gardner might be guilty of nothing more than being a liar or scammer. Second of all, we've made—I've made—good progress in *catching him*, as you say."

"How so?"

"All those phone numbers on his card? The ones that were disconnected? I mixed 'em up a bit—you know, put the local exchange of one with the last four numbers of the other—and voilà!"

"Voilà, you found him? That simple?"

"Okay, I had a little help. Police stuff. Too complicated to explain now. But I've got some men staked out where I think he's living. We'll want you to do an ID, of course, so be prepared to come in whenever—"

"And you couldn't tell me this in ten seconds or less on the sidewalk in front of my office? I'm a busy person, you know. I'm *not* just sitting around waiting for your call, I mean, waiting for you to—"

"Yeah, so busy I hear you haven't been in to see Tina again." He grabbed a handful of fries, and I reached over and took one myself.

At the mention of the beautiful Tina, I wondered if he'd ever brought her to Fuddruckers; then I reminded myself that this was hardly a damn date. "Well, if you're about to bring him in, why do I have to—"

"We *haven't* brought him in yet."

"Well, *I* don't do the sketching. If you think you got a lousy sketch, maybe you oughta blame Tina—"

"Valerie, Valerie." He gulped the last of his hamburger and shoved his chair back. "Let's go do it. Now."

Well, I wanted James Gardner caught as much as—no, more than—anyone else, and so I decided to cease and desist with the cat-and-mouse game I was so poor at, anyway. "Fine." I scooted my own chair back before he had a chance to help me.

***

My second encounter with the sketch artist (as I preferred to call her) was frustrating. It was warm and muggy inside the police station, the air conditioner obviously straining to cool things down. I noticed that most of the guys not in uniform, including Culotta, had loosened their ties and rolled up their sleeves. The sketch artist, who was wearing a tight linen skirt (totally free of wrinkles) and a pink sweater with the sleeves rolled up (wool, for Pete's sake), looked as cool as if it were snowing outside. She had her hair knotted casually at the back of her head, and I stared in awe at the tendrils that framed her face.

I resisted rolling my eyes as she set to work, asking me the same questions about Jim Gardner's appearance. When she was done, I was prepared for our second collaboration to produce a replica of the first sketch. However, when she printed it and held it up against the first one, I could see they actually looked quite different.

"I think this one is probably more accurate." She smiled as Culotta appeared and snatched both sketches from her. I wanted to ask her how she could possibly know that, but I was thrown off when she added, "Good job, Valerie."

Feeling like a kid who'd just received a gold star from a teacher, I raced out of the station, skipping the office and returning instead to the sanctuary of my apartment. Then I began to clean it. Long overdue, anyway.

When my marriage to David was falling apart—when I could no longer hide it—cleaning became the outlet for my depression. I even let my cleaning lady go. I'd always thought I needed one for the Big House. And I did, until my life had shrunk from a million activities to just staying home feeling embarrassed and sorry for myself. I knew everyone figured I was the last to know about David's serial infidelities, but the truth was, I'd probably always known. But once they were *out there*, thanks to his ever-more-daring escapades, I remained inside—often cleaning, hunting down every speck of dust in the house and scrubbing the counters and floors alike until my nails were obliterated.

It didn't take me nearly as long to clean my apartment, and the adrenaline that energized me was coming from fear, not anger. But still, when I climbed between my clean sheets at bedtime, there was a moment or two when all I thought about was the peaceful, contented pleasure only clean sheets can bring.

And then my phone rang.

CHAPTER FIFTEEN

A re you okay?" It was Culotta.

"I'm fine. Tell me what happened."

I heard him sigh, and I pictured him scratching the back of his head, something he did whenever he wasn't sure what to say next.

"Just tell me."

"He never showed. I've still got a couple of guys at his house. But I figure he made us and skipped."

"Oh." I scratched the back of my own head. "That's not good, right?"

"We don't even know if he's the guy we want. The thing is—"

"He's out there somewhere. And he knows where I live."

I heard a laugh and wasn't sure if it was genuine or if he was trying to make me feel better. "Why don't you go and stay with Kit for a couple of days? Just till we get this guy and clear him."

Okay, this definitely was not making me feel better. "I'm fine here. Really. I have a gun and—"

"Whoa. You have a gun? Do you have a permit to go with it?"

"Of course," I lied. How stupid of me to mention the Glock.

"Okay. Good. But please, do me a favor. Be alert and careful. I don't think you are in any danger. It doesn't appear, so far, that you are even his target."

"Right."

"But just be careful. Promise?"

"Promise."

"Okay, I gotta go." He broke the spell, and I imagined him driving over to Tina's fabulous condo, somewhere on water, the two of them locked in each other's arms.

"Bye," I said, and hung up.

***

When I got to the office the next day, Perry was already at his desk, wearing a purple shirt and yellow bow tie with white polka dots. "Val, before you say anything, let me tell you what the plan is. We're meeting T. L. at Buster Brown's for lunch. It's her favorite place. She'll be there at twelve thirty, so we can't be late. We're lucky she can get away. Friday is a busy day at the library, and of course she runs that whole place. Like clockwork, I might add."

I sincerely doubted Perry even went to a library, much less knew anything about the workings of such an institution. "Buster Brown's?" I said. It was a fun eatery, the last place I would have pictured T. L. enjoying.

"Are you planning to wear that?" He scanned me from the top of my head down to my shoes.

"No. I was planning to have Ralph Lauren whip something up on his sewing machine." *Was he kidding?*

We arrived at Buster Brown's at twelve thirty on the dot. Perry had insisted on driving, and even though we got there fifteen minutes early, it took him that long to find a suitable parking spot for his Corvette. Suitable meaning he took up almost two spaces. I smiled as I recalled the time he came into the office, indignant about a note he'd found on his windshield: *Learn to park, idiot.* Apparently, he hadn't.

We went inside, with Perry panicking that we were now late. When he realized we weren't, his eyes lit up with excitement. We found a table at the back of the large room and took the laminated menus as big as billboards from the hostess.

While I studied my billboard (for such a large selection, there was little that wasn't fried), I heard Perry's ringtone. Johnny Cash singing "I Walk the Line" was barely audible over the rock music flooding the restaurant.

He answered it immediately. Elbows on the table, he pressed the phone to one ear while plugging the other with an index finger. "Hmm. Yes. No problem. Yes, we can wait. Yes, Valerie is with me. Okay; drive carefully. Oh, and parking is a bitch. You'll have to drive around a bit." He smiled into his phone as he ended the call. "That was T. L."

"No kidding." I finally spotted a grilled-chicken salad in tiny print at the bottom of the menu.

"She's running late. Had a problem at the library."

"Really?" I turned the menu over and perused the twenty million fruity drinks offered. "Someone trying to use a fake library card?"

"She didn't say. Probably a confidential matter. She said we should order." Poor Perry; he looked disappointed, but I'd already decided that since I was here, I might as well partake of the jumbo deep-fried shrimp that came with fries.

Our waiter, who was heavily into goth, hovered nearby, and I waved him over. I tried not to look at the multiple piercings on his face, but I did admire the way he'd applied his eyeliner.

Twenty minutes later our food arrived. Perry had the grilled chicken, and he ate slowly, his eyes watching the door. "Gee, I hope she can make it."

"Don't worry, Perry. If she can't get away, we can do this another time." I took a sip of my mango-strawberry slush. It had seemed silly to order a Diet Coke.

"Darn it." He sounded disappointed, like a kid at the circus who'd just found out the clowns were on strike.

Twenty minutes later Perry's phone rang again, and he gave me a look that implied *what are you gonna do?* What he said into his phone was, "Yes, yes, please don't worry about it; no, we'll definitely do it again; really, you are so sweet." He sadly shut off his phone. "She can't get away. Big emergency at the library."

"Ah." I drained the remains of my slush through my straw. "Did she discover a book with two pages stuck together?"

"Why are you so mean, Val?" He sighed, looking disappointed in me.

"Sorry."

Now I was disappointed in me too.

***

Back at my desk forty minutes later, I called Deanna Finkelmeyer, and we agreed to meet at her house on Windjammer Drive at four. She asked if I was bringing Tom with me, but I steered her in another direction. Tom rarely made house calls.

Next, I called Kit and told her about my conversation with Culotta the night before. I glossed over the fact that Jim Gardner was officially a person of interest and out there somewhere on the loose, since I knew she'd bug me to move to her house.

"How'd Culotta find him, anyway?" she asked.

"Police stuff. Plus, he played around with the telephone numbers."

"Hmm. Hard to believe. So, Jim Gardner doesn't live in Utah," she added, more to herself than to me.

"That's what the police are thinking."

She changed the subject abruptly. "Larry and I are taking Wendell Fullerton to dinner tonight. You should come with us."

"Wendell Fullerton?"

"Right. Hubby of Christine. Victim number three?"

I hated the way she said it, making it somehow sound like a live game of Clue. Next we'd stumble across Colonel Mustard in the dining room with a dagger. "Whose idea was that?"

"I suggested it. Ya know, to support him and all that crap. Plus, it'll be good to get his perspective on things. Really, you should come with us."

"No, thank you. I'm meeting Deanna Finkelmeyer at four, and then I'd like to get home and catch up on paperwork. I've got a mountain of work to do."

"Okay, I'll call you when we get home if there's anything good to report."

"Go easy on him, Kitty Kat."

***

Deanna Finkelmeyer lived in a sprawling white colonial. A Realtor's dream. It looked as if a decorator had just finished setting the rooms for a photo shoot. All soft, beige leather furniture and shades-of-mocha accessories.

"Your home is beautiful," I said, snapping pictures with my phone.

Deanna was wearing a loose tiger-skin-print blouse over black leather pants, way too tight and way too rock-and-roll. "Thanks." She looked pleased at the compliment. "I did all the décor myself." She winked at me and smiled. "Hard to believe, eh?"

"Not a bit," I said, thinking exactly that.

"I have a degree in design from The Illinois Institute of Art. You've heard of them?"

"Of course." I loved working with their graduates, and this was no exception.

"So, how much do you think we can get for this little shack?"

"Two million, easy. We'll start at two million five."

Deanna looked satisfied, and later, after she'd given me a tour and I'd taken more pictures, she hugged me at the front door. I promised to come back with signs the next day.

"Tell Tom hi," were her parting words.

***

"Deanna Finkelmeyer signed a contract," I told Tom. I was back in my car and excited about the Finkelmeyer house.

"Good deal."

"She specifically told me to tell you hi, by the way. In fact she really wanted you to come with me to view her house. You obviously know her."

"Hmm," Tom said. "What's the house like?"

"Oh, it's pretty fabulous. So, you are old friends?"

"Something like that."

"She said she graduated from The Illinois Institute of Art. Pretty impressive."

I heard Tom break out in a guffaw. "That's a good one."

"Hard to believe, really."

"You bought it? She no more graduated from the Institute than Perry was chosen a Rhodes Scholar. When I knew her, she was working at a run-down Indian casino in Southern Illinois. But she was good; I'll give her that."

"I'm surprised."

"She's a con, Val."

"No, I mean the part about you being in a run-down Indian casino."

"Yeah, we all have a few things we'd rather forget. What does she look like these days?"

"She's colorful."

"That's the word, all right, Pankowski. Colorful."

***

I stopped at the office before returning home. Billie's car was the only one parked in front of the building.

"Bill, it's me," I said, unlocking the front door.

"Hey, Val," she said from her desk. "How'd it go with Deanna?"

"Good. She's quite the personality. I like her." Billie got up and walked slowly toward me as I collected some files from my desk drawer. "She knows Tom," I said idly.

"No doubt. She's got quite a history. Her last husband is in prison for fraud—"

"Wait. *Last* husband? How long has she been married to the present one?"

"About eighteen months."

I wondered why Kit hadn't mentioned this, and at the same time, why it seemed important.

"Well, I like her," I said, as if the fact that a short marriage was a reason to *not* like a person. I gathered up some more paperwork and shoved it into an empty manila folder.

Billie slumped down into my visitor's chair. "So tell me, how did lunch go with Perry and Miss Sears Catalog Circa 1960?"

"She didn't show; apparently, there was a shakedown at the library."

"Interesting," was all Billie said, as I closed my desk drawer and waved good-bye.

***

I stopped at the deli close to my apartment on the way home and bought an Italian beef sandwich. Somehow, my enormous fried lunch had left me hungry. I also stopped at the liquor store and bought two bottles of cheap pinot.

121

Armed with my food, drink, and stack of paperwork, I was ready to slip into my pj's and spend the evening on my couch catching up on my job. I was feeling confident I could make a quick sale on the Finkelmeyer house.

Once inside my apartment, I put the wine in the fridge and the Italian beef on the kitchen counter. In my bedroom, I unbuttoned my blouse and opened the top drawer of my dresser to locate my pj's. The contents of the drawer, with its two stacks of clothes (T-shirts on one side and nightwear on the other) were slightly disheveled. Like I'd dug into the bottom layer of each stack. I pulled out what I was looking for.

Next, I went to my closet and slid the mirrored door to one side. All the clothes on hangers had been pushed to the right, leaving a big gap between the hangers and a plastic shoe rack. I tried to remember if I'd moved the hangers myself, looking for stray shoes at the bottom of the closet. I couldn't remember. I'd left in a hurry that morning.

An uneasy feeling washed over me. A little unsteady, I left the bedroom and entered my tiny living room, glancing around, taking everything in. Nothing seemed disturbed. Magazines were in a pile on the coffee table, cushions on the couch in their proper place. CDs stacked where they should be.

I shrugged. I was getting paranoid, and the smell of the Italian beef was calling my name. I walked into the kitchen, took a bottle of the pinot out of the fridge, and pulled open the kitchen drawer that housed all sorts of junk, including the corkscrew.

I stopped. All the various utensils had been pushed to the back of the deep drawer. As if a hand had shoved them. Had I done that? It was entirely possible. Who remembers stuff like that? Or had I maybe just closed the drawer too hard, causing the contents to shift?

Shaking my head, I removed the cork from the bottle and poured some wine into a new wineglass I'd bought at Target. Standing in my kitchen entrance, I surveyed the living room area again. One of the advantages of a small apartment is that it's easy to take it all in at a glance.

After a few more sips, the uneasy feeling started to leave me. I turned toward the counter to open the wrapped sandwich, touching the inside contents with my fingertip to determine if it needed a blast from the microwave. It did.

While I waited out the thirty seconds I'd punched into the timer, I noticed the calendar lying on the counter next to the coffeepot. Its six-inch square pages were held together with curly wire. As you flipped each page over, the top half revealed a different scene from New York, one for each month. The bottom half held a square the size of a postage stamp for each day of the month. When I'd left that morning, the picture was of the Brooklyn Bridge. But now a close-up of the Statue of Liberty's face filled the top half of the calendar. It was a gorgeous picture, showing her strong features in detail, but I wasn't ready for it. We still had fifteen days of the Brooklyn Bridge to go before we progressed to Lady Liberty.

There was no doubt about it. Someone had been in my apartment.

CHAPTER SIXTEEN

I remained standing in place for a few seconds, although it felt like an hour, a creeping fear paralyzing me. *Why* hadn't I listened to everyone? Why hadn't they *made* me listen? Dennis was a cop, for Pete's sake. He should have known. And Kit was my best friend. She should have *insisted* I leave. She should have *made* me move in with her and Larry.

For one crazy second I wondered if Kit or Dennis had staged this intrusion, just to scare me into staying somewhere else. It was wishful thinking, I knew, but it would have worked.

I couldn't get out fast enough, as soon as I could get my legs to move.

I grabbed my purse, only because it was on my way out the door, and then I moved faster than my ex chasing a new skirt.

I called Dennis first, as soon as I was safely in my car and on my way to Kit's.

"Culotta," I heard him answer his phone, and I felt better—safer—already.

"Someone's been in my apartment. *In* my apartment. It wasn't you, was it?"

"Whoa. Valerie?"

"Yes, of course." *How many women did he* have *with potential intruders? This was Downers Grove, not Miami. Or even Chicago.*

"What do you mean, have I been to your apartment? Of course—"

"No, I mean when I wasn't there? Did you go through my stuff, try to scare me—"

"Val, slow down. Make sense. And if you're driving, pull over. You're in no condition to drive; do you hear yourself?"

"Of course I hear myself. I'm scared, not deaf." But I swung my Lexus into a Burger King that materialized as if ordered up by Culotta. And I congratulated myself at how easily I parked it in a much smaller space than Perry required for his Corvette. SUV and all. "Okay, I'm parked now. *Did* you try to make it look like someone broke into my apartment? To make me move out?"

"No, I did not. But maybe I should have . . . I really didn't think you were in danger." I'd never heard him sound so . . . downright humbled by his own lapse in judgment.

I would have said *I told you so*, but I hadn't. I'd been scared, but obviously hadn't *really* thought I was in danger, or I would have moved out.

" . . . are you listening?" I heard him break through my scattered thoughts.

"What? No, come again."

"I said, get to the station right now. Do you think you're being followed?"

I glanced over one shoulder and then the other. It was growing dark, which didn't help a thing, my vision or my fear. I saw a couple of teenagers get out of the car that had just pulled in next to me, but other than that, just a bunch of empty vehicles. "No, I don't think so. But I'm not coming to the station; I'm going to Kit's. Can you meet me at my apartment in the morning, so I can get some things?"

"Sure. We'll check it out right now—I'm already on my way. I'll be back there at eight tomorrow morning."

"So will I. And Dennis?"

"Yeah?"

"Thanks."

"Just doin' my job."

Of course he was. I hit the button to end the call, and put my car in reverse. As if to spite him, I started to drive before I got Kit on the phone.

"You win," I greeted her.

"What? Val?"

"Why is everyone having so much trouble recognizing my voice? Sheesh."

"No, I knew it was you. But I don't know what you're talking—"

"Got a toothbrush I can borrow?"

***

Kit not only had a toothbrush I could borrow, but also silk pajamas with matching robe and slippers, and a room with a view of her backyard, the water in the pool softly illuminated by pale-blue lights. I immediately wondered why I'd balked at going there.

After we'd caught up over a glass of wine, she helped me settle into "my" room—across the hall from Sam's-room-turned-Kit's-office, which was right next door to what was now "my" bathroom. It was pitch-dark, but the twinkling lights scattered around their pool area and strung on the backyard trees made me feel I was in a fancy hotel.

And better than chocolate on my pillow, Kit had left a Waterford candy dish full of dark, milk, and white chocolates on the bedside table—right next to a stack of tempting books, with the TV remote on top.

126

I grabbed the remote and tuned in to a *Law & Order* episode. Maybe I'd visit her copy of *The Great Gatsby* tomorrow night. I remembered having read and liked it years earlier.

But even before I could drift off—which usually takes ten minutes, tops (it's later in the night that I typically awake and have trouble getting back to sleep)—I heard Kit chewing Larry out about something. I felt bad, although I didn't know which one of them to feel bad for. Was she picking on him, or had he done—or not done—something he deserved to be scolded about? Either way, it upset my newfound sense of peace.

I awoke the next morning to the same sounds, this time coming from the kitchen. It made me so uncomfortable, I didn't go down for the cup of coffee I would have preferred to start out with.

Instead, I went ahead and got cleaned up (though not dressed; I'd need Kit to dig for something that was loose on her). By the time I got out of the shower and blow-dried my hair, I heard only quiet from downstairs.

I hurried to the kitchen, knowing I'd have to gulp down my coffee while getting dressed so that I could meet Culotta on time. I felt lost with so many of my things still back at my apartment, from my paperwork to my own underwear (cotton Jockey instead of silky Calvin Klein that Kit would likely offer up, but at least they fit me).

I barely had a foot in the kitchen doorway when Kit spoke, skipping the *good morning* or *how'd you sleep* I'd been expecting. "Ya know, Val, I've been thinking. Your James Gardner was late meeting you that night on purpose."

"Yeah? And why do you say that?"

Since it was obvious she was too engrossed in her thoughts to do it, I grabbed a cup from the rack and poured myself some coffee. I sipped the hot magic potion carefully and felt myself grow alert. I knew it had more to do with Pavlov's law than any real properties of the caffeine. But hey, whatever works.

"Think about it. Obviously, Daphne was what—sorry, who—he was after, not the house. So he had to make sure she'd return home, thinking the showing was over. Then he could meet her."

"Okaaaay." I took another drink as I tried to follow Kit's thinking. "If it was only Daphne he was after, and not me, then how do you explain my intruder last night?"

"Do you think your intruder was James Gardner? Or do you think maybe it was Culotta, to force your hand, get you to the safety of our house?"

"That's ludicrous, Kit." Even though I'd had the same thought, now that Kit said it aloud, I realized how ridiculous it sounded.

"I suppose."

"Speaking of Culotta, I gotta meet him at my apartment . . ." I peered at Kit's microwave clock. "Yikes. In a half hour. Do you have anything I can wear? Anything big enough?"

"Oh yeah, like you need a tent." She shook her head in mock disgust. "Follow me."

In twenty minutes I was out the door, looking and feeling almost as elegant as Kit in my borrowed black leggings and camo-print silk blouse from Neiman Marcus that she hadn't even worn yet. No one could ever question Kit's generous nature—if only she'd lay off my friend Larry.

***

I'd never been so happy to see Dennis Culotta's car as when I saw it in my parking lot that morning. Still, I felt the fight-or-flight instinct deposit butterflies in my stomach as I made my way into the building and up to my apartment.

I didn't know if I was relieved or disappointed that there was no yellow crime-scene tape blocking my entrance. The door was ajar, but I played it safe—and dramatic. I called out, "Dennis? Are you in there?"

"Yeah, c'mon in," he called back. I felt embarrassed as I realized by the sound of his voice that he was back in my bedroom or bathroom. Was my bed made? Did I have underwear lying around on the floor? Toothpaste in the sink? How *had* I left it, only about fifteen hours earlier? I couldn't remember.

As I made my way through my apartment, which took about half a minute, I saw nothing amiss—unless you counted the strange man in my kitchen swirling a brush over the cabinets, leaving powdery marks as he moved along.

"There's no sign of forced entry," Culotta greeted me as he emerged from the bedroom. "Can you tell if anything's missing?"

I gave a sideways glance toward the man in my kitchen, who hadn't even acknowledged me.

"Joe Printer," Culotta said. "He's dusting for prints."

"Wait." I went closer to him, out of earshot of the other man. "Your fingerprint guy is named Printer?"

Culotta looked up from his notebook. "Yeah. So?"

"Nothing. Hey, maybe the intruder's name is Joe Intruder?" I thought it was amusing, but judging from his pained expression, I could see he found it less so.

"Very funny," he said, but he wasn't laughing. "Would you just take a good look around and tell me if anything's missing."

"I didn't notice anything last night." Of course checking for missing items had been the last thing on my mind when I'd grabbed my purse and fled the building as if it were on fire. I suspected Culotta realized this.

"Please make sure. Take your time and look carefully."

"Okay." I complied and slowly started an inspection of my small home.

Joe Printer stood and shook his head as I reached to open a kitchen cabinet. "Don't touch anything; we don't need any more prints."

I pulled my hand back, and Joe Printer obliged by slowly opening the door for me, his hands covered in blue rubber gloves. The cabinet was empty, but only because of my lack of grocery shopping, not because an intruder had been there looking for something to eat.

"Who else has a key to your apartment?" Culotta asked. He stayed in the doorway of the tiny kitchen, which was good, because three people were three too many in the small space.

"Dennis, no one I *know* would come in here without my knowledge." I was offended for whomever I'd given a copy of my key to. And just who *was* that? I'd have to think.

But first, I continued through my apartment, opening doors and drawers using the tissue Joe had handed me as if I were about to sneeze. In the bedroom I could see that he'd left a dusty white trail on the furniture.

"I can't see that anything's missing. It's not like I had any jewelry hidden or anything." I paused and thought for a moment. "The only thing of real value, and only to me, is my client list."

I made my way to the coffee table in the living room for the manila folder of paperwork and the notebook that held my client list. Only the notebook wasn't there. "Hmm . . . I'm sure I had it with this folder. It's important stuff."

"Just what is your client list? Can't anyone get that information off MLS or something?" Culotta didn't seem too worked up about my list being missing. But I didn't appear to have anything else to report, so he'd have to settle.

"It's actually a wish list, *potential* clients, and a lot of information I've gleaned about them that I'm sure they'd rather not even *I* know, let alone whatever nut must have taken it."

"Like what?"

"Like . . ." This was almost embarrassing. " . . . just little things about them, what they like, what their moving plans might be, what I think might inspire them to change houses . . ."

"Sounds creepy."

I didn't like his condescending smile or the way he dismissed the seriousness of that information floating around town. But I *was* glad to see he was willing to drop the subject. Now, if only that notebook would turn up at my office, I could perhaps have a good day befitting my fabulous outfit.

Back in the bedroom, I packed a bag with some clothes, shoes, and cosmetics to take to Kit's. I planned to drop them off at her house before going to the office. Culotta stood in the doorway, watching me closely.

"So there's nothing missing? Seems odd someone would break in and not take anything—"

"Except my client list. It's very important."

"Yeah, so you said." He'd taken out his own little notebook and was writing something down.

I zipped the bag closed and took a look around the room. And then a chilling thought hit me. I quickly opened the drawer of the bedside table. "The gun." I turned toward Culotta, who was still writing. "The gun, Dennis. It's gone. I keep it here and now . . . it's gone; oh crap, it's gone . . ."

He was suddenly behind me, pushing me gently aside and checking out the small drawer himself.

"And you're sure you put it here?"

"Well, of course. You think I'd drop it in the laundry basket, for Pete's sake? I never really wanted it in the first place, but Kit insisted. I doubt I'd even be able to shoot the damn thing. I've been putting it in my purse when I leave the house, but I guess I forgot to take it yesterday—"

"You *guess* you forgot—and what do you mean, *Kit* insisted?"

"Okay, okay, it's Kit's gun. And I forgot to take it with me yesterday morning. So shoot me."

He let my poor choice of words pass. "So every day you walk around with a gun in your purse, one that isn't even yours, one that you don't think you can even shoot—"

"Is that important right now? The thing is, it's gone." My voice had risen, and I knew I sounded a little loony.

"Okay, calm down." He paused, and I waited for a lecture on proper gun ownership, but he probably figured *what's the use*. Instead, he said, "So, every morning you put the firearm in your purse?"

"Well, obviously not *every* morning."

He shook his head, wrote something else in his damn notebook, and then said, "Was it loaded?"

I nodded.

***

When I pulled in Kit's driveway a half hour later, I was surprised to see Larry's car.

I was even more surprised to hear raised voices coming from inside the house when I approached the front door. So rather than get in the middle of their argument, I turned around and tiptoed back to my car, as if they could hear me if I walked normally. It was like when I had a big van years ago and drove it into parking garages; I couldn't help but scrunch down over the steering wheel, as if that could keep my van roof from scraping a garage ceiling.

As I drove to work, I tried not to think about my makeup bag and the imminent melting of my solid foundation and boiling of my mascara remover. After parking my car, I cracked open my windows and then headed into the office.

Perry handed me a pink message slip that made walking into an argument between Kit and Larry sound like a relaxing afternoon in an overstuffed chair at Barnes & Noble.

"The Utah state police? What do you mean, the Utah state police want me to call them?" I slammed my file folder down on my desk, which somehow reminded me to look for my client list. I grabbed drawer handles on my desk and pulled at them, but no sign of my green spiral notebook, aka my client list, appeared. "Why do they want me to call them?"

"I wrote down everything they said." Perry motioned toward the pink paper in my hand and then returned to his computer, as if the success of Haskins Realty depended on it. I knew, however, he was more likely to be immersed in bow ties than houses.

I picked up the message slip I'd set on my desk. "Have you seen my green spiral notebook, Perry?"

"Your client list?"

"How did you know—"

"Because it says *Client List* on the cover. But it looks like it's more of a *potential* client list."

"Perry!" I said, before returning my attention to the message in my hand. *Call them about James Gardner*, I saw, scrawled in Perry's flowery handwriting. I almost expected to see it followed by a few smiley faces. But instead I read *ASAP*.

Crap.

***

Larry's car was still parked in the driveway when I returned. Of course I hadn't been away from their driveway long enough for my makeup to get warm, let alone damaged.

I hoped they were finished bickering, but I couldn't wait. I needed to bounce my concerns off someone before I phoned the Utah authorities. I knew Culotta should be my expert of choice, but somehow I trusted my friends more. They'd be sure to put *my* best interests first.

I stood at the front door, ready to ring the bell, but was stopped by their voices and the sound of my own name.

CHAPTER SEVENTEEN

What's going on?" I finally pushed open the unlocked front door. Kit and Larry were standing in the hallway, toe to toe, Larry's heavy golf bag slung over his shoulder. They stopped talking as soon as they saw me, like two kids caught in the planning stage of some dastardly act.

"I think you might be safer if you left town for a while." Larry came toward me, dropping his golf bag. Then he put an arm around my shoulder.

"That's just ridiculous." Now Kit approached and took the bag I was holding. "She's safer here, with us—"

"You mean with *you*—"

"I mean with both of us, where we can keep an eye on her—"

"All I'm saying is, she'd be better off in, say, Door County. With her mother—"

"Right; no one would ever find her in Wisconsin, and her ninety-year-old mother is a trained assassin—"

"All I'm saying is, I think she'd be safer far away from here right now."

"How would she be safer? There's a serial killer out there. You don't think he has a car, for crying out loud?"

"I just mean until this business is over—"

"*Stop.*" I extricated myself from Larry's arm and took a step back. "First of all, my mother is not ninety, and she'd kill you if she heard you say that. And second, I'm not going anywhere. If you guys are uncomfortable with me around here—"

"No, no, no," Larry said. "I'm just thinking of your—"

"And *of course* she's not ninety," Kit said. "That was a slight exaggeration to make this one come to his senses." She jerked a thumb in her husband's direction. "See, Larry? See what you've done now? You've gone and upset Val." She threw a menacing glance at him and then put an arm around me. "Honey, Larry is being overly dramatic, as usual. You're perfectly fine, and—"

"Me?" Larry looked astounded.

"I can go to a hotel," I said. "In fact, I *will* go to a hotel." Now I pulled free of Kit's arm.

"*Absolutely not,*" they said in unison.

"Larry, go play golf, for crying out loud." She returned her arm to my shoulder. "Val is not going anywhere. She's staying right here, and you and I will keep her safe."

Larry shrugged in defeat.

I gave him a kiss on the cheek before he left, and he hugged me hard.

"Whew," Kit said, as we heard his car back out of the driveway. "That man has some harebrained ideas. Now, here's what I'm thinking. What we need to do is borrow Roscoe for a few days."

"Who's Roscoe?" I knew full well who Roscoe was, but I hoped there was *another* Roscoe on the planet.

"You know Roscoe, the Larsons' Rottweiler. Larry loves him. We both do. Remember, we kept him over Christmas when they went skiing in Colorado?"

How could I forget Roscoe and his sabbatical at Kit's? It was a nightmare. He was as big as a horse, with an overly large head and two piercing brown eyes that seemed to focus on me the whole time. No matter how many times I tentatively tried to pet him, I always expected to lose a finger or, worse, a whole hand, even though Kit assured me he was really just a baby and completely harmless.

I particularly remembered one night when I was staying with them during the Christmas holidays. I could hear Roscoe's nasally breathing coming from outside my bedroom door, where he'd apparently set up camp. I was too terrified to make the trip across the hall to the bathroom. In the morning I'd called Kit from my cell phone in the bedroom, and she answered from the kitchen.

"Kit, could you get this dog to move? He's blocking my bedroom door."

She laughed, but I soon heard her outside the room cajoling the dog to come have the delicious pancakes she'd made just for him.

"Please, please, please don't bother the Larsons," I said now. "We don't need Roscoe." The truth was, I'd take my chances with a serial killer any day, rather than face down that Rottweiler.

"What can it hurt? He's a bab—"

"I know, I know, a hundred-pound baby that always looks like he wants to rip out my throat."

"That's ridiculous. He's completely harmless, and at least he'd watch over us. I'm telling you, he'd be good to have around. He's a baby, Val."

"Well, if he's such a baby, what good would he be?"

"He'd alert us—at night, when we're all asleep."

"Well, I'm scared of him—"

"And don't you think a murderer might be afraid too?"

"Hardly. Promise me you won't call the Larsons."

"I'll just see what Roscoe's up to."

"*What he's up to?* Is he working security at a Kanye West concert?"

"Let's at least see if he's free for the next few days."

"You've gone completely insane. You do realize he's a *dog*, not a freakin' secret agent, don't you?" I'd had enough of this conversation. "I'm going to work. I just stopped by to drop this stuff off."

So much for my asking her guidance about the Utah police. Her inane suggestion that we bring in Roscoe gave me just the excuse I needed to not deal with Utah right now. "Please don't interrupt your precious Roscoe's schedule," I said, as I headed toward the door. "We don't need him."

"And please, don't *you* go anywhere unusual without calling me first."

"Right. I'll text Roscoe." She and the dog had a thing going on; that much was obvious.

"And Val, don't forget you're armed, right?"

"Hmm," I mumbled, opening the front door and making my exit.

***

I waited until I was in my car and had driven out of Kit's street before I called her.

"About last night . . . ," I began.

"Yeah, tell me what Culotta said about it this morning."

"Well, for starters, my client list seems to have been stolen."

"Is that a big deal?"

"Yes. It has a lot of information I've accumulated for a long time about prospective and current clients; it'll be hard to replace it. I've had that list for—"

"Forget about it. I'll get all your info back in twenty minutes on the Internet. Probably more than you had in the first place. Why didn't you tell me you needed client stuff—"

I interrupted her egotistical rant, although the truth was, she probably did know, or at least could find out, as much information on local buyers as I could. "There's something else missing."

"What? You don't have anything worth stealing. Do you?" I could almost hear her mentally running through my home. "It's not something I gave you, is it? Wait—did they take that crystal Lalique vase I gave you two Christmases ago?"

"No." I didn't have the heart to tell her the precious vase was still in its box, stored on a top shelf in my bedroom closet. As lovely as it was, it looked out of place with my IKEA furniture. Luckily, she hadn't spent enough time in my apartment to realize it wasn't on display. "Something else."

"Well, Val, you don't really *have* anything else valuable—"

"The gun."

"How could that be? Don't you keep it in your purse?"

"Always. Generally. But I forgot it yesterday. First time ever. Promise. It was in my bedside table when I left for work yesterday. And . . . well, this morning it was gone."

"Oh, Val."

I thought she sounded so disappointed, I almost wanted to cry. "Sorry, Kit. I know you were trying—"

"So some lunatic has your—my—gun. Big deal. He's not the only criminal in Chicago with a gun. Don't worry about it."

I sighed with relief. Mainly because she'd taken it so well. "Thanks for being so understanding."

"At least the Lalique is safe."

***

When I returned to the office for the second time that day, I could see through the glass entrance that someone was sitting in my visitor's chair.

Shirley Herzog. I recognized her hair, which was again pulled back into a tight ponytail. She turned toward me when I walked through the door, and I saw that she was again wearing an oversize white T-shirt, this one featuring an

SPCA logo and an adorable mutt holding a US flag between its teeth. Her ensemble was completed by baggy shorts, and I was reminded what good legs she had.

"Hi," I said.

"Hi, yourself." She smiled. "I was in the area, and I thought I'd stop by and see if you've heard anything about . . . you know."

"No; nothing."

"Did the police ever locate that fiancé of Juanita's? The guy in the picture I gave you?"

"No, unfortunately." I glanced at Perry, who was typing furiously but not hiding the fact that he was listening to every word.

"Shirley, can I get you some coffee?" I hoped she would say no, since Billie was not in the office and it would mean I'd have to maneuver the cappuccino machine alone.

"Nah." She held up a Styrofoam cup I hadn't noticed before. "I'm good."

"Are you still looking at houses?" I sat down and needlessly straightened out a stack of files on my desk.

"Yeah, still got my eye on poor Juanita's place. But there's all kinds of red tape and stuff till her will is straightened out. But it's perfect for me."

"Ugh."

We both looked over at Perry, who was shuddering. "What's your problem?" Shirley asked him, her tone a little threatening.

"I could never live in a house where someone had been murdered."

I watched as Shirley crumpled the Styrofoam coffee cup in her hand. She looked angry. "Someone will, eventually, and it might as well be me. I'd take care of the place." She rose, reminding me how short she was.

I rose too. "If you need any help with anything, let me know." I watched her look around, the crumpled cup in her hand, and I took it from her. "Let me get rid of this for you."

"Thanks." She took a ring of keys from her pocket. "Take care."

Perry and I watched her leave the building and climb into an enormous black Ford truck.

As I headed toward the kitchen to throw away the crumpled cup, I noticed for the first time the logo printed on it: Cyral's, The World's Best Gyro.

Instead of disposing of it, I took a paper towel from the holder on the counter that held the cappuccino machine, as well as reams of printer paper, and carefully wrapped it around the cup.

"Wow, she's scary," Perry said, as I returned to my desk.

"No, she's really nice." But I wasn't so sure. "By the way, how long was she here before I arrived?"

Perry, who'd stopped his fake typing, leaned back in his chair and folded one arm across his chest, cradling his chin in the palm of the other hand. He studied me closely for a few seconds.

"Val, I'm loving this," he said.

"What? What are you loving?"

"This look." He waved his finger up and down in the direction of my torso. "The blouse is fabulous. Where did you get it?"

"Oh." I looked down at Kit's clothes. "It's old; it was stuffed in the back of my closet. And you didn't answer my question. How long was she here? And did she touch anything on my desk?"

Perry returned to his typing. "Didn't notice. I'm very busy."

"Right."

"But you really should shop at Neiman's more often, Val."

"How did you know it was from Neiman's?"

"Class. You can always tell."

***

When I got back to my new lodgings at the end of the day, Kit was busy in the kitchen. An enticing aroma filled the room, as I perched on a stool at the counter.

"Hiya." She placed a wineglass before me and poured from an open pinot bottle. "How was your day?"

"Are you and Larry speaking?" I took a sip.

"Phew." She waved a hand in the air. "Of course we are. Ya know, he's only thinking of *you*."

"Well, I know *that*." I felt annoyed that she would think otherwise. In her clever way, she made it seem like *I* was the problem, and she had to come to Larry's defense.

She took a sip of her own wine and then put on some rather chic black oven mitts. Next, she removed a large cast-iron dish from the oven and placed it on the counter.

"Wow," I said. One of the best arguments for staying at Kit's was the fabulous food I was about to enjoy. "That's some dish."

"I know. Le Creuset," she announced. "On sale this week at Sur La Table. You should stock up, Val."

"Yeah, right, because my Cheerios would taste so much better. What I meant, dummy, was what's inside it."

"Veal cannelloni."

"One of my favorites. When do we eat? I'm starved."

"Unfortunately, it's not for you. We're taking it over to Wendell Fullerton's."

"Huh?" I felt disappointed.

"Yes. I called him this afternoon and told him I'd bring something by for him to snack on."

"Hey, didn't you guys have dinner with him last night? I completely forgot."

"Yes, we did." She removed the mitts, carefully, like a surgeon who'd just performed heart surgery. "But your dear pal Larry has absolutely forbidden me to ask any questions. My shin looks like a hockey player's from him kicking me under the table."

"Where's Larry now?"

"Where is he always? On the golf course."

"Still?"

"Honey, it takes them forever. Why do you think they have the term *golf widow?* But we don't have time to chitchat. Even Larry comes home eventually, and we need to be gone. I can make a quick snack first, if you like. I have some goose-liver pâté, and I think there's a few shrimp left."

Before I could respond, I heard the sound I'd been dreading. Four feet padding across the tiled kitchen floor from the direction of the living room. I watched on full alert as the huge black-and-brown beast made its way slowly into the kitchen. He lifted his oversize head and stared up at me; his soulful eyes bore into mine.

"Kit," I whispered, "I thought I told you not to invite him." I pointed down at the Rottweiler, who was now seated comfortably at my feet, still staring at me.

"We were lucky," she whispered back. "The Larsons are going away for a few days, and they were delighted when I called. Just give him a chance. He's a baby."

"If you say *baby* one more time, I'll kill you. He's terrifying."

"Insulting him won't help. And he can hear every word you say." She'd removed the pâté from the fridge and set it on a plate with some homemade crackers.

"Even when we're whispering?"

"Oh, what a good, good boy," she said in a normal human tone, looking over the counter at the beast. "See? He's happy to be here."

I took a cracker from the plate she'd set before me and scraped some of the pâté across it, purposely keeping my eyes away from Roscoe.

But suddenly he leaped up. I had to admit, it was a graceful movement for such a large dog, and even though I was prepared to let him eat all the pâté he wanted, he instead ran through the kitchen and into the hall, stopping at the front door. His bark was low and growly, and I felt sorry for anyone on the other side.

"See?" Kit said. "He's been here only two minutes, and already he's protecting. There must be someone at the front door for you."

"Me? How do we know it's for me? It's more likely—"

"Oooh, let's hope it's Tom Haskins. He'll definitely be afraid of Roscoe."

"In your dreams. Tom won't be afraid of him, and besides why would Tom be here?"

"Let's find out." She walked slowly into the hallway. Although the doorbell had not rung, Roscoe now stood close to the front door, each bark louder than the last, lifting his two front legs off the ground.

"Good Roscoe." Kit took hold of his red leather collar. I was amazed at her bravery. I'd never really thought of Kit as an animal lover, and if I'd had to choose, I would have picked a Yorkie or Chihuahua for her, some breed in the designer category. Watching her now with Roscoe was impressive.

She opened the front door with her free hand, but there was no one outside. Roscoe's barking only increased, and when Kit let him go, he ran immediately to something lying in the middle of the driveway. He began a sloppy sniff and then looked up at us. It was a bouquet of flowers. Expensive. Roses and tulips.

Laughing, Kit bent down to retrieve the flowers encased in a woven basket.

"Val," she yelled, even though I was standing right behind her. "They're for you."

We looked up and down the street, but it was empty. So Roscoe and I followed her into the kitchen, where she put the bouquet on the counter.

"Good boy," Kit said to Roscoe. "What a clever dog you are." There was a white envelope stuffed into a plastic cardholder, and Kit ripped it out and handed it to me.

Carefully, I opened the tiny envelope. The first thing I noticed was that the delivery had come from Juanita's Flowers. Second was the message. *Enjoy your new home.*

I dropped the card on the counter and sat down on the stool. Before I knew it, I was stroking the top of Roscoe's head. He was looking up at me, and for the first time we made eye contact that seemed nonthreatening.

Kit put on her reading glasses, grabbed the card from me, and began studying it. "Is Juanita's shop still in business?"

"I would have thought not."

"Ya know what this means? The killer knows you've moved in here. Who did you tell?"

I removed my hand from Roscoe's big head. "No one, really. Billie, Perry. Not Tom yet, but I will. That's it. Oh, and of course Culotta knows."

"I suppose the killer could be following you. That would make sense—"

"*None of it makes sense.*"

"Okay, calm down. We just have to remember the killer knows you're here. Now aren't you happy we have Roscoe? Good boy!"

Crap!

We moved the flowers into Larry's office, out of sight, and I tucked the card into my purse.

Kit took Roscoe out to the patio, where he lay soaking up the late-afternoon sun. She placed a soft, plush toy—a red ladybug—in front of him. It was a sweet picture—such a large animal with a small, cuddly toy—until he lunged his head forward and half of the ladybug disappeared into his mouth. From the safety of the living room, I gave Roscoe a wave.

"That's his baby," Kit said. "Isn't it cute?"

"I thought *he* was the baby."

***

As we set off for Wendell Fullerton's house, I remembered Shirley's coffee cup still untouched in my purse.

"We need to make a stop first. At the police station. I have something to give Culotta."

"What?" she asked. Not so much a *what do you have to give him*, more of a *what the hell happened that you haven't shared with me*.

With the veal cannelloni safely packed in an insulated bag on the floor of the car, Kit changed direction, heading toward the police station, and I filled her in on Shirley Herzog's visit earlier.

"So, what are you thinking?" she asked. "Fingerprints on the cup?"

"Exactly. Or DNA. Even though I kinda like her, I was a little surprised at how angry she can get."

"Didn't you say there was a guy taking fingerprints at your apartment this morning?"

"Right. Joe Printer. He was dusting th—"

"Wait. The fingerprint guy's name is Joe Printer?"

"Yeah. So? And don't ask me if I think the intruder is called Joe Intruder."

"Of course not; that would be stupid."

When we pulled into the parking lot, I hoped Kit would stay in the car. Of course that didn't happen. And now, with the cup still wrapped in a paper towel in my purse, I felt *really* stupid. What was I thinking? The police had undoubtedly questioned Shirley, and if they deemed it necessary, they would have taken their own set of prints from her. Was I really just looking for an excuse to see Culotta?

"How do you know your dream man is here?" Kit asked, in that uncanny way she had of reading my thoughts.

"I don't. And it doesn't really matter. I can leave it with anyone."

Now I was hoping Culotta *wouldn't* be around, and for once my wish came true. The guy at the front desk, a grandfatherly type who looked a little too old to still be on the force, assured me he'd take the cup and have Detective Culotta call if he had any questions.

"Don't you have a plastic bag you can put it in?" Kit asked. "Val, if you'd told me about this before we left the house, I could have given you a Ziploc."

Gramps smiled at Kit. "We have our own bags, ma'am." He gently took the cup from me, being careful not to disturb the paper towel. "I'm sure Detective Culotta will be very grateful for your assistance."

We left a few minutes later, but not before Kit had instructed the elderly officer to be sure to lock the evidence up safely. He smiled at her with twinkly eyes, but for all I knew, he was going to dump the cup into the trash.

"Are you sure we're doing the right thing, visiting Wendell Fullerton?" I asked, once we were back in the car.

"Of course. Everyone loves my veal cannelloni."

"Not that. I mean stopping by. What did he say when you called?"

"He didn't. I got his voice mail. But I called his office, and they said he wasn't expected in for the next few days. Where else would he be?"

"Well, he could be anywhere."

"So if he's not home, we'll just have a look around."

"Kit, I don't think this is such a good idea."

"I'm not suggesting we break into his house. We'll just see what happens. Really, if he's not home, we'll leave."

"Promise?"

"Promise. We'll just go home and take Roscoe for a nice, long walk."

But it appeared that Wendell Fullerton was home. And not alone. There was a black Ford truck parked next to his Jaguar.

The same truck I'd seen earlier that day.

CHAPTER EIGHTEEN

What the—" I stared at the truck, my mouth agape.

"What?" Kit asked.

"That's Shirley Herzog's truck. What's *she* doing here?"

"What are we waiting for?" Kit got out of the car, opened the back door, and took out her dish of veal cannelloni. "Let's go find out."

"Maybe it's not her truck," I said, as we started walking up the driveway.

"Is it or isn't it?" Kit stopped by the truck and awaited my answer.

"Well, I suppose there *are* a lot of black pickup trucks."

"Ya think?"

"But this *looks* like the one she had parked in front of the office today." While I was looking for any distinctive features on the truck that might call up a memory from the vehicle I'd seen earlier, the front door opened and out stepped my answer.

"What the—" This time it was Shirley asking. "Why are you girls looking at my truck?" She was wearing a simple white cotton blouse, and below it cropped jeans. But I wasn't struck so much by her choice of clothing as I was by the pink lipstick and hint of mascara.

"I was just wondering if it *was* yours." I followed Kit up to the front porch, where she handed Wendell the veal cannelloni.

It seemed no one was eager to speak, not them and not us. Kit and I hoped they would say something first, something revealing. Like why the hell Shirley was visiting Wendell. What was *their* connection?

I, of course, broke the silence first. I think it's a birth defect of mine, feeling I have to fill any lull in a conversation with my babbling. "Shirley, I didn't know *you* knew Wendell."

He looked at me as if I were missing a body part. Like a brain. But then he softened his expression and extended his free hand. "I'm Wendell Fullerton. And you must be a friend of Kit's."

I nodded, and we shook hands. "Valerie Pankowski," I said.

Then he gave Kit a one-armed hug. "Shirley was just leaving; why don't you ladies come in?"

I smiled at Shirley as she nodded her head, but it was a forced smile. I didn't want to offend her, but I also had grave suspicions about her. Not to mention I was a little afraid of her.

"How do you know Shirley Herzog?" Kit asked Wendell, as he closed the door behind us.

"Oh. She's a patient . . . let me put this in the fridge." He indicated the cannelloni. "Can I get you ladies something to drink?"

I wondered if he was telling the truth. Didn't dentists have one of those confidentiality agreements with patients? Could he just label her one like that? Then again, who cares who gets a cavity?

"Do you use makeup when you visit your dentist?" I whispered to Kit, as Wendell disappeared into the kitchen.

"Makeup? I use Xanax. Why?"

"Well, this is the third time I've seen Shirley, and she was scrubbed clean the other two times."

"Yeah, I don't usually make house calls to my dentist, either . . . oh yes, we'd love a drink," Kit's voice returned to normal as Wendell reappeared. Without consulting me, she accepted his offer, and we followed him down a long hallway and out to a patio as elegantly appointed as most people's living rooms. Lush foliage all but enveloped outdoor sofas and chairs, and yellow blooms of sunflowers and snapdragons adorned glass-topped tables.

I tried to remember from the gory photographs I'd been shown by Culotta exactly which chair his dead wife had been found in and eventually chose the one farthest from the patio door. His backyard seemed as isolated as a jungle, and as I sat on the edge of a chair, I was amazed to see Kit looking so relaxed.

"How are you doing, Wendell?" she asked, as he returned carrying a tray with three glasses of what looked like lemonade.

One thing Kit had been right about: Wendell was indeed handsome. If you liked a man tall, with classic features, square chin, blond hair expertly cut, and an athletic build underneath a white T-shirt and khaki shorts. Me? I preferred someone a little less perfect.

"It's tough, Kit. I'm not going to lie. I think I'm just in shock, and that's the only thing that allows me to put one foot in front of the other. I just miss her . . ." His voice cracked, and he lowered his head to his hands. I could see his shoulders shaking, but I was disappointed I couldn't see his face and check for *tears*. Was he the brokenhearted young widower—or a good actor?

Kit got up from her chair and joined him on the love seat. She patted his back and murmured words of sympathy, even though I felt certain she was more suspicious of him than I was. Wasn't she? Wasn't that why we were here? Then again, Kit would deliver veal cannelloni to a guy on death row.

While I was busy silently conversing with myself, Wendell had raised his head, and he and Kit had begun a real conversation. " . . . would want to kill Christine?" I heard Wendell asking. "And why was your business card at the scene?" He looked at me as if I'd put it there.

I let out an offended sigh. "That's what *I'd* like to know. I have no idea." Now my voice broke, and Kit was immediately by *my* side. I pushed away her attempt to hug me. I wanted to keep a clear view of Wendell when he answered my next question. "You told the police you were at the country club when your wife was murdered, but that's not true, is it?"

But Wendell was saved by the bell. My ringing telephone, to be exact. Okay, so the *Law & Order* theme song I have for my ringtone isn't exactly a bell. But Wendell took advantage of it to avoid my question without looking suspicious. We all three looked at my purse by my feet, the source of the ringing phone, until at last I reached in and plucked out the offender. I debated only briefly once I saw it was Culotta calling. Then I swiped to answer as I rose and went to the far end of the patio.

"This isn't a good time," I said, dispensing with any form of greeting.

"Oh, it isn't, is it? And I guess it's not a good time for you to return phone calls to the police in Utah, either, huh? Or even tell me they're trying to reach you? You don't think that's something I should know?"

"What? How did you—"

"Valerie, this is a murder investigation you're mired in. Why would you keep *anything* from me?"

"I wasn't keeping anything from you. For Pete's sake, I just got the message to call them this *morning*. I haven't had a *chance* to call them back."

"Oh, the house business is that brisk, is it?"

"It's not going to be brisk if you don't find out who's after me." My voice cracked again. I mustered control and continued. "Someone left me flowers."

"What? Speak louder."

"Someone left flowers for me in Kit's driveway. The card said *enjoy your new home.*" I said it so loudly, I could see Kit and Wendell turn their heads toward me. And I saw Kit raise a finger to her lips. I lowered my voice. "Whoever is doing all this knows where I am. We've got to catch him, Dennis."

"No, *we* do not have to catch him. *I* have to catch him. Now, about the Utah—"

"Yeah, what do they want?"

"It seems they received a bizarre delivery: a box of your business cards with Jim Gardner's name included. They tried to contact you, and when you didn't return their call, they phoned the Downers Grove police."

***

You'd think that getting my client list back would have turned my bad day good. Or at least better. And it might have, if not for the *way* I got it back.

The office was empty by the time Kit and I arrived there after leaving Wendell's. She stayed in the car while I ran inside to get some signs I needed for the next day's open house. And I saw it right away. A FedEx envelope on my desk. Always intriguing. I noted an unfamiliar return address as I pulled the cardboard zipper open.

Inside was my green spiral notebook. And nothing else.

I knew this was bad news. It was a message of some kind from *him*. Whoever he was. Or she. There was nothing in the notebook to identify it as mine, so whoever mailed it back to me must have taken it from my apartment.

I'd learned my lesson, so before running out to tell Kit, I phoned Culotta to let him know about my client list.

***

I knew I wouldn't sleep until I got my talk with Tom over with. So I got settled in the bed in Kit's guest room, nestled among the pillows and comforter in a fort as good as any Emily and David had ever made together. Then, feeling literally fortified, I placed a call to Tom. Doubtful that I'd find him home on a Saturday night, I mentally prepared the message I'd leave.

But the man himself answered, rather coldly, I noted. "Hello," he said. No *Hi, Kiddo* or *What's up, Pankowski?* Just *hello*. Then I remembered. His caller ID would tell him it was Kit calling him, and she wasn't one of his favorite people on a *good* day. And I knew this whole murder thing had him as upset as it did me. He probably forgot I was staying there.

"Tom, it's me."

"Oh yeah. You're at the dingbat's house."

"Tom, that's mean. She might be saving my life."

"Larry's probably capable of saving your life. Not Kit."

"Plus, we have Roscoe," I said.

Roscoe and I had come to sort of a truce. We both avoided eye contact, but I never really felt comfortable in Kit's house unless I knew exactly where the beast was. When I'd said good-night to Kit and Larry earlier, Roscoe was curled up on the sofa between them. Larry was stroking the top of the dog's giant head and reading aloud from a golf magazine, and Kit was explaining to him the intricate plot of a PBS murder mystery she was watching. Roscoe seemed bored by both activities and more interested in the rawhide bone he was slobbering over, so I felt safe in retreating to my bedroom.

"Roscoe?" Tom asked.

"Forget it. I'll explain later. I'm calling about the open house tomorrow."

"Yeah, I tried calling your apartment about that. Forgetting you weren't there. I don't think you should go."

"I'm not."

"Good. All settled, then. It's just too risky."

"But Tom . . ."

He gave me an unusually long time for a man who lacked patience as much as he did, but when I still didn't continue, he said, "What? But Tom what?"

"I quit." And I started to cry.

"Aw, Kiddo. Don't do this. Not over the phone. You aren't quitting."

"Yes, Tom, I—"

"No, you're scared shitless, and who wouldn't be? I am. For you, of course. But Culotta'll catch the guy. Or maybe you and your ditzy pal will." He snickered.

"Tom, I know I'll never, ever feel safe going into a house by myself again. I don't know if I'll even be able to move back to my apartment."

"Oh yeah, give yourself a few days with Kit, and I promise, you'll be dying to move back. Sorry, you'll be *eager* to move back home."

I prayed he was right.

"Just take some time off. Perry can take over your listings. I'll help him, see to it he doesn't do irreversible damage. You just catch up on your sleep and *Law & Order* shows." Again, a chuckle that wasn't mean, although it did make me feel defensive.

But I was too tired to defend. "Thanks, Tom."

"I think you should go to Door County and stay with your mom. Or why don't you visit Emily in LA?"

"LA in July? I don't think so."

"Door County in July is perfect."

"A little isolated for someone being chased by a murderer, don't you think?"

"You got a point there, Pankowski. Okay, stay with Kit and Larry. But don't go *anywhere* alone."

"Okay, Boss."

We hung up, and I felt much better than when I'd placed the call. Tom could drive me crazy, and more often than not, I hung up exasperated with him. But he could also make me feel more secure, as he just had. And that wasn't an easy thing for anyone to do right now.

CHAPTER NINETEEN

"Waffles or eggs?" Kit stood at the stove, a spatula held up in one hand, a cup of coffee in the other.

"These look heavenly." I took a seat at the counter and eyed the plate of waffles before me.

"Those are for Roscoe. But I can easily make another batch if you—"

"Roscoe? Are you kidding me? And where is the hound of the Baskervilles, anyway?"

"He likes to walk before breakfast, so Larry's taking him around the block. And he doesn't like syrup on his waffles."

"Larry or Roscoe?"

"Roscoe, of course, and really, I can make some more if you—"

"Kit, you realize he's a *dog*, right?"

"Exactly. It wouldn't be natural to put syrup on waffles—"

"Oh, for Pete's sake. Just let me get some coffee—unless, of course, Roscoe doesn't approve of coffee before walking."

"Val, what's your problem? You're in a horrible mood."

"I know. I'm sorry." I reached for the coffee cup she handed me and took a long gulp. "It's Sunday, Kit. I haven't slept this late on a Sunday since, well, I don't know how long. I should be preparing for an open house. Tom wants Perry to do it, but I know he'll screw it up."

"That's not your problem, ya know; that's Tom's. Why don't we do something fun today instead?"

"Fun?" I almost threw the coffee cup at her. "There's a killer out there, dropping my name, sending me flowers, mailing my business cards to Utah, of all places. What the hell could be fun? And if you're suggesting we take Roscoe to the circus, I truly will strangle you."

We both grew silent at the word *strangle*.

And then Perry's neck came to mind. "Kit, you don't think any harm will come to Perry, do you?" As I said it, I took my cell phone from where it was charging on Kit's counter and scrolled for Culotta's number. The call was answered on the first ring, only it wasn't him.

"Hi," said a chirpy female voice. Damn Tina. I immediately ended the call.

"Here, give me the phone." Kit snatched it out of my hand. I watched her redial Culotta's number, a stern look on her face, but underneath that, I could see she was enjoying this. "Hello," she said, disappointed when the call was obviously answered this time by the great detective himself. "Kit James here. Yes, yes, that was Valerie who just called . . . yes, yes, she tripped and dropped the phone . . . yes, yes, she's okay. Here, you can talk to her now."

I took the phone she handed me, mouthed the words *thanks for that little image*, and wandered into the hallway. "Sorry to bother you, but you seem to have a need to know everything," I said.

"What's up?" He sounded impatient.

"Well, I just had a thought. I was supposed to have an open house this afternoon, but Tom Haskins has forbidden me to—"

"Forbidden?"

"Okay, he suggested it might not be safe. Perry—remember his nephew?—well, he's going to do it, and I just thought—"

"It's under control."

"How do you mean?"

"We have it covered. You just stay put and enjoy your Sunday."

"Oh. You too." Was he planning a day of his own fun with the delectable Tina?

"By the way, your business cards sent to the Utah cops came from a post office box here in Downers Grove. We're checking it out."

"Okay. Good. Well, call me if you have any more news. And please . . ."

"Yeah?"

"Please watch over Perry. He's an—"

"Yeah, you told me already. He's an idiot, but he's *your* idiot. Oh, how was your trip?"

"Huh?"

"Your friend said you tripped."

"Oh, she's another idiot."

***

When Larry returned from his walk, with Roscoe in tow, he looked as though he'd been as far as the Wisconsin border. Roscoe had hardly raised a sweat and ran straight to the kitchen, where he sat back on his haunches, eyeing the waffles.

"Gooooooood boy." Kit grinned. "See, Val, he loves his waffles." She set the plate down on the floor, and Roscoe slobbered over them, finishing his breakfast in a few hearty chomps.

157

"That's disgusting," I said, then regretted it immediately, as Roscoe turned his face up toward me. "Oh, goooooood boy," I mimicked Kit. "Good boy."

Our day of fun consisted of first going out to breakfast, Kit's treat, and then to her favorite day spa, where we had manicures and pedicures. I felt uneasy the whole time. It wasn't because I hadn't enjoyed such a luxury since I'd gotten my divorce (I'd splurged a couple of times at a cheap nail salon, where I once left with bleeding cuticles). And it wasn't because Kit insisted on paying for the whole thing. It was because I couldn't stop thinking of Perry. He was an innocent who wouldn't recognize an oncoming strangulation if he'd been given a written notice beforehand.

"Wanna drive by the Harper house?" I asked Kit when we emerged from the spa, both wearing heavy paper flip-flops on our feet.

"What's the Harper house?"

"It's where the open house is being held. Should be starting just about now. No need to go in; we could just drive by, see how Perry is doing, see if any prospects have come by . . ."

I wasn't even finished with my reasons for going before Kit was in the car and asking me how to get there.

***

The Harper house was on a nice street, located in a good area on the outskirts of Downers Grove. Although I never really saw much value in open houses, the owners had been keen on having one. The first thing I noticed was Perry's Corvette, parked at a diagonal in the driveway, forcing any would-be buyers to park in the street. Next was the sign. He had stuck it in the front yard behind the trunk of a large tree, making it all but impossible for any passing traffic to see it.

"Good grief," I said, as we slowly drove by. "He really is an imbecile. Should I get out and move the sign?"

"Definitely not. There are way too many people watching."

"What are you talking about?"

"I can see at least two cars parked with someone inside. One guy's reading a newspaper, and the other's on a cell phone. Probably Culotta's guys. And look; see that man over there mowing his lawn? What's he doing?"

"Looks like he's mowing his lawn."

"Or staking out the Harper house. Geez, Val, don't you learn anything from all your *Law & Order?*"

"Have you seen him talking into his wristwatch?"

"Not yet. But I have a feeling you and I shouldn't be here." With that said, she plunked her flip-flopped foot down on the gas pedal, and we sped away.

***

We pulled into Kit's driveway next to a white Mercedes convertible, top down, that I didn't recognize.

"You have company?" I asked, as we removed our paper footwear before getting out of Kit's vehicle.

"That's Deanna What's-Her-Name's car. I wonder what she's doing here."

When we got inside, Deanna was sitting on the couch in the living room beside Roscoe, gently stroking his head. The dog was so at home in Kit's house, I almost expected him to be wearing glasses and reading the *Chicago Tribune.*

"Hey, girls." Larry came from the kitchen with two glasses of wine, one of which he handed to Deanna. To my surprise the second glass was for him, not Roscoe. "Look who stopped by."

"Deanna!" Kit leaned over and gave her a peck on the cheek.

"Sorry to barge in. I was hoping to speak to Val. I heard she's staying here for a few days."

"Yes. Her place is being fumigated," Kit said, taking Larry's glass of wine from him and handing it to me. "Fleas.

The place is crawling with fleas. Larry, would you get me one of those?"

"How horrible," Deanna said, although her tone implied she'd come across a flea or two in her time. Roscoe yawned and actually looked bored by the conversation. Apparently, fleas were of no threat to him. "Have you had any bites?"

"Oh no." I resisted the urge to scratch and reminded myself to kill Kit later. "The bug people have it all under control."

Deanna laughed. "No, honey, I meant on my house. Anyone interested yet?"

The truth was, I really hadn't had much time to devote to her home, but now that I at least had my client list back, I was determined to give it my best. I'd already retired my idea of quitting. As always, just waking up the next morning made things seem better. And I knew *not* working wouldn't make me feel any safer and would just allow me to think too much. "I have a few prospects," I lied.

"What about an open house?" she suggested.

"Well, open houses can be good—"

"Let's do one next Sunday. Charlie will be gone all day, and I can make myself scarce. That's generally how you do it, right?"

"Right. Okay, if that's what you'd like, I'll set it up. But in the meantime, if I come across any interested buyers, I'll let you know."

"I hear you gals stopped by Wendell's yesterday," she said. "What did you think?"

"He was upset, of course." I gingerly took a seat on a chair across from the couch, willing Roscoe to stay put.

"Shirley Herzog was there," Kit added, taking the glass of wine Larry handed her. "Actually, she was leaving just as we arrived. Do you know her?"

"Shirley? Hell yes, I know her. She used to work for Wendell. Back in the day. Now she's a rugby player or something like that."

"He didn't mention she worked for him. He said she was one of his patients."

"She sure could be. Personally, I only go to female dentists. They understand me." As proof, she gave a glistening smile that showed off a full set of capped teeth.

"Your teeth are beautiful," I said.

"Should be. Cost Charlie a damn fortune." She downed her glass of wine and stood up, pulling at her too-tight polka-dot top edged in glitter. "I gotta go. Bye, doggy." She gave Roscoe a pat on the head, and we all walked her to her car.

"Look, Val," she said, when she was sliding into her Mercedes, which, like her clothes, seemed too small for her body. "I know you've had a rough time lately. Word gets around, but I want you to know, it doesn't bother me a bit. Okay? I'm no stranger to trouble."

"Okay. Thank you."

"Oh, I got a feeling *I'll* be thanking *you*." She put on a pair of gold-rimmed sunglasses, and we waved as she backed out of the driveway.

"Give my love to Tom," we heard her yell over the sound of her engine. "Tell him to stop by and see my place. I'd like to know what he thinks."

***

Later, Kit whipped up an enormous salad that included bacon and fried garbanzo beans, and Larry grilled four T-bone steaks (one, of course, for Roscoe), which we ate at the kitchen table. When we were done, Larry took Roscoe for a stroll around the block, and Kit insisted she didn't need help cleaning up the dishes, so I took my phone out to the patio to call Culotta.

"Hi," he answered, and I was so glad to hear him and not Tina.

"Just checking in with you. Anything happen at the open house?"

"Nope. One couple with a baby, another with two small kids, two guys, and some middle-aged woman. Perry made it through without a scratch."

"Oh good. Kit and I drove by—"

"What—"

"—but we didn't stop. Promise. I was nervous, that's all. But we saw your guys."

"What guys? What are you talking about?"

"Didn't you have two guys parked in the street?"

"Valerie, this is Downers Grove, not Beirut. I had one guy posted inside the house. Out of sight."

"Oh good. That makes more sense." I didn't mention Kit's suspicion of the guy with the lawn mower.

"Look, any time you're planning to show a client a house, or whatever you call it, let me know, okay?"

"Okay. I will. I'm gonna get busy tomorrow. I have a very good house to show."

We said our good-byes, but before I could set down the phone, it rang again, and Perry's face appeared on the screen.

"Hey," I said, happy to hear from him. "How'd it go?"

"Val, it was an amazing success. I was rushed off my feet. Hardly a moment to breathe."

"Really?" I would have suspected him of exaggerating even without Culotta's report. Usually, I found open-house traffic slower than Chicago's at rush hour, and I generally used the time to catch up on my personal e-mails.

"Oh yes. I know you don't think much of open houses, but it's all in the approach. I think I got a few interested people."

"I heard you had a cop there."

"Yes, but I handled it smoothly. He stayed out of sight in one of the upstairs bedrooms the whole time, and no one knew he was there."

"So you never actually took anyone upstairs?"

"Val, I did such an awesome job showing the first floor, no one needed to go upstairs."

I sighed, ready to put an end to Perry's boasting. "Well, I'm glad it all went so well for you."

"A triumph, Val. Uncle Tom stopped by for a few minutes, and I could tell he was pleased."

"Did he move the sign?"

"He suggested I move it; you know, in that funny way he has. He also suggested I move my car into the street. But only for safety reasons."

"Of course."

"And the best part was T. L."

"T. L.?"

"Yes, she stopped by, just for a few minutes. I guess she wanted to see a Realtor in action."

CHAPTER TWENTY

I said good-bye to Perry and was still smiling at his last remark when my phone vibrated in my hand. A picture of my daughter, Emily, resplendent in a Regency-style dress and bonnet from the 1800s, filled my screen. Emily is an actress, living in LA with a husband who's almost as determined as she is to make a success of her career.

The picture was taken when she had a small part in a movie last year. It was a Jane Austen wannabe, and Emily played the cousin of the best friend of the leading lady. She'd been on the screen for a total of eleven minutes (not that Kit or I had timed it or anything) and delivered her dialogue (twenty-one words) in an impeccable English accent. The fact that the leading man had chosen not to share his country manor and yearly stipend with Emily, we attributed to bad writing.

My stomach swayed as I wondered if I could talk to my daughter without divulging what was going on. "Hi, Em."

"Mom! Where are you? I've been trying to call you for two days, and I've left messages—"

"I didn't get any messages or see any missed calls—"

"I'm talking about your landline. Have you been out of town?"

"Why wouldn't you call my cell?" I was stalling, hoping I could keep her from pressing me about my whereabouts, hoping I wouldn't cave if she did.

"Don't we usually have our long chats when you're home? I figure if you're available only by cell, you're working or busy. But I left a message on your home phone to call me when—"

"Oh . . . well . . . yeah. I haven't been home for a couple of nights."

"Why not? Mom, you sound funny. Have you got a guy?" Her voice was suddenly relaxed, full of mischief and . . . hope?

"No, Em, I don't have a guy. I'm at Kit's . . . she just wanted my company."

"Oh. Is Uncle Larry gone or something?"

"Yes." *Something*, I thought.

I felt only slightly guilty about my white lie. I'd told it for the same reason I didn't go stay with her—or my mother—while waiting for the murderer to be caught. I didn't want to worry the people I loved most or put them at risk.

"Well, you're not going to believe the part I'm about to get, Mom. I just know I am." My daughter's excitement was contagious, and soon we were both squealing with the glee that only the thought of being up close and personal with Ryan Reynolds could bring.

***

Tom was in a foul mood when I arrived at the office early the next morning. My showing up only made it worse. "I thought I told you to take some time off, Val." It was awfully early for him to be chomping on a cigar, even if it wasn't lit.

I knew he was shook up about something—probably worried about me. I felt a tenderness begin to swell in my chest, but then I had to ask. "Is everything okay, Tom?"

"No, it's not okay. My mother just called."

"Oh no. Is she all right?"

"Yes, she's all right."

"Your dad?" I set my purse and briefcase down on my desk and rubbed my neck. I had slept funny last night and was paying the price today.

"He's fine, Pankowski. Let's just get to work."

"Well, you're the one who told me your mom called with bad news. It's not like I was prying." I headed toward the kitchen, hoping to find Billie there and fresh coffee on the way.

"Did I say bad news? I don't think I mentioned news of any kind. And what are you doing here, anyway?" I heard him say to my back. He wasn't going to let me off the hook. "You're putting us all in jeopardy by being here. I don't want you to—"

I stopped in my tracks and turned to face him. He was rummaging around in Perry's desk and looked up at me when he realized I was staring at him. "What?" he asked, shifting his cigar around the word.

"Tom, I'm pretty sure I'm the only one at risk, if anyone is. And I am *going* to continue my work. If I had to spend all day with my nut-job friend, as you call her, the way she's worrying and calling in the dogs—literally—well, *I'd* become a nut job—"

"Fine, fine, whatever." He obviously had bigger worries than our safety. "Hey! You wanna go to a concert tonight?"

I felt my spirits lift. The last time he asked me that, he proceeded to give me two tickets to The Rolling Stones. Kit and I had danced the night away with Mick, Keith, and the boys to tunes like "Brown Sugar" from our teenage years. In fact, I think we might have actually invented twerking that night, although of course no one was paying any attention to us. "You've got concert tickets?"

Billie suddenly appeared at my side, handing me a cup of coffee. The smell alone lifted my spirits even higher.

"Yeah, I've got concert tickets." He took the cup of coffee Billie handed him, and we both told her thanks and then took grateful sips. "And unfortunately, I've got to go to it," he said. "Wanna come with me?"

I paused only long enough to picture sitting at Kit's with her worrying about me and me worrying about Roscoe. "Sure. Who are we going to see?"

"Perry and the Hinsdale Male Chorus. How can he be singing in it already? He just joined."

"I don't think it hurts to have an in with the director," I said.

"I'm assuming she's smart enough to make sure the others drown him out. Ah, here they are." He picked up an envelope addressed to *Uncle Tom* and stuffed it into his jacket pocket. Then he removed the cigar from his mouth and grimaced. "My mom's insisting. We'll go. The four of us." His grimace turned to an almost smile, as if by including me in his dreaded evening, he'd cut his misery in half.

I supposed I should be flattered. Plus, it confirmed that his phone call *had* been bad news. His mommy was making him go listen to some tunes.

An evening apart from my neurotic friend and the beast didn't sound so bad.

***

I was sitting at my desk, finally focusing my thoughts completely on something other than murder—my own or anyone else's—when a call from Culotta yanked me away from my work on Deanna Finkelmeyer's listing.

"What's up?" I asked, as soon as he identified himself.

"Whoa. I catch you at a busy time? Gotta get right down to business?"

Actually, it was a pet peeve of mine, to be greeted on the phone with a *what's up?* Might as well be an *I'm too busy to talk to you; get to the point.* Which, come to think of it, was exactly what I did want to convey to Detective Womanizer Culotta. I don't have to be fair or accurate in my thoughts. "Yes," I said, "I'm rather swamped right now. I've been distracted lately, as you might imagine, and neglecting too many things. Are you any closer to taking care of that for me? Did you check that coffee cup for fingerprints? Or DNA?"

"Sorry to be such a disappointment to you. But I figured you and your friend would have solved the case by now."

"Make up your mind. First you want us to butt out, now you want us to do your work—"

"Make no mistake about it. I *do* want you to butt out."

"Well, anyway, what'd you find out about the fingerprints? Do Shirley's match the ones found in my apartment?"

"What part of *butt out* do you not understand?" He paused, but before I could justify my curiosity as my right to know, he continued. "Is that what you thought? That Shirley's the one who—that Shirley's our murderer?" He sounded as shocked as if I'd named *him* a suspect. And then he let out a derisive laugh.

"No, I don't think Shirley *is* the murderer," I said. "But I think she *could* be."

"Nah, I don't think so. In general, women tend to use poison or a gun; they don't strangle people."

I racked my brain for a *Law & Order* episode to prove him wrong, but none came to mind. "So you're not going to check her prints?" I wasn't about to agree that he was right. I felt certain I could find an exception to his rule, given some time with my new BFF Google. I gave thanks almost daily that it had come along just as my memory was beginning to take periodic vacations. "Did that old guy even tell you I dropped it off?"

"Yeah, I saw a note to that effect. You brought it in on a weekend—"

"Well, it's Monday now."

"Yeah, but maybe you're the only one who thinks it's a priority. I'll see how busy the lab is. And I'll think about it."

"Then why did you call, if not to report on the prints?"

"I called to remind you to call *me* before you go to any showing alone."

"I will. Look, I gotta—"

"Yeah, I know. You're busy."

And the phone went dead in my hand.

Asshole, I thought. And I punched in Kit's number.

" . . . good boy; just let me take this call," I heard her murmur. Then, "Hello?"

"Kit, sorry to interrupt you and Roscoe, but—"

"Oh, Val, you should see him; he's so cute. This morning after you left, he came into the kitchen with one of your shoes in his mouth. It was adorable—"

"Wait. Not my black patent leather pumps—"

"No, one of those ratty old flat things you bought at Target or somewhere—"

"Oh no, not my new Nine West ballet flats." I'd bought them on sale at DSW, marked down to half price. So far, I'd worn them only in my apartment, since they felt like sharp knives strapped to my feet. But I loved the way they looked and was convinced that one day they would magically transform into comfy slippers.

"Why did you buy green shoes, for crying out loud? Who wears green shoes?"

"Just tell me they're okay."

"Stop panicking. Roscoe dropped the shoe as soon as he saw his waffles."

"I knew that beast had no eye for fashion. Kit, would you close my bedroom door, at least."

"Calm down, Sarah Jessica Parker; your shoe is safe."

"Good. Now listen, I want to go to Aurora, to Cyral's. You up for a drive?"

"I'll be ready. Just honk. But why? Never mind. You can tell me in the car."

And again the phone went dead in my hand. But it didn't make me mad when Kit hurried off. I knew it was so she could get ready for me to pick her up. Culotta hurried off without saying good-bye because he was a jerk.

***

Kit came trotting down the sidewalk as I pulled into her driveway, proving her timing was as impeccable as her makeup, hairdo, and attire. But although I didn't mention it, I couldn't help but notice that she was wearing purple suede ballet flats. Not dissimilar to my green Nine Wests. Although hers were at least two sizes smaller than mine and appeared to be comfortable.

"What's up, Val? Why are we going to Cyral's? Did something show up with Shirley's fingerprints?"

"Oh, who knows. Detective Asshole hasn't checked yet. He's not sure it's necessary. He says women don't kill someone by strangling them."

"Hmm. Because they're not strong enough?"

"That's probably his theory. I think it has something to do with not looking a person in the eye, you know, while you strangle them."

In one quick movement she leaned over toward me and with an imaginary rope in her hands, pulled my neck backward. "His theory sucks. Wasn't a rope or something used? I could have killed you just then, Valley Girl. From behind."

"Good to know."

"He's still on your shit list, I see." She pulled down the visor and looked in the mirror, as if to make sure she hadn't come undone during her faux attempt at strangling me. "So why are we going to Cyral's, then? Not that I mind a chance to see that gorgeous Greek guy again."

"Well, I'm curious as to why Shirley was there."

"Can you blame her? I mean, besides the fact that she wants the house of the dead shop owner next door; wouldn't *you* enjoy having coffee with that guy? So what if you have to pay for the experience?"

"Way to be sensitive, Kitty Kat. And the Greek guy is a little too pretty for my taste."

"So you're thinking Shirley might be the . . . what is it you say? Perp?"

Kit loved making fun of my *Law & Order* watching. And I loved ignoring her. "Yes, I'd say Shirley's a suspect in my mind. If I had to pick from all the people I know. She . . . she just seems a bit *off*."

But if we went to Cyral's to learn more about Shirley, we *left* knowing even more about the gorgeous (according to Kit) Giorgos.

CHAPTER TWENTY-ONE

Giorgos, this looks divine." As she said it, Kit actually clapped her hands in delight. She's a gourmet cook, but generously compliments any other foodies she comes across. And the two plates Giorgos set before us certainly looked deserving.

Since the restaurant still smelled fishy and the plastic menus were still covered in some sort of greasy substance that displayed a million fingerprints, I was amazed when Kit agreed to let Giorgos pick something for us to actually eat. I guess his good looks outweighed the poorly maintained restaurant.

"It's called papoutsakia," he said.

"Eggplant stuffed with ground beef, cheese, and . . . and . . . let me guess . . ." Kit snapped her fingers.

"Béchamel sauce," Giorgos supplied the last ingredient.

He was wearing a crisp white shirt and formfitting black pants, the same uniform we'd seen him in when we first met. His hair appeared as glossy and black as ever, and his bright-white toothy smile hadn't changed.

"To what do I owe the pleasure of two beautiful ladies coming to visit?" He pulled out the vacant chair at our table and sat down.

It was lunchtime, and as I glanced around the dingy restaurant, I saw a few other diners who'd ventured out to partake from Cyral's menu. I was happy for Giorgos (unless, of course, he was the murderer).

"Val's podiatrist is in Aurora, so I tagged along for the ride," I heard Kit say.

I stopped chewing my stuffed eggplant. *Where had* that *come from?*

"Yes." Kit patted her mouth with a paper napkin. "Bunions. Cheap shoes. But since we got here too early and we both love Greek food, we thought we'd stop for an early lunch first."

"So glad you did." He smiled his million-dollar smile, after a discreet glance down at my feet to check for any deformities.

Kit moved on. "Have the Aurora police had any success with Benita—"

"Juanita," I corrected her.

"Juanita's murder?" she smoothly continued.

We watched Giorgos cross himself, put his hands together in a prayerful position, and then look up. For a moment I expected to see Juanita herself perched on one of the blades of the dusty fan hanging from the ceiling. "No. Not a word. It's so horrible. She was an angel." He leaned back in his chair and crossed his legs. "So, you don't live in Aurora?"

"Downers Grove," I said.

"Really? And you come all this way for a podiatrist?"

"Explain." I motioned to Kit. It seemed only fair, and I was looking forward to what she would come up with.

"Speaking of feet, doesn't papoutsakia mean *little shoes* in Greek?" she asked.

"Exactly!" Giorgos beamed.

"Business seems good," she said.

"Good days, bad days. For a Monday, not so bad."

"Do you know Shirley Herzog?" Kit asked. "She was bragging about your coffee."

"Shirley? Yes, yes. I know her. She's the lady who wants to buy Juanita's house." He stopped briefly and looked at the ceiling again. "You know her too?"

"No," I interjected, before Kit had time to fabricate a story around Shirley Herzog. "Not well, anyway. She was in my office recently, and I noticed she had one of your coffee cups."

"Yes, she's a big fan of Cyral's. She seems like a nice lady. When all this business is done, maybe she will be my neighbor."

"What? I thought it was Juanita's *house* she wanted!"

"Yes, yes, house. But also the flower shop next door. Wasn't your husband Juanita's accountant? He should be aware."

Kit and I chewed on our little shoes, digesting not only the good food but also the fact that Shirley Herzog was interested in a little more real estate than she'd let on.

While Giorgos left us for a few minutes to tend to the needs of another customer, Kit leaned over and asked, "Did you notice all the family pictures on the walls?"

Indeed, I couldn't miss them. Unprofessional color photographs in cheap frames covered the long walls. "I think it's typical of a family restaurant," I said. "Usually they have one or two celebrities thrown in."

"In Aurora?"

"It's possible."

"Somehow I can't see George Stephanopoulos hanging out at Cyral's. Do you think the bathroom is clean?"

"Well, since I've never used it, I can't say for certain. But if you've had all your shots, you should be safe."

"I'll risk it." Kit got up and took the long walk to the restroom at the back of the restaurant.

While she was gone, I perused the array of family photos. In every one, Giorgos stood out as if he were the visiting celebrity. In several of them he was with a large lady about his age and not very attractive, but with the same shiny black hair.

"Ah, you see my wife, Antheia." He said it proudly, returning and looking at pictures of the woman.

"She looks nice."

"A saint," he confirmed, as Kit came back to the table, her hands grasping the purse straps that hung on her shoulders.

"We really need to get going, Val," she said, interrupting my picture gazing. "You have that appointment. Don't want to mess with your bunions."

"Right." I took my wallet from my purse. "How much do we owe you, Giorgos?"

"Please." He looked offended. "Lunch is on me."

"No, really, let us pay—"

"You pay by coming back again, and maybe you bring some of your friends with you."

"Okay, well, thank you," I said. "And yes, we'll certainly be back."

He kissed us both on each cheek, as if we were close friends, and walked us to the door, where he watched us until I was backing out of the parking lot.

"Phew. That was odd," Kit said, as I turned onto the road.

"I know. Why didn't Shirley ever mention she was in the market for the flower shop as well as Juanita's house?"

"Much more important, look at this." She unzipped the top of her leather purse and removed a five-by-seven-inch framed photograph.

I swung into the next row of shops I came to, far enough away that Giorgos couldn't possibly see my car. Pulling my spare pair of reading glasses from the visor above my head, I took the photo from Kit. It showed a group of people, with Giorgos in the center, his large wife next to him. On either side of the Greek couple stood several adults, all smiling, all with their arms around each other. I scanned their faces, hoping to see what had caused Kit to steal a picture, presumably from the restroom.

"See?" She tapped the glass. "Juanita and the guy next to her."

"Her fiancé." It was Jim Gardner, or his possible look-alike. But definitely Juanita's fiancé.

"Of course I never saw that picture Shirley gave you, but that's gotta be him. And Giorgos said he'd never met him, right?"

"Right."

"This looks suspicious."

"Sure does." I didn't even bring up the fact that she'd stolen the photograph. I was well past chastising her.

"But not half as suspicious as the bathroom," she said. "Let's stop at the first Starbucks we see, Valley Girl. I still have to go."

***

I met Tom and his parents at Hinsdale Central High School. They were waiting outside, and I spotted them immediately. I'd met Tom's parents when I was a teenager and saw them occasionally through the years. I'd always liked them. Tom's father was what you might expect: an older, faded version of his son. The same bald head, the same craggy good looks. His mother was petite and pretty. In her late seventies, she was stylishly dressed, with her gray hair cut fashionably short.

"Valerie." She held out her arms as soon as she saw me. "Good to see you. Isn't this exciting, Perry making his debut?"

I walked into her hug, and over my shoulder I saw Tom and his dad exchange glances with identical raised eyebrows. "It is exciting," I said, when Tom's mother released me. "You must be very proud of your grandson." I looked at

Tom and his father for a reaction, but now they were both intently studying their shoes.

The auditorium was packed, and we took the last four vacant seats in a row close to the front. With her back to us, I noticed T. L. first. She wore a long, flowing black robe, which made her look like a judge. In front of her, on four different levels, was the Hinsdale Male Chorus. About forty men who, with the exception of Perry, seemed to be fifty and older. Behind them was an enormous sign extolling the benefits of buying a car at McVaughn Chevrolet.

T. L. had stuffed Perry on the second level in the center, and he stood out like an adorable lamb in a herd of sheep. It wasn't so much his youth, his good looks, and his obviously highlighted blond hair that I noticed, but more the black suit and tie he wore. I'd never seen him in such conservative dress. As soon as he spotted us, he gave a tiny wave, whispered something to his seventysomething colleague next to him, and then flashed us a wide smile.

Tom's mother grasped my hand in delight. It took me back to the millions of school plays I'd attended over the years, where a young Emily had reacted the exact same way when spotting her parents in the audience. Of course the older Emily had become far too sophisticated to give her parents any such recognition.

When the audience quieted down, we watched T. L. raise her arms slowly, a baton in her right hand. The chorus responded by singing "Leaning on Jesus," with a solo from a tenor in the front row who looked to be in his midfifties. I kept my eyes glued to Perry. I wasn't sure if he was actually contributing any sound, but he certainly was mouthing the words.

After a few more religious-themed songs, T. L. turned to the audience and bowed gracefully at the applause. Then she turned back to her guys and once more raised the baton. There followed a selection of songs from several classic American musicals. As the chorus launched into *Oklahoma!*, I glanced down the row to see Tom. He had his elbow on the armrest of his chair, his face hidden by his hand, and I couldn't tell if he was appreciating the tribute to the American heartland or if he was asleep.

Less than an hour later, T. L. took her final bow, and the chorus filed off the stage. We worked our way to the exit and were soon met by Perry and T. L.

"That was beyond beautiful." Tom's mother wrapped her arms around her grandson.

I watched Perry turn his attention to his uncle, who gave a slight smile but apparently had nothing to say.

"You were marvelous," I said for him. *Was Tom really not going to comment?* After all, as choruses go, they were pretty good.

"Uncle Tom, what did you think?" Perry asked, not willing to let it go.

"Nice suit," Tom replied.

"He loved it," I said on Tom's behalf.

"Really? I'm so glad." Perry looked delighted. "And it's all thanks to T. L." He wrapped his arm around Judge Judy's black-robed shoulders.

"Val, you should join a chorus; you've got a great voice," I heard Tom say. Not only was that not true, but to my knowledge, he'd never even heard me sing.

"I'm sure she does," T. L. said. "To hear Perry tell it, she's good at everything. If we ever get a female chorus going, I'll let you try out." She still held the baton, but now she was using it to tap the palm of her left hand.

"I'm a horrible singer," I said, embarrassed, "so you don't need to worry."

"I'm not a bit worried," T. L. said. Then, in what seemed like a shocking move, she planted her thin lips on Perry's cheek. "You must excuse me. I have some other people to talk to." And she disappeared into the throng of people, her black robe billowing out behind her like wings of a crow.

***

When I got back to Kit and Larry's, I let myself in with the key they'd given me when they first moved there. I went to the living room, feeling like I was sixteen and coming home from a date, knowing my parents would be waiting up for me and I'd have to recap every detail for my mother. Usually, my father went straight to bed as soon as he knew I was home.

Larry was in the recliner in front of the TV, his eyes closed, a magazine open and lying on his chest. Kit and Roscoe were curled up on the couch together, reading her Kindle. She snapped the e-reader shut as soon as she saw me, and Roscoe turned his giant head in my direction. He looked pissed (didn't he always?), and I found myself hoping they'd at least reached the end of a chapter before I'd interrupted them.

Kit sat up and patted the empty cushion on the other side of her, but I took the vacant armchair across from Larry. "How was it?" she asked.

"Pretty good. Nice to see Tom's parents again."

"How are they?"

"They're great."

"What was his mom wearing?"

"A nice dress and jacket." This was *exactly* like my mom's interrogation after a date. Next, she'd be asking me if Tom acted like a gentleman.

"Did Tom misbehave?"

I filled Kit in on the evening, including T. L. kissing Perry on the cheek before flying off.

"A little possessive, don't ya think?" She vigorously rubbed the top of Roscoe's head, and I wondered if the question was directed at me or him.

"Could be."

"Hey, maybe she was trying to make ol' Tom jealous. Let's face it, she's more his age than Perry's, right?"

"That's crazy talk."

"Val better be careful. She might lose her boyfriend Tom." Okay, now she was *definitely* talking to the dog.

I said my good-night. Larry had already woken and, seeing that I was home safe, promptly left for bed. Roscoe hadn't moved, and I hoped he'd stay put until I was in my bedroom with the door shut.

Once I was settled—pj's on, makeup removed, teeth brushed—I crawled into bed and turned on the TV. But a chirping sound coming from the general direction of my purse made me jump up and dig for my cell. I hadn't checked messages all evening; very unlike me.

There were two voice mails.

First one from Perry: *Hi, Val. Two things. First, OMG, I'm on cloud nine. Can you believe the performance? T. L. thinks it's one of the best ever. And she should know, right? And second, I'm thinking of growing a beard. What do you think? T. L. says go for it. Think about it and let me know. No rush. Oh, and hope you got home all right. Love ya, kiss kiss.*

I hit the button for the next message.

It was from Deanna Finkelmeyer: *Val? Sorry to phone so late, but I just got a call from someone interested in my house. Not sure how they got my number, but I told them I'm listed with you and they should call Haskins to set up a time to visit. I wanna play fair with you guys. So why don't you or Tom give me a call tomorrow, and we'll talk. Oh, and tell Tom hi from me.*

As I hit the *end* button, Tom's name appeared on an incoming call.

"Tom!"

"Hey, Kiddo. Just making sure you're okay, that you didn't slash your wrists or anything."

"I thought the chorus was pretty good."

"Yeah, you'll have to tell me all about it someday. Good to know I didn't waste any favors with McVaughn."

"Say, I just listened to a message from Deanna Finkelmeyer. Looks like we got someone interested in their house. They want to see it."

"Anyone we know?"

"She didn't say. But she told them the house was listed with Haskins and they'd have to call us to set up a viewing."

"Man or woman?"

"She didn't say. But she did want me to tell you hi."

"She's a piece of work. Okay. Don't even think about leaving Kit's house. I'm calling Culotta now."

He ended the call without saying good-bye, and I sat with the phone in my hand for several seconds. Then I hurried out of bed and slipped on my robe. I needed to talk to Kit, just to be reassured I wasn't alone.

When I opened the bedroom door, I nearly tripped over the big black-and-brown mass lying there. Roscoe. If I hadn't been so wary of him, I would have patted his head. Instead, I carefully stepped over his bulk and said, really meaning it, "Good boy."

CHAPTER TWENTY-TWO

I awoke at ten the next morning, stretched out my arms luxuriously, and then scrunched down in the bed. After thinking about the events of the night before, I reached for my phone on the bedside table. I called Tom and then Culotta, but ended up leaving voice mails.

After lying there a while longer, I began to wonder—if they were so concerned about me, insisting I had to stay home—why they didn't answer my calls or at least return them immediately.

I felt relieved when the phone rang, but it was neither of my so-called protectors. Putting on my glasses, I saw Deanna Finkelmeyer's name flash on the screen.

"How's it going with our potential buyer?" she asked, as I sat up in bed and pushed the glasses farther up my nose.

I couldn't be honest with her; I couldn't tell her *the police* were involved, not if I wanted to keep her listing. "I'm waiting to hear back," I said, glad I didn't have to lie—yet.

"I don't want to be pushy, but they sounded really eager, in town for just a couple of days, from Colorado or somewhere. One of those states out there on the left side of the country."

A jolt ran through me as I thought of *Utah*. "Um, I'm getting another call, Deanna. I'll get back to you as soon as I know anything, okay?" Again, it wasn't a lie, because I was getting a call-waiting, accompanied by the flashing of *Dennis Culotta* on my screen.

I cut Deanna off and switched to the detective. "Dennis?"

"You okay?" he asked, and I had to admit I liked the concern I heard in his voice. This was more like it. But at the same time, it scared the hell out of me.

"Yes. Why shouldn't I be okay? I'm at Kit's, like I'm supposed to be."

"You sounded weird. I thought maybe you were crying . . . or choking."

"Choking?"

"Sorry; wrong word. Are you afraid?"

"*Should* I be afraid?"

"Nah. Careful, yes. Afraid, no. Tom told me about the potential buyer. Probably on the up-and-up. But just so you know, Tom plans to show the house instead of having you do it. Just in case."

"Will Tom be alone?"

"Don't worry about Tom. I'll be there too."

"What about Deanna? Does she know—"

"All she needs to know is that someone from Haskins will be at her house to meet a prospective client. We'll let her think it's you, and we'll ask her to leave the house early so she won't run into Tom."

"Good luck with that," I said. "She's got the hots for him, so if she thinks he might be in her house, she'll stick around."

I heard Culotta chuckle. "Yeah," he said, in a lazy, sexy voice, "the ladies all love Tom."

"Not even close," I said, as if I had to defend my boss. From what? The ladies? Deanna? "Well, it sounds like you have it all planned out. Why are you calling, then?" I asked. "Just to tell me that?" I still felt the sting of his nonchalance, if something as mild as nonchalance could sting. But then he surprised me.

"What do you say we forget about all this . . . murder stuff . . . and have dinner tonight? Just pretend we're two people who want to talk over a good meal?"

"Talk about what?" And what the hell did he mean *pretend?*

"I don't know. We didn't seem to have trouble finding things to talk about the last time we went out together."

Went out? This was sounding more and more like a date. I started feeling what my mother used to call gaga. *Oh, Valerie, don't tell me you're gaga over that boy with the severe case of acne,* I heard her say more than once, probably because most fifteen- to seventeen-year-old boys *were* pimply faced. And she didn't like a single one of them.

I almost asked if he wasn't afraid of upsetting Tina by having dinner with me, but I suddenly realized I didn't want to remind him of anything that might stand in the way of our dinner. I didn't know if it was because I wanted to be with him or because the thought of another Roscoe-free evening sounded so good. Then I realized it didn't *matter* why. "I'd like that. Pick me up at seven? At the James house, of course."

"Of course. But I'll be there at seven thirty."

Damn him.

***

When I stepped out of the shower thirty minutes later, I could hear Kit talking to Roscoe in the kitchen. It sounded like she was reading to him from *People* magazine. There'd been no sign of the beast as I'd made the perilous journey across the hall from my bedroom to the bathroom. Even though I appreciated Roscoe's protective tendencies, I still didn't trust him.

I dried off and stepped into some baggy shorts and a T-shirt and then made my way downstairs for coffee.

"Good morning," I said, as I entered the kitchen.

"Hey, Val. Sorry I didn't leave a note—I thought of it as I was driving away. And I didn't want to call and risk waking you. I'm glad you could sleep."

"Who was sleeping? I didn't feel I had much to get up for, but I certainly wasn't sleeping. You went somewhere?"

"Aww, poor baby." She was patting Roscoe's head, so once again I wasn't sure if she was talking to him or to me. But I supposed of the two of us, *I* was the poor baby. Although I did have that dinner date coming up. What was Roscoe doing this evening?

"Where'd you go, anyway?" I asked, hoping to hear *grocery store*. But I had a feeling . . . I poured myself a cup of coffee that had just finished brewing, and then I took a stool at the counter.

"I went to see Shirley."

"Shirley who?"

"Shirley Feeney of Laverne and Shirley. That's right, Val. I dropped by to have a beer with the girls."

"Okay, funny lady, you stopped at Shirley *Herzog's* house. But what the hell for?"

"Settle down, Val. We've got detecting to do. Your life might depend on it. And *you* can't leave the house."

"Why did you go see Shirley?" I dismissed Kit's dramatic explanation, concentrating instead on why she had gone anywhere without me. I was thrown back to our fourteen-year-old selves, when I had mono and was housebound and had to hear all the latest school gossip via my totally biased best friend. Never the preferred way to get the real story.

"To find out why she didn't tell us she was interested in buying Juanita's flower shop, of course."

"So you just stopped by her house to ask her that?"

"Yep," Kit said, her back to me as she removed what looked like pork tenderloin from the freezer.

At the sight of the meat, Roscoe began prancing in place, practically on top of Kit. Could he smell frozen meat? Was he really that good?

"And? Did you find out?" I asked.

"I found out, all right. She wasn't."

"She wasn't . . . ?"

"You seem a little dreamy this morning."

Dreamy? Was my upcoming dinner date showing? "I'm not dreamy. I just can't for the life of me think why you went to see Shirley." *Without me*, I didn't add. "But tell me what she said."

"I did tell you. She *wasn't* interested in buying the flower shop. She didn't have a clue what Giorgos was talking about. That's what she calls him, by the way. Giorgos. I'm tellin' you, something is up between those two. One of them, at least, is lying."

"Well, that's what *we* call him, just Giorgos. What *is* his last name, anyway?"

"I don't know. But we gotta find out. That and a whole lot more. About both Giorgos and Shirley."

I heaved a sigh worthy of Atlas anticipating the load he was going to carry. Number one, I felt so helpless, housebound as I was. And number two, I just wanted to think about having a tasty dinner and stimulating conversation with a handsome man.

"You hungry? I can whip up some eggs." I watched as she removed some items from a grocery sack I hadn't noticed before. A package of prosciutto and some mozzarella wrapped in cellophane.

"Are we having a dinner party?" I asked, as she put the items in the fridge.

"No, why?"

I'd forgotten that Kit and Larry ate like this on a daily basis. How Kit stayed so slim was due to the miracle of genetics. "Looks like you're planning to make something fabulous." I crossed my legs and then uncrossed them at the sight of some cellulite poking its ugly head from under my shorts. Proof that eating Cheerios for dinner did nothing to quash fat cells.

"This?" Kit indicated the tenderloin. "It's nothing that special."

"Well, I won't be home for dinner. Actually, I have plans."

"Hmm." Kit leaned on the counter, across from me, a bag of baby spinach in her hand. "Not with the boy who sacks groceries at Dominick's, I hope. I hear he lives in the fast lane."

"And he has his own car." I smiled and then took a sip of my coffee. "Actually, Dennis Culotta invited me out."

Kit stood up. "Good. You can find out what the police are doing. If anything. I can't wait to hear. Want me to straighten your hair?" I watched her take eggs from the fridge, and I was surprised, or maybe hurt, that she didn't place more importance on my seeing Culotta.

"No, thanks," I said. "So you just showed up at Shirley's house and questioned her?"

"That's right. I made up a tiny lie and told her we were having a little memorial dinner for Juanita, and we'd love her to come. Then the subject just naturally got around to real estate."

"Naturally. Memorial dinners and home buying. I can see that. But I wish you had let me know. I'd have gone with you on your little escapade."

"Oh, that's not all. I also swung by Wendell Fullerton's house on the way back. Seems Deanna was correct. He's a hound dog, all right. And I'd say it was a motive I saw leaving his house."

"Huh?"

"A woman, Val, a woman. Looking like she'd slept in her clothes, although I'd bet Larry's life she removed every stitch at some point during the night. She was definitely what your mom and mine would call a hussy."

"And you know all this because . . . ?"

"Because I drove up just before she came out the front door. So I watched her leave. And then I had myself a chat with Wendell. I told him we were planning a little memorial dinner for Christine. One thing led to another, and I found out, among other things, why Shirley no longer works for him."

"So this time you went from memorial dinner to past employee? Another perfect segue." I let her refill my coffee cup. I was in awe that she had accomplished so much without me, and I shrugged off my left-out feeling.

"And?" I said, when she didn't continue.

"And what?"

"What happened?"

"He fired her."

"Well, it must have been friendly fire. They seemed pleasant enough when we saw her at his house."

"I know, right? So, what have *you* been doing, if you didn't sleep?"

I filled her in on my two phone calls that in comparison to her efforts, not to mention her imaginary little memorial dinners, seemed hardly newsworthy.

***

I tried calling Tom so many times throughout the morning that when I finally heard his unrecorded voice answer, I was almost too shocked to respond.

"Valerie? Are you there? You left me about a hundred messages; you better have something to say now."

I tried to bring my mind back from its mulling over all that Kit had told me. I'd hit the redial over and over while pondering her report. "Tom?"

"Yes, it's Tom. *You* called *me*. Whaddya need?"

"I need to know what's happening with the person who's interested in the Finkelmeyer house. Dennis said you were going to show it."

"Yeah."

"And?"

"And what?"

"Well, did they like it? And *are* they from Utah?"

"I don't know anything about friggin' Utah. But we're meeting at the house tomorrow morning."

"Oh. Not until tomorrow?"

"Do we have a bad connection? You sound like you're in a fog, Valerie. What's your friend feeding you over there?"

"Sorry, Boss. I'm not going to relax until I know how your showing tomorrow turns out." *But I'm gonna try like hell to relax with Culotta tonight,* I thought.

"You're not that hard up for a sale. You've actually had a good month."

"I'm not worried about the sale. I'm worried about *you.*"

He chortled. "I'm a big boy. I can take care of myself. And you too."

CHAPTER TWENTY-THREE

We dined at Mancino's. It was an Italian restaurant owned by Joe, a friend of Culotta's. We'd eaten there together only once, in what seemed like another lifetime, but when Joe Mancino appeared at our table, he greeted me like a friend who stopped by every week.

"Valerie," he said, reaching down and taking my hand to his lips. "*Bella signora.*" His broad Chicago accent disappeared into the language of his heritage. Following a snap of his fingers, a waiter appeared with a bottle of Laetitia Pinot Noir, which he dutifully poured into our empty wineglasses.

"So, what are you in the mood for tonight?" Joe cocked his thumb toward Culotta. "If this one had let me know you were coming, I would have prepared something special."

"You got any fish back there?" his friend asked.

With his eyes on me, Joe laughed. "Fish, he says; you think this is Long John Silver's? But yeah, I got fish. I got pesce spade al pomodoro. The finest Pacific swordfish flanked with eggplant involtini filled with spaghetti and topped with crab."

"Sounds wonderful," I said, as I watched Joe put his fingers to his lips and kiss them in the universal sign indicating the upcoming meal would be paradise. I was just glad I wouldn't have to dig out my reading glasses in order to read the menu.

"So," Culotta said, when we were alone, "what shall we drink to?" He raised his glass and held it toward me.

"I dunno." I raised my own glass. "How about me selling the Finkelmeyer house and making an obscene commission."

He tapped his glass against mine. "Sounds good," he said. "To Valerie making lots of dough. *Salute.*"

Our waiter brought us a basket of bread and a small dish of olive oil and herbs for dipping. Culotta held up the basket in my direction, and I took a slice.

"How do you like it at the James household?" He broke off a chunk of bread and dipped it in the oil.

"Fine. I'm glad I went there."

"Shouldn't be for too much longer." He nodded. He was wearing a blue shirt under his jacket, but it was no match for the hue of his eyes, illuminated by the soft light from the candle between us. Now, *they* were some kind of blue.

"Really?" Although I had promised myself I wouldn't bring it up, the confidence he showed in predicting a quick end to the ghastly murders made me more than curious. I was able to hold off prompting him for a few seconds, but when he didn't continue speaking, I couldn't resist. "You think the guy from Utah, or wherever he's from, is the one?"

I watched him wipe his lips with a white linen napkin, then carefully place it back on his lap. "So far, he's our only lead, but I don't know . . . we'll have to wait and see."

"See what? If he does indeed show up tomorrow morning, he's not gonna pull anything with Tom."

"How d'you figure that?"

"Well, so far, each of the victims was murdered when she was alone," I said. "Surely, if there's a pattern here, Deanna is the target, not Tom."

"And he could just be getting the lay of the house and then come back, when Deanna Finkelmeyer is there alone? Kinda like you and Jim Gardner?"

"Exactly; just like Jim Gardner."

"What do you think about him?"

"Me?" I wiped my own mouth. "You've checked him out, right? Along with the others?"

"What others?" His blue eyes twinkled. "There are others that I should be aware of?"

"Huh," I said. "There's definitely a few others you should be considering."

"Tell me."

"Okay. But let's start with Jim Gardner."

"Okay. Let's start with him."

"Well, he may or may not be the guy coming to see the Finkelmeyer house tomorrow. If he is, then he's gonna have to be really disguised. Right? I mean, since I was with him at Daphne's. Plus, he may or may not be Juanita's fiancé. Either way, he's worth considering."

"That's a lot of *may or may nots*."

"Well, *you're* supposed to sort them all out."

He nodded slowly but not necessarily in agreement. "Okay. Who else you got?"

"Well, there's Shirley Herzog. She's suspicious."

"How so?"

"Okay." I stabbed another piece of bread into the olive oil. "She's the one who had the picture of Juanita's fiancé; plus, she's desperate to buy Juanita's house. And there's something going on with her and Giorgos—"

"Giorgos?"

"Yeah, the guy who owns the restaurant next to Juanita's flower shop. They have a connection. He seems to think Shirley wants to buy the flower shop as well as—wait!"

You know about Giorgos, right? You've spoken to him, haven't you?"

"Not personally. The Aurora police did. It was in a report somewhere."

I opened my eyes wide in shock. "In a report somewhere? Geez, I thought you were more on top of it than that."

"Don't worry. I'm on top of it. What else you got?"

"Okay, well, something else about Shirley. It turns out she has a connection to Wendell Fullerton as well." I waited for some reaction, but he continued to stare at me as if I were telling a not-very-funny joke and he was waiting for the punch line.

"*The dentist!* Husband of the third victim. Christine," I reminded him.

He nodded. "Got it. What about him?"

"Well, turns out Shirley used to work for him. Years ago, I think. But they do have a connection now too."

Culotta opened his own eyes wider, looking surprised.

I was on a roll. He seemed impressed with how much I knew, but I was alarmed at how much *he* apparently *didn't* know. "Wendell is already seeing someone else, so soon after Christine died. Deanna Finkelmeyer confirmed he was a serious player—"

"What about Deanna? Think there's anything there?"

I didn't answer immediately. The memory of previous times spent with Culotta suddenly washed over me—when he'd appeared in my life investigating the murder of Susan Reed, a woman who'd worked for Larry James. Back then, while I was dreaming of how good it might feel to kiss the detective, he was busy picking my brain for anything I could add to the investigation.

I took a long sip of wine, leaning back in my chair and watching him closely.

"Deanna?" he asked again. "You think she's okay?"

I waited a few more seconds before answering. "I wouldn't know. Isn't that your job to find out?"

He wiped his mouth again, needlessly.

"Okay, Valerie. You're absolutely right. It is my job. But right now I'm off duty and having dinner with a gorgeous woman, so if you don't mind, let's not talk about the case anymore."

Damn him. He was good. "I think that would be best."

"How about those Cubs?"

We continued chatting, making small talk. He asked me what Emily was up to, and I filled him in on her career, embellishing just a little. He asked about Kit and Larry, and I told him about Roscoe, a slightly altered version of the truth in which I was firmly in control and Roscoe was my lapdog.

Then I excused myself to use the restroom. When I returned, I found Culotta writing something in his little leather-bound notebook.

"Are you kidding me?" I asked in disgust.

He quickly closed the book and shoved it into the inside pocket of his jacket. He then stood up until I was seated, an old-world gesture that I'd seen from only my dad and Tom Haskins.

"Should I order another bottle of wine?" he asked, after he sat back down.

"I don't know; you're the policeman. Wouldn't that put you over the limit?"

"Are you angry? You seem angry."

And then the proverbial clincher happened: his phone rang. It had been lying on the table by his plate, and I'd paid no attention to it until it started a vibrating dance and Tina Reilly's face filled the screen in all her blond gorgeousness. She was now the third person at our table.

We both looked at the phone, and then I looked at Culotta, who appeared sheepish.

"Aren't you going to get that?" I asked the sheep.

"No. Of course not. It can wait." Wait for what? Wait until he had everything he needed and could then dump me? The sheep disappeared, replaced by a wolf. He pressed a button on the side of the phone to turn it off and then shoved it inside his jacket pocket. He obviously had reinforced pockets in that jacket of his.

Up until then I'd managed to not even think of Tina, but now with her lurking inside his coat, my anger began to bubble.

"Sorry about that," the wolf said, not looking a bit sorry.

"Was this evening just to interrogate me?"

"Don't be silly, Valerie. We're old friends, and I just wanted to have a nice time catching up."

"We're hardly friends—"

"But isn't this how we become friends . . . doing stuff like this?"

"Were you writing down everything I just told you? Geez, I can't believe—"

"Hey, get over yourself. First of all, you haven't told me anything I didn't already know—"

"Really? You knew all about Giorgos Whatchamacallit *and* that Wendell Fullerton was playing around?"

He quickly whipped out his notebook again (leaving Tina firmly ensconced in his pocket) and flipped through the pages.

"I shouldn't really be telling you this," he said, "but your Greek pal Giorgos—sorry, can't pronounce his last name—has got form. That means—"

"I know what it means."

"Okay. He just finished two years for ADW. That means—"

"I know what it means: assault with a deadly weapon."

"Er, okay, the *lady* knows what ADW means—"

"Is he married? Just tell me that."

"Not unless he got himself hitched in lockup. He's a good-looking guy, so maybe—"

"But I saw a picture of him and his wife."

"Probably a sister; he's got like a dozen of them."

"Okay, so he served time; doesn't mean he strangled anyone." Why I felt the need to defend Giorgos was a bigger mystery than the real friggin' mystery at hand. "Anything else in that little book of yours?" I asked.

He flipped a few more pages and began reading again in a monotone voice. "Christine Fullerton filed for divorce six days before she was murdered. Dr. Fullerton moved out of the residence and was not living there permanently at the time of his wife's death."

"So I guess they weren't selling in order to upgrade, but probably to go their separate ways. But . . . but he said he came home and found her . . . why'd he say he came *home*, if he wasn't living there?"

"He says he stopped by to get some things."

I nodded; that made sense. But what didn't make sense was why Kit hadn't uncovered any of this stuff.

"You ready to order?" I heard him ask, and I watched him shove the book back in his pocket.

"Are you sure?" I asked.

"Yes, I'm sure. I think Joe's fish sounded—"

"I mean about Giorgos and Wendell Fullerton, for Pete's sake."

"Oh yeah, I'm pretty sure. I checked the prison records on Giorgos, and I saw the petition filed in court by Christine Fullerton, unless of course you think they were fakes." He smiled that smile that made me melt and feel foolish at the same time.

"Okay. Let's order." I leaned forward in my chair. "And please, let's not discuss this business anymore."

"Fine with me. I never wanted to discuss it in the first place. It's just—"

I reached across the table and put a finger up to his lips to silence him. And he gently took it and kissed it.

Crap!

***

Dennis Culotta delivered me back to Kit and Larry's front door at ten thirty. I didn't invite him in since he claimed he had an early start in the morning. He wanted to be at the Finkelmeyer house long before Tom and the prospective buyer showed up. More important, I wanted to fill Kit in on what I'd learned.

He walked me to the doorstep and then held out his arms to give me a hug. It was nice; it was friendly. It was the kind of hug you give your sister or your grandmother or your colleague at work who's retiring. Certainly not the kind of hug you give a person whose finger you kissed so intimately earlier that evening. But I held him just a little longer than necessary, more for Tina lurking inside his pocket than for my own enjoyment.

As soon as he was gone, I fumbled with my key. When I finally got the door opened, I was confronted by Roscoe, sitting in a perfect doggy pose in the hallway. He looked like he should be the cover dog for a Rottweiler calendar. I closed the door behind me and leaned against it, averting my gaze while being hyperaware that he was staring at me. (I'd read somewhere that dogs interpreted eye contact as a challenge, and I had my hands full fighting people right now.) I called Kit's name, and she came into the hallway.

"What are you doing?" she asked.

"Nothing." I wasn't about to tell her I was afraid to move.

"How was your evening. Was it fun? Did you go somewhere nice? Why didn't he come in? Did you discuss the murders? Did you learn anything new—"

"Oh yes, Kitty Kat . . ."

"What's wrong with you? You look strange. Did something happen? Did that damn Culotta upset you?"

I inched past Roscoe, who immediately turned and padded his way after us. "There's nothing wrong. We had a perfectly lovely evening."

"Good. You want a drink?"

"Nope. Think I'll just go to bed."

She and Roscoe followed me up the stairs and into the bathroom and watched as I took off my makeup. Then I crossed the hall, changed into my pajamas, climbed into bed, and began telling Kit about the ex-con Giorgos and the Fullerton divorce.

She sat on the edge of my bed and listened in silence as she patted my legs through the covers with one hand and Roscoe's head with the other. "He's very cagey," she said, after I'd told her all I knew.

"Right." I slid farther down under the lightweight duvet. "How did he keep that a secret? Even Deanna didn't seem to know—"

"Not Wendell. *Culotta*. Way too cagey."

CHAPTER TWENTY-FOUR

I sat straight up in bed, which caused Roscoe to go on high alert. Or had he maybe heard something in the house? Maybe an intruder . . . I realized Roscoe might be scaring me as much as protecting me. "Why do you say Culotta's cagey? I mean, of course he is, but why do you say that? Now?"

"Down, boy; it's all right." Kit seemed more interested in soothing Roscoe than me, and my resentment of the dog went up a notch. "Think about it, Val. Who's really getting hurt in all these murders? I mean, yeah, of course the dead people are. But what's the one constant among them?"

"Kit, I'm having real trouble putting two and two together here." I flung the covers off to relieve my sudden hot flash.

"Having a hot attack?" Kit smiled, but although I usually chuckled at her word choice, I didn't find it funny now.

I watched her continue to pet Roscoe's head, only slightly mollified since she also kept giving my leg the occasional pat of comfort.

"I think Culotta withheld the fact that he's focusing on you," she said at last.

"You think he thinks *I'm* the murderer?"

"No, but I think he wanted to probe for why someone would want to hurt you. You're the common denominator in all this. Why else would your card be left at each scene if not in an attempt to hurt you?"

"You're saying *I'm* responsible for all the deaths? That three people were killed because someone would want to hurt me?" I felt like throwing up. Because I felt like she might be right.

I also thought she might be right about the reason Culotta asked me out. I realized now how my wine-loosened tongue had wagged on and on about myself, with only occasional nudging from the man I'd hoped was interested in *me*, not the reasons someone would want me dead.

"Why don't they just kill *me*, then, if I'm the one they want to hurt?"

"*They*? Hmm . . . I suppose there could be more than one."

"Focus, Kit. It wasn't a literal *they*. I meant, why didn't *he* just kill *me*, if I'm the one *he* wants to hurt?"

"Ya mean *he or she*."

"Actually, I mean *he*. Remember, Culotta says women don't strangle."

"Huh. A woman can do anything a man can. She just might have to find a different way to accomplish it. If you recall, I could have easily strangled you when you were driving."

"Yes, you proved your point. But why me?"

"I'm guessing that's what your detective wanted to find out tonight. Did you tell him?"

Again, my thoughts went back to my conversation with Culotta. But I was afraid the same wine that had me spilling my guts probably also dimmed my memory for what I'd spilled.

"Maybe," I said. "He did ask some questions along that line. Oooh, you're right. He *is* cagey. He asked about us going to high school here. He asked if you, with your brash ways—sorry; his words, not mine—had made any enemies back in high school. And then he even asked if I had maybe inadvertently stepped on anyone's teenage toes."

"And? What did you tell him?"

"Man, he really had me babbling then. All my high school memories . . . well, it was fun to talk about them; I mean, how many people who didn't go to high school with us ever want to hear about those years? So yeah, I told him everything I could think of . . . you know how one memory leads to another."

"Hmm. So he probably wondered if maybe someone from your long-ago past has been nursing a grudge and decided to complicate your life. Not a bad thought."

"Kit!"

"I mean, it's a horrible thought, that someone would do that. But he might be on to something. Think. Who might that someone be?"

She sounded desperate, and I knew she wanted to figure it out before Culotta did. I was too tired and too scared to care *who* discovered the murderer's identity. As long as he—or she—was caught. And soon.

I shook my head. "Sorry, Kitty Kat. Can't think of who it could be. And anyway, you'd be as likely to know as I would." If I hadn't been so scared, that would have been a pleasant thought, how we'd been so close through all these years. "But let me sleep on it. Or just let me sleep." I nestled back down beneath the covers and breathed a sigh of relief after she kissed my forehead and left the room with Roscoe.

And then it hit me. I knew who might want to hurt me.

***

I didn't sleep much that night. Big surprise. Between wondering about my *who* and worrying about Tom showing the house the next morning, my mind was awhirl all night long. I dozed off a couple of times, only to have a dream—a nightmare—about my *who* or Tom. At least they weren't one and the same person, I thought ruefully, as I climbed out of bed at first light—which comes early in July.

Then again, although they weren't one and the same person, I had a strong feeling they might be connected.

I grabbed my phone and opened the bedroom door a crack, and Roscoe's head popped up as if it were connected by a string to the doorknob. Then he unfolded himself from his prone position and stood staring at me. I couldn't read the expression in his sleepy brown eyes. Was he daring me to even think of leaving my room, or was he offering to safely escort me to wherever I wanted to go?

I took my chances on the latter and swung the door open wider. Then I crept past him, trying not to make eye contact. He stayed closer to my side than I would have liked (why couldn't he fall in behind me like a good doggy?), but the one time I whispered *heel*, I felt him tense up. So I *shut* up.

As I'd feared, Kit wasn't awake. At least she hadn't been to the kitchen yet. I pushed the coffeemaker's *on* button, knowing she'd loaded it with water and coffee beans the night before. All the better to not have to fully awaken until ground and brewed coffee could be consumed. I sat on a stool, tucking my feet under me in the age-old kindergarten position, which rendered me only slightly unsteady—less of a risk, I determined, than having my feet dangling too close to Roscoe's slobbery mouth down below. Then I checked my phone for messages—phone, e-mail, *or* text. No voice mails. No new e-mails. But *bingo*. A text from Culotta.

Thx for fun night. Maybe do again soon? Tomorrow?

Yeah, right, I thought. Apparently, I hadn't given him what he wanted. Well, I felt pretty certain I *had* uncovered what he wanted, but I wasn't about to give it to him. Yet.

Instead, I sent a text to Perry, which I knew he wouldn't read for a few more hours. That was okay. I felt better as soon as I pressed *send*.

***

"What're you doing up so early?"

I jumped at the sound of Kit's voice, which sent me wobbling on the stool, my right leg falling down precariously close to Roscoe's mouth. She was wearing a black silk robe belted tightly around her slim waist. Resting across her forehead was a red satin night mask embroidered with the words Dreaming of Paris. "Well, right now I'm reading the latest garbage on Miley Cyrus."

"You saying *she's* garbage, or what they're writing about her is garbage?" I was glad she didn't wait for an answer. Instead, as she poured herself a cup of coffee, she said, "Ahh, glad you got this started. I need it faster than usual. I didn't sleep well last night, thinking of—"

"Paris?"

"No. Thinking of you . . ." She removed the mask and tossed it on the counter.

"*You* didn't sleep well thinking of me? How do you think *I* slept?"

"Um . . . not at all?"

"You got it."

She leaned over the counter and patted my hand. Then she heaved a big sigh. "Don't worry. I'll think of something for us to do next."

In our biggest role reversal ever, I answered her. "I already have."

CHAPTER TWENTY-FIVE

We left Roscoe watching a recorded episode of *Downton Abbey* (Kit had somehow discovered that he was a big fan) and headed for my SUV.

"Okay, so let's hear this idea of yours," Kit said, as I pulled out of her driveway.

"Well, I've gone through everyone I know, or knew, and, if I do say so myself, I've led a pretty exemplary life—"

"Yes. You're a saint—"

"So then I concentrated on newbies—people I've recently met. Someone within my current circle who might want to do me in. And the only person I can think of is Deanna Finkelmeyer—"

"This I have to hear."

"You will. Just give me a chance."

"But you'd never even met her until I introduced you."

"Correct. I didn't know her, but that doesn't mean she didn't know *me*. Or should I say know *of* me?"

"Okay, go on. You've surely got more—"

"Well, think about it. She told you she'd had her house on the market. Did you ever see a sign in her yard?"

"No . . . but I was hardly driving by—"

"Well, I texted Perry this morning and asked him to check with Harris-Wiggins—that's who she told me she'd been listed with. It occurred to me that since they're an excellent outfit, probably the best real-estate company in town, with ten times the sales Haskins has, not to mention a staff of dozens, it didn't make sense for her to switch midstream. Especially since she didn't know me at all—"

"You're right. That doesn't make sense. I know they'd be the ones I'd call—"

"Oh great. Good to know my best friend wouldn't even call me if—"

"Kidding."

Only I knew she probably wasn't. I don't believe Kit has ever considered my employment at Haskins a serious career.

She waved her hand in my direction. "Continue."

"Okay. Let's face it; my only recommendation was from you, and you couldn't even remember Deanna's last name."

I stopped talking for a while, realizing that as I spelled my theory out, it sounded weak. Flimsy. Lame.

Kit, however, seemed to be lapping it up. "Okay; so far, so good. Go on."

"Well, then I realized something else. She may not know me, but she certainly knows Tom. Or did at one time. In fact, she's a little obsessed with him. Every single conversation we've ever had has ended with her mentioning him, asking me to pass on a greeting—"

"Wait . . . obsessed with Tom? Now you're losing me. Why would anyone be obsessed with Tom Haskins?"

"Some women find him very attractive, Kit."

"No way—"

"You'll have to trust me on that."

"Okay. Let's say in some other universe Tom Haskins is considered attractive, but where do *you* come into the picture?"

I sighed. My flimsy theory was now sounding slightly insane. "They have a history. Tom knows her, although I'm not sure how well or why, but he claims that a lot of the stuff she told me about herself isn't true. Apparently, they first crossed paths at an Indian casino in Southern Illinois, where—"

"Oh, *now* it makes sense. Tom Haskins in the glow of a twelve-foot neon Illini Tribesman . . . who *wouldn't* fall in love with him? But I still don't get why you'd be a target."

"Jealousy?" I mumbled.

"Huh?"

"Jealousy," I said, a little louder.

"Are you saying what I think you're saying? Deanna is jealous of your close, personal relationship with the man of her dreams, and she's what? Trying to spook you? Scare you out of town? What? Tell me what."

"It sounded so good in my head. I was thinking who would want to hurt me . . . and that's what I came up with."

"Val, honey, you're sleep deprived. You're scared out of your wits. But honestly, I don't—"

I held up my hand to stop her speaking. My phone had pinged, indicating a text message. I pulled into a vacant parking space in a strip mall and retrieved my phone from my purse. Putting on my glasses, I saw Perry's name on the screen.

Val I chkd with harris-wiggins they never heard of Deanna Funkelstein and house on Windjammer Dr never one of their listings and don't forget I need ur thoughts on my beard so get back to me oh and hope you r safe

He ended his message with three smiley faces.

Okay, so he got her name wrong, and his concern for my safety took second place to his potential beard. But he had the street name right. I held up the phone to Kit's face, proof that I wasn't totally losing it.

***

I drove past the Finkelmeyer house, where Tom's Mercedes stood in the driveway, and I parked a few houses away. I spotted Culotta's car parked discreetly down and across the street.

"So what's our next move?" Kit asked, as I put the gearshift into *park*. It was strange hearing this from her; usually she was the one with the next move. And several more moves after that.

I hesitated before responding. "Well, I'm not sure. Tom and Culotta are already here—"

"Yeah, just great. Frick and Frack." She shook her head in dismay.

"No, this *is* great. I'm glad Culotta's here."

"But please tell me why *we* are here."

I reached for my phone and dialed Tom's number. "Let me just get the lay of the land," I said to her, covering what I assumed was the mouthpiece of my phone, although I wasn't totally sure. "Tom, it's me," I said, as I heard him say "H'lo."

"Yeah, I can see that, Pankowski. Where the hell are you? You should be safely tucked up in your pal's house watching television."

"I am. Well, near enough. Just wanted to know what was happening. Is the Utah guy there?"

"No, and he's late."

"Tom, when you called to make the appointment, was it a him or her?"

"What are you talking about?" He sounded impatient, and when I looked down the street, I saw him come out the front door and take a cigar from his pocket. Slowly, he began the arduous chore of lighting it with one hand.

"Well, I just had a thought. When you called to set up—"

"It was a guy." He hesitated, and I watched him take several puffs of his cigar. "Or a broad with a throaty voice. I don't know; what are you getting at?"

I pressed the phone flat against my chest for a moment, hoping Tom couldn't hear me, and repeated his words to Kit in a whisper.

"Geez," she responded, in a louder-than-normal voice. "What kind of moron can't tell the difference between a man's and a woman's voice?"

"Val?" I heard Tom say as I put the phone back to my ear. "What's going on?"

"Look, this is just a hunch, but I'm a little concerned about Deanna Finkelmeyer. If she shows up there, call Culotta right away—"

"Too late," I heard him say, as I watched him stroll down the driveway, puffing on his smoke. "She was supposed to be gone, but I guess she couldn't resist seeing me in action."

As he said it, the front door opened and Deanna Finkelmeyer filled the doorway. Even from a distance I could see some sparkly stuff on her low-cut, too-tight top as the sun bounced off the sequins, or whatever the hell they were.

"What time is the client supposed to show?" I asked.

"Nine." Tom turned and looked at Deanna. He gave her a slight wave with the hand holding his cigar, then pointed to the phone, as if she wouldn't be able to figure out he was on a call.

"It's nearly nine forty-five," I said. "Do you think he's going to show?"

"How the hell would I know?"

"Don't move," I said, shutting off the phone before he could question me. "Deanna is there," I said to Kit, who was also watching and could clearly figure this out for herself.

"So what do we do?" she asked.

"I think we should call Culotta. He's parked over there." I indicated his blue Ford.

"There's no one in that car, Valley Girl."

I gave his vehicle a second look and saw she was right. "Okay, so he's somewhere in the house. Or maybe he's crouching down and we just can't see him—"

"What would be the point of that? Surely if he's gonna offer any kind of protection, he should be able to see—"

"Kitty Kat, I don't have all the answers; I'm just nervous for Tom, that's all—"

"According to your own theory, ya know, old Deanna wants a roll in the hay with lover-boy, not a rope around his neck."

"Exactly." I grabbed my purse and opened the car door. "C'mon; let's make sure neither one happens."

***

An hour later we were back in my car, headed toward the nearest Starbucks. My rush to save my boss had done nothing but irritate the hell out of everyone. Tom was furious with me for leaving the safety of Kit's house. Culotta was furious that I had jeopardized the whole thing, claiming that if the Utah guy was going to show, and he was our killer, I'd probably scared him off.

But Deanna was the most furious of all. In all our previous encounters, admittedly not many, she'd always given me the impression she liked me, or at least had no problem with me. When I appeared at the end of her driveway, however, I heard her say, in a loud voice, "Shit, what's *she* doing here?"

Although it hurt my feelings, it did at least make me think my theory wasn't completely off the charts.

I sat at a table while Kit purchased our beverages. When she joined me and put my vanilla latte in front of me, I smiled up at her. "I feel stupid." I took a sip and then wiped foam from my top lip with a napkin.

"Oh, don't feel stupid." She took a sip of her own drink. "You had a good hunch."

"Really? You think so? It seems all I did was ruin any possible chance that the Utah guy might show. I suppose I should have thought it through more. Now it seems ridiculous that Deanna would be involved."

"Man, you're not her favorite person. Especially when Tom is around."

"No kidding. But at least I was right about that."

"Look, Val, it's possible you're on the right track. Perhaps not with Deanna, but with someone else. You—we—just went about it the wrong way."

I was grateful she was including herself in my failed scheme. "You think so?"

"Yes. Clearly someone wants you out of the way."

"Duh! But why not just kill me and be done with it?"

"Too simple. This person enjoys seeing you squirm."

"Squirm?" I said, way too loudly. "You call this squirming?" Out of the corner of my eye, I could see a woman at the table next to us remove a muffin from her overweight child's mouth, midbite, and usher him and their belongings to another table farther away.

"Sorry," I said, my voice returning to a normal pitch, addressing mother and child. The boy followed his muffin to the safer region of Starbucks, but not before throwing me a look that suggested I was probably a child-killer.

"Calm down," Kit said to me, not even registering the chubby kid. "We'll figure this out."

Even though she dismissed my need for histrionics, I managed a sigh of relief at having her back in the driver's seat.

"There's something we need to check out," she said, downing the rest of her coffee.

CHAPTER TWENTY-SIX

Grab your cup. Let's roll," Kit said, and I followed her out of Starbucks.

I had to trot to catch up with her, once we were out on the sidewalk. I figured whatever idea she had cooked up must be really good, and I felt hopeful and excited. "What is it?" I asked, breathless, once I was beside her.

She waited until we were both in my car before she answered me. "Your suspicion about Deanna was good. Someone is jealous of you and wants you either in prison or at least out of . . . I don't know . . . out of the realty world? Out of Downers Grove? Or, as you suspected, out of Tom's life?" She shook her head hard, and I knew she was still having trouble believing anyone would care about—let alone be jealous of—any relationship of Tom's.

My hands rested on the steering wheel, waiting direction from my crime-fighting partner. "So who? If not Deanna, who do you think it might be? And why?" I asked.

"If we figure out who, we'll know the why. Or if we could figure out why, we could deduce the who."

Deduce? She was getting way too full of herself in her role as detective, I feared, but I didn't want to say anything that might prevent her from sharing her brainstorm with me. So I sat quietly and looked at her while she apparently sorted her thoughts.

At last she spoke. "How about another cup of coffee?" was the brilliant remark she finally came up with.

"Kit! I haven't even finished this one—"

"Greek coffee."

"Wha— Oh, you mean a cup of Cyral's coffee?"

She pursed her lips and raised her eyebrows in an expression that said *ya think?* "Yeah, Cyral's. More to the point, a cup of coffee served up by Giorgos, maybe along with a little truth. For a change. C'mon. What are you waiting for?"

I wasn't sure *what* I was waiting for; I just knew I wanted more. But I started my car and pulled away from the curb as soon as the traffic ebbed momentarily. "Why Giorgos? I'm a little afraid of him, now that—"

"Ex-con, ex-schmon. He's not gonna hurt us in the middle of the morning in his own restaurant."

I wished I could share her certainty. "But why go see him?"

"Because he lied to us. About having a wife. And not telling us he just got out of prison."

"That's not a lie."

"By omission, it is."

"Kit, I hardly think we could expect anyone to announce they'd done time. It's not even relevant."

"Oh, the shop owner next door gets murdered, and it's irrelevant that Giorgos did time for assault with a deadly weapon?"

That shut me up, and we rode in silence. It could hardly be called a comfortable silence, since I felt certain we were both entertaining pretty grisly thoughts. But it was the

silence that marked our friendship: we neither one felt the
need to say something just to be saying something. Ever.

Happy to see other cars (protection?) in the parking lot,
I pulled into an empty spot and then followed Kit into the
restaurant.

Giorgos was in his usual place behind the counter,
looking like the winner of a beauty contest among his dowdy
customers. All I could think of was the deadly weapon he'd
used in the assault that had landed him in the clink. The
weapon I felt certain was right now below the counter he
was leaning on.

He stood up straight and flashed his brilliant smile as
soon as he saw us, but I noted one of his hands hung by his
side, no doubt so he could easily reach his gun. I glanced
around, not happy to see that the several customers in the
place all looked old enough to be paying for their early-bird
lunches with Social Security money. Not a robust one
among them. We were on our own, if Giorgos started
shooting.

Instead, he came from behind the counter (weapon-
free), his empty hands outstretched.

"A pleasure once again. Ladies, please, take seats; I'll
bring you menus."

"Just coffee." Kit sat down at the table closest to the
door. "But only if you'll join us. And could you put it in to-
go cups? We can't stay long."

"Ah," Giorgos said mournfully, looking down at my
feet. "More trouble with the bunion?"

"Yes, and inflamed corns." Kit sighed and also gave my
feet the once-over.

"Then I'm lucky your foot doctor is so close to my little
restaurant." He patted my shoulder, as if assuring me I was
doing the right thing and matters of the feet should not be
ignored. I had a horrible vision of him in prison, his smile
gone, a machete in his back pocket.

Then, as if plagued with the same vision, he quickly
returned to the counter, where he grabbed three paper cups

from beside his coffeemaker and filled and delivered two of them before going back to get his own.

"Giorgos, we were wondering . . ." Kit paused, as if wondering what she was wondering. Then she looked up and appeared to be studying the framed photographs on the wall. Next, she actually rose for a second to get a closer look. Giorgos and I silently watched her. He was no doubt as confused as I.

Soon she returned to her seat and finished her thought. "Why did you tell us you were married, Giorgos?"

He was smooth; I'll give him that. Without hesitation, he smiled widely, flashing his pearly whites, and punched his chest lightly with his fist, as if conveying *mea culpa* in a game of charades. "Ah, you found out my little secret. It's just something I'm used to telling women. Keeps the stalkers away, you see?" He made it sound so innocent, I was almost ready to forgive him.

Kit, however, was not. "Oh, I see," she said, in an *I see, all right* tone of voice that finally seemed to fluster Giorgos just a tad.

I didn't like thinking of an armed man feeling flustered. "Kit, we really should be going." I stood up from my seat, but she didn't budge.

"Giorgos, while you're fessing up, is there anything you haven't told us about Juanita? Your relationship with her? Or your relationship with Shirley Herzog?"

I was dismayed to see that her questions didn't seem to alleviate his flustered state.

"What are you talking about, Miss Kit?" he asked. If anything, his *I'm so offended* face was more endearing than his dazzling smile. I wondered how a jury had ever found him guilty of anything and sent him to prison. "I have no relationship with a Shirley Herzog. I had no relationship with Juanita. She was just a friend of mine. If you call that a relationship, then so be it."

"Hmm." Kit seemed to be processing his heartfelt response when all of a sudden her hand flew to her face, knocking over the coffee cup Giorgos had just set down. "Oh, I'm so sorry." She immediately grabbed his cup with one hand and a fistful of napkins from the nearby holder with the other. She mopped up the hot liquid, all the while continuing to apologize profusely.

Again, Giorgos and I watched, seeming to share a sense of embarrassment for her. "No need to worry," he said.

But I *was* worried. Kit was up to something, which didn't usually bode well for me.

She finally finished cleaning up the mess, with help from Giorgos, who rushed to the counter and returned with a towel, probably the one he used to clean his gun. Then she rose and said, "Yes, Val, we do need to get to your doctor. Those corns won't remove themselves. Sorry, Giorgos, for the mess and for bothering you. We were just in the area, and I wanted to ask you about that. About why you lied to us. I thought we were friends, ya know, so—"

"We *are* friends," he said. "At least I like to think we are."

As Kit made a beeline for the door, and I followed, we both gave him little waves on our way out, not really caring if he removed us from his Christmas-card list.

"What in the hell was that all about?" I asked, as soon as we were in my car and safely pulling out of the parking lot. I couldn't get away quickly enough.

"I just have a hunch, Val. I'd like to check the DNA of our Greek god."

And then I saw it. The coffee cup Giorgos had drunk from, the one she'd spilled. She'd pulled it out of her purse with one of the napkins she'd also pilfered, and was holding it like it was a Ming Dynasty vase she was afraid of breaking.

"*Of course*." I slapped my forehead with the palm of my hand. "And we'll use the DNA-comparing machine Larry bought you for Christmas—"

"Obviously, we'll take it to your pal Culotta—"

"But why? I don't get it. If he's been in prison, then surely they already have—"

"Maybe. But I'd like to see how it matches up with the DNA from the cup you already gave them. Ya know, from Shirley Herzog."

"Okay. I'm slow this morning. Must be my corns. But why do you think there is any connection between Shirley and Giorgos?"

"Because I'm pretty sure Shirley Herzog's picture is in one of those awful frames he has plastered on the walls. Don't you get it?"

"Enlighten me."

"Family, Val. Family."

***

"So I guess this means you're not still mad at me?" I asked Dennis Culotta, as soon as we'd been seated at our table for two, quite cozily in a corner, I might add.

I'd assumed the invitation he'd texted late the night before was rendered null and void by my shenanigans at Deanna Finkelmeyer's house. But here we were, ten hours later, looking like any normal couple enthralled with each other. (*A contradiction in terms?* I wondered, thinking of all the dinners David and I'd had in later years, when I considered us normal; we'd usually felt more irritated than enthralled. I decided—wishful thinking?—that Dennis and I looked like a *dating* couple, rather than a *normal* one.)

He'd asked me to dinner when Kit and I stopped by the station with the DNA-laden cup in the middle of the afternoon. He took the evidence from Kit's hands and started to ask how we'd gotten it—then, shaking his head, he obviously decided he'd rather not know. I was glad he acted like nothing unusual had happened that morning and told me in a rush that he was *on a case* (mine, I hoped) and couldn't talk, but could I please meet him at Chantal at seven o'clock. "Pretty please?" he'd added. *That* sent Kit's eyebrows up to her hairline, and it made me giggle nervously.

216

I told myself I agreed to dinner only because I wanted to know once and for all if his interest in me was strictly professional. Of course I knew that made no sense because if I didn't care about him, then what difference did it make what his interest was?

"Nah, I'm not mad." He looked up as the waiter appeared, and then took the proffered menu. After ordering a bottle of wine, he turned his attention back to me.

"But you *were* mad," I said, when he appeared to forget what we'd been talking about.

He nodded. "Yes, of course I was."

I cursed myself for reminding him, as I could see his ire returning. "Well, sorry. I know that was stupid of me. Can I blame it on cabin fever? I've been cooped up—"

"Doesn't matter. Turns out your guy—or gal . . ." He paused to snicker, and I felt *my* ire begin to form. "Tom says you think it might be a woman we're after. I told you—"

"I know, I know. Women don't strangle."

"That's right. Anyway, it turns out your prospective buyer called Tom and postponed the showing until tomorrow morning. So no harm, no foul."

"Oh good." It was an enormous relief. I had felt sick to think our guy—and I was thinking guy again; it only made sense that Utah was our perp—had gotten away. Especially if it was my fault. "So, the plan for tomorrow morning—"

"Is none of your business," he said, but not in his Detective Culotta voice. Instead, he sounded and looked like datable Dennis, his eyes twinkling and his voice soft, if slightly teasing. "Now. Can we really have a normal dinner? With normal dinner conversation? No offense, but I need a break from your case."

"*My* case? I haven't been murdered or murdered anyone. How can it be *my* case?"

"You know what I mean."

"Not really—oh, just one more thing." I raised my index finger. "The cup we gave you this morning . . . did you learn anything?"

"About your case . . ."

"Okay, it's my case, only as far as I seem to be a victim. But back to the cup—"

"What do you want to know?"

"Well, Kit . . . we . . . had a hunch that it might be important . . ."

He leaned back and laughed. "That Kit's really something."

"But did it prove—"

"Not a lot we didn't already know."

"Oh." I felt disappointed. More for Kit, really, than for me.

"Seriously. Could we not talk about it for . . ." He looked at his watch. "Three hours? Just give me until ten o'clock with no talk of *the* case. Fair enough?"

"Fair enough. If you promise to turn off your phone so Tina doesn't join us again."

"Can't. Gotta keep my phone on. You never know when there might be a murder in this sleepy town." He gave a rueful half smile. "But it won't be Tina. She's . . . um . . . we . . . she's out of the picture."

I took my napkin and looked down as I opened it onto my lap. I didn't look up until I'd erased the big grin off my face.

"Oh, and one last thing," I heard him say. "Shirley Herzog and Giorgos the Greek are brother and sister. But I guess you already knew that."

I didn't, of course, but I was silently impressed by Kit's hunch. Although what it meant in the great scheme of things, I wasn't sure. And anyway, it hardly seemed important. The big news was that Tina was no longer in the picture.

***

I glanced at my watch as Dennis escorted me to my car following a leisurely and crime-free dinner. No crimes committed, no crimes discussed. But now I noted it was ten fifteen, and so I leaned against my car door before he had a chance to open it for me.

He dropped his arm to his side and looked at me, his blue eyes showing off their color with the help of the light pole I'd parked under (my mom always told me that was the safest place to park). He looked at me quizzically, and I realized he probably thought I was giving him an invitation to kiss me. Not that it sounded bad, but there are things more important than a kiss, even to a love-starved divorcée like me. So I asked him. "*Do* you really have hopes of solving the—"

"Valerie."

"It's after ten."

He looked at his watch. "So it is. I'd forgotten. I guess I hoped you'd also been distracted—"

"Oh, I was, Dennis. It was a lovely dinner, really. But I'm sure you can understand my obsession—"

"Yes, of course. I suppose I better get to work—forget about you until this is all over."

"Forget about me? This is *about* me, isn't—"

"I mean in a . . . um . . . personal way. But maybe then, after someone's behind bars, you can give me your full attention?"

Now I really was gaga.

CHAPTER TWENTY-SEVEN

I took my key out of my purse and watched Culotta amble down the path to his car. He was jingling his car keys in his right hand; I guess even the police don't leave keys in a car, if only for a few minutes.

I was laughing as I let myself in and then stopped immediately at the sight of Roscoe sitting in the hallway on his haunches, his tongue hanging out. He cocked his head slightly and seemed to be peering past me to the outside.

"Good boy." I eased past him, shutting the door behind me. "Good boy."

Kit appeared in the entrance to the living room, glasses resting on the end of her nose, her Kindle in her hand. "Geez." She glanced at her wristwatch. "Ten thirty! You guys really know how to paint the town red."

"He's going back to work." I hurried past her and into the safety of the living room.

"I ask myself *why*. Seems like we do all the work for him."

"Well . . ." I plunked down on the couch, and Roscoe jumped up on the middle cushion next to me. "You'll be happy to know that Shirley and Giorgos are brother and sister."

She removed her glasses and took a seat across from me. "I know. Her real name is Sibilla. She divorced Reginald Herzog twenty years ago. Apparently, she and baby brother are close—"

"Wait, how do you know all this?" Roscoe turned his head quickly in Kit's direction, obviously waiting for her to explain herself.

"Oh, a bit of this, a bit of that, a lot of Internet. Point is, why the secret? Why not admit it?"

"Maybe if your brother is a felon, you don't go around broadcasting it."

"Hungry? You want me to cook—"

"Kit, I just had dinner."

"How was it? I've never cared for Chantal; they tend to overcook everything. And their wine list is dismal. What did you eat?"

For the life of me, I couldn't remember. "Er . . . something good; I dunno. Thing is, Tina and Culotta are apparently on the outs."

"No kidding? Did her high school principal call?"

"No, she—"

"Speaking of calls, you had one from Deanna Finkelmeyer." I sat up straighter as Kit continued. "She said she wanted to thank you for the red scarf . . . something about it looking good on her neck . . . hides the wrinkles . . ."

"I have no interest in speaking to her. She has what she wants. Tom will be back there tomorrow for Utah guy—if he shows. And besides, she was rude—wait!"

"Red scarf?" Kit said, at the same time I was thinking it.

"Red scarf! I never gave her a red scarf. I don't even own a red scarf."

"Nor should you; red is not your color—"

"Kit, shut up and listen. Tell me exactly what she said."

"Hmm . . . it was hard to hear . . . Roscoe was watching *Antiques Roadshow*, and I didn't want to turn down the volume." Kit stood and moved over to the empty couch cushion beside Roscoe as she spoke, and began tenderly stroking his head. "Plus, there was a lot of background noise. But she said you should call her when you got home, no matter how late. She said it was very important. She asked where you were, and I told her you were having dinner with a friend—"

"Did she ask who?"

"Yep, but I didn't mention any names."

"She thinks it's Tom."

"You don't think—"

"Well, I know I didn't give her a damn red scarf, so why would she say that?"

"I'll drive." Kit jumped up. She disappeared for a few moments and then met me at the front door.

Before we left, we took one look backward. Roscoe had followed us and was sitting in his normal position, tongue drooling, head slightly lopsided.

"Daddy will be home soon." Kit knelt to his level. "He'll read to you."

But as soon as I opened the front door, Roscoe darted (who knew he could dart?) past me, stopping at Kit's car in the driveway.

"Looks like he's coming with us," she said proudly.

"Okay," I agreed. "But he sits in the back."

As Kit pulled out of her driveway, both Roscoe and I swiveled our heads to check where she was going.

"So what are we thinking here?" I asked.

"I'm thinking this is showtime, Valley Girl. The call was to lure you over there. It's all very literal, don't you think? She doesn't have much imagination."

"On the contrary, I'd say she has too much. Red scarf . . . blood . . . neck. I'm calling her." I pulled my phone out of my purse and punched in her number. The call went straight to voice mail.

"Call Culotta," Kit said, when she heard me leave a message for Deanna to call me back.

I hesitated. I'd already blown his proposed sting operation; it seemed foolish to call him again.

"Do it," Kit said, reading my mind.

"But what do I say? Deanna wants to return a scarf I never gave her in the first place, and this must mean she's a serial killer? Tell me again what she said."

"I already told you, it was hard to hear her—"

"Oh, right, because Roscoe is such a fan of PBS. And anyway, why did she call you and not me?"

"I don't know; maybe she did call you, and you didn't hear it ring because you were soooo busy with your dreamy boyfriend."

I looked down at my phone and checked calls received. There was one from Deanna's number that I had indeed missed. "Crap! You're right. She did call me. So what's the plan?"

"First and most important, we tell the police where we're going. Then we confront her. Val, she's not about to kill *you,* for crying out loud."

"How can you be so sure? She's obviously deranged, not to mention really pissed off at me."

"Call Culotta."

Reluctantly, I pulled my phone from my purse once again. "Okay. But if this turns out to be nothing, I'll feel like such a fool."

Culotta's phone also went to voice mail. I left a message telling him I was going over to Deanna Finkelmeyer's house and would appreciate it if he'd meet me there. Something had come up, and it sounded strange. I could imagine his reaction. The only thing that sounded strange was *me.* At least I hadn't told him I was accompanied by Kit and a Rottweiler.

***

At the Finkelmeyer house, all the lights were out. I checked my watch under the glow of the light shining above the front door. It was after eleven, a time for any normal person to be in bed.

"Kit, this is stupid. Let's just leave. There's absolutely no reason for us to be here."

Kit's response was to reach past me and ring the doorbell.

"What if she's in bed?" I whispered.

"Then she'll have to get up to answer the door. Will you calm down?"

We listened to the chimes echo throughout the house, but heard no movement.

"Okay," I said. "She's either asleep or not home. Could we just go now?"

But Kit was already fiddling with the lockbox attached to the heavy metal door handle. "I hope you have a key for this thing," she said, ignoring my request to leave.

"You're not thinking of going inside, are you?"

"Of course I am. How else are we gonna find out if she's home?"

"Kit, really, this is such a bad idea on so many levels—"

"Key?" she said, her palm outstretched. Roscoe, who remained at her side, looked up at me, his expression clearly asking *what are you waiting for?*

I dug into my purse and produced the key. She took it from my hand.

"It's breaking and entering—"

"Don't be crazy; what are we breaking? We have a key, right?"

Before I could reply, she'd opened the door, and once again Roscoe went into his darting routine, disappearing into the house. Triumphantly, he returned and stopped in the hallway, his look and almost-silent half growl urging us to follow. It was like he wanted to communicate to us on the q.t. It seemed only right that we let him lead the way.

It was dark. It was silent. The three of us walked slowly through the long hallway into the kitchen. I thought I heard a scraping sound, then a sort of muffled cry, and then Kit switched on the light.

Sitting on a kitchen chair, with what looked like fifty feet of duct tape wrapped around her body, was Deanna Finkelmeyer. Her mouth was bound with a red scarf, her expression wild. More than being shocked at the sight of the bound woman, I was astounded to see that the scarf was indeed mine. Something I'd bought a million years ago and stuffed away in some bag with other things that no doubt needed to go to Goodwill. I don't know what outraged me more: the fact that Deanna was trussed like a turkey or that someone had been to my apartment and removed my beloved if forgotten scarf.

And then Roscoe, from his place in front of us, turned and broke the silence. A bark. A loud, raucous sound that seemed to shake the whole house. Following Roscoe's gaze, Kit and I turned in alarm and saw another item stolen from my apartment: Kit's Glock. And the weapon was pointing straight at us.

CHAPTER TWENTY-EIGHT

She waved the gun in the air, much like I'd seen her waving the baton at the Hinsdale Male Chorus. She indicated she wanted us to stand behind Deanna. Kit and I both took several steps backward, but Roscoe remained stoically in place, not budging an inch.

"T. L.!" I said, as Deanna struggled within her bindings, thrashing her head from side to side. I put my hand on her shoulder, silently urging her to remain still.

"Who's this?" T. L. spoke, pointing the barrel of the gun in Kit's direction. "I should have known you wouldn't have the courage to come alone, Valerie."

"She's a friend of mine . . ." My mouth was suddenly dry.

"Kit James," my pal spoke up in a loud voice. I worried Kit would hold out her hand in greeting and invite T. L. to dinner.

"No matter. I can take care of her as easily as I can take care of you two."

Deanna began squirming again, and then started rocking her body from side to side. Roscoe remained motionless, his eyes defiantly fixed on T. L.

"The police will be here any minute," I said, as T. L. moved the barrel of the gun in my direction.

Now that she had us lined up where she wanted, she cupped her left hand under her right one, exercising proper gun control. "No problem. I don't need much time."

"Could you at least tell us why?" Kit asked. "What this is all about?"

"It's about *her*." She fixed her eyes on me. "Someone has to put an end to her. It's time she stopped stealing Perry's thunder."

I almost laughed. There were a lot of ways to describe Perry, but having thunder wasn't one of them.

"What do you mean?" Kit asked. "Val has done nothing but nurture and help Perry."

"Oh yeah? He doesn't need her *help* anymore. Perry will finally be able to shine on his own, and that fool uncle of his will recognize who's really the brains in that office of theirs."

"Look, you don't have to do this," I said.

"Do what?" T. L. actually laughed a little.

"Whatever the hell it is you're planning here," Kit answered for me. "Val has no quarrel with you—"

"But I have one with *her*." T. L. had stopped laughing, and her face had taken on a hard, crazed look. "I'm sick of Tom's little princess bullying Perry, stealing clients from him, getting all the credit for his hard work. Oh yeah, Perry has told me all about you—"

"That's not in any way true, T. L.," I said. "Everyone, including Tom Haskins, knows Perry is running that office. I've learned so much from him . . . I'd be lost without him . . ." Oops; wrong thing to say. Never a good idea to show admiration toward a serial killer's object of affection.

T. L.'s eyes scrunched up, and she put her left hand to her temple and began to rub, as if at a spot she just had to get rid of. Then she took a step backward.

Was that good or bad?

Well, it turned out bad—for her. At her movement, Roscoe suddenly leaped in the air toward her, his teeth bared, a vicious growl coming from his throat. He hurled his heavy body at her as she raised her arms, and the gun flew out of her hand.

"Get him away from me!" T. L. screamed. But she was now pinned up against the kitchen wall, her arms over her head as if she were the victim of a holdup. Kit rushed to retrieve the gun, which had landed several feet across the floor, while Roscoe remained in his vigilant position, his front paws firmly holding T. L.'s shoulders in place. His head was almost level with hers, and if it weren't for the sheer terror on her face, it would have looked as though they might be doing a crazy Latin dance.

When Kit had control of the gun, she turned it on T. L. and reached over to touch Roscoe's back lightly. He dropped his front legs to the floor but continued his watchful stance and deep growl.

With the gun pointing firmly at T. L., Kit knelt down and rubbed his head with her free hand. "Oh, Roscoe," she said into his silky ear. "You really, really are a good boy."

CHAPTER TWENTY-NINE

W ho's this Roscoe? I heard he knocked the gun out of the crazy broad's hand," Tom said.

"He's a dog. A brave, enormous, wonderful Rottweiler, to be exact. He belongs to Kit's neighbors, but she borrowed him for . . ."

"For?"

"For protection. But he was so much more than that."

Tom took a cigar out of a leather holder lying on his desk in front of him. Slowly, he picked up a cutter and made a show of snipping off the end.

"So, this T. L. broad did it all for Perry? Is that what happened?"

"Yes." I nodded, as Tom slowly shook his head.

"Remind me never to check a book out of the library."

"Oh, I think we're safe there."

"She *was* a librarian, right? *And* a choir director?"

"Yes. But not just in Downers Grove. She was sentenced to six years in a mental-health facility up north—"

"A nuthouse—"

"Tom! It used to be for the criminally insane—"

"So she was an inmate?"

"Yes. Kit checked her out on the Internet—"

"Speaking of the insane—"

"Oh, shut up. Kit has been fantastic throughout this whole nightmare. And yes, T. L. was confined. But she did work in the library there. And direct a choir. They put her on some kind of release program in Downers Grove."

"You're sure it was really because of Perry?" He shook his head again.

I nodded again.

After T. L.'s arrest, Perry had taken some personal leave to get over the emotional trauma he'd apparently suffered. When I stopped by his apartment to check up on him, he was as disheveled as I'd ever seen him. Dark circles under his eyes, hair needing a cut, a growth of stubble covering his face. But hey, he still looked like he could give Bradley Cooper a run for his money.

I sighed now and leaned back in Tom's visitor's chair. "Seems she had a crazy fixation on him, and she believed I was holding him back. Stealing his referrals, that sort of thing."

"Where'd she get that idea?"

"Where do you think?"

"From Wonder Boy himself would be my guess."

"Mine too."

"I should kick his ass—"

"Tom, don't be too hard on Perry. Honestly, I think this is the first time anyone has shown a real interest in him. He's not used to be being adored—"

"Except by himself."

"He got carried away with the attention and couldn't help boasting—"

"I should still kick his ass."

"You don't have to kick anything. He knows you're mad at him, and that's probably punishment enough."

"You're way too forgiving, Pankowski."

"I don't think so."

"So her insane idea was to dispose of all those poor women and leave your business card at the crime scenes to . . . what? Implicate you as the murderer?"

"That seems to have been her plan. As you said, it was insane."

"And she did it because Perry's such a great guy?"

"To her, yes."

"And getting you out of the picture leaves Perry as top dog around here?"

"Seems that was her motive. I'm thinking that when Perry and I were supposed to meet her for lunch, and she didn't show, she used that time to break into my apartment and steal my stuff—worst of all, the gun." I shuddered.

"So all those ladies died to get rid of Valerie Pankowski. It would have been easier to just shoot you." I don't think I'd ever seen Tom look so sad.

"Well, thanks for that thought. Unfortunately, Daphne, Juanita, and Christine just put their houses up for sale at the wrong time."

"Any good news in this pile of crap?"

"Well, *you'll* probably think so. We got the listing for Juanita Perez's flower shop. Larry James knows the executor of her will. We even have a buyer."

"Tell me."

"Shirley Herzog. Turns out she and her brother Giorgos plan to be the largest Greek restaurateurs in Aurora. They're going to buy the property on both sides of Cyral's and expand the place. Larry recommended us for the listing, and I told Shirley we'd give her a good deal—"

"What?"

"She deserves it. Her brother too. He's trying to turn his life around. I like him."

"This brother and sister—they got the finances?"

"Oh yes. In fact, Shirley has recruited Wendell Fullerton as an investor in their little scheme. They have a history together—she worked for him until he had to let her go, but it was all very friendly. Apparently, they were discussing the property on the day Kit and I stopped by his house and saw Shirley's truck parked outside."

Tom put the cut cigar in his mouth but didn't light it. "So T. L.'s as crazy as batshit? Boy, Perry can sure pick 'em."

"Tom, I think T. L. picked *him*, not the other way around. She's convinced he's a genius."

"Has she *met* Perry?"

I ignored Tom's remark. "It's a tragedy. A huge freakin' tragedy." I felt a lump form in my throat, and I stopped talking for a moment to gain control and stop any tears. The lump had become familiar to me during the past week, now that I knew I was safe, but at such an enormous cost.

"Okay, Pankowski, looks like you'll be doing the work of two people while Perry, the genius, recovers from his pain and suffering. You can follow my lead with the Finkelmeyer house." Tom winked as he said it, finally striking a match to the end of his stogie.

To everyone's surprise, the prospective buyer, who ended up meeting Tom at Deanna's house a couple of days after the incident, turned out to be a *she* from California who bore no resemblance to Jim Gardner. The Californian had succumbed to Tom's charm, and the deal was closed in record Tom-time.

"Yep, I can see where Perry gets his smarts." I winked back.

"One other thing. Your business cards being sent to Utah—what was that about?"

"Well, our elusive Jim Gardner appeared to be from there, and so T. L. sent them to the Utah state police, with his name written on one of the cards."

"How'd she even know about Jim?"

"You have to ask?"

"Perry."

"Right. Perry was blabbing every detail of what was going on around here. My guess is, T. L. wanted to get Utah involved and confuse the issue."

"But Jim Gardner wasn't even from Utah?"

"Right. He's a local guy. But T. L., or I should say Perry, didn't know that at the time. Culotta uncovered Gardner's past as a thief, a professional who stakes out homes to rob by posing as an interested buyer. Oh, and he was never Juanita's fiancé, although he did bear a resemblance to the guy in Shirley Herzog's murky photo."

"And the client list?"

"Right. T. L. returned that to me in a FedEx envelope, not using her own return address, of course."

"Geez, Pankowski. You really got yourself in the middle of a pile of horse—"

I held up a finger to stop him from finishing his thought. "I know. You don't have to remind me. None of it my fault, however. But there's one other thing I need to ask you."

"Shoot."

"Deanna Finkelmeyer. What's the deal with her? One thing Perry did do right was confirm she'd never had her house listed with Harris-Wiggins."

"And . . . ?"

"Well, my guess is that she really wanted your attention. Listing her house with us but then getting me as the agent must have been a big disappointment for her. Do you two have a past?"

"I told you . . . I met her years ago when she was working at a casino—"

"What was she doing there, anyway? A dealer, waitress, what?"

"Let's just say she was a working girl and leave it at that."

I was glad to do so. When Deanna had been released from her duct-tape prison and my red scarf had been removed from her mouth, she let forth a tirade of abuse in my direction. It was clear she had no intention of hanging out with me and doing gal stuff anytime soon.

"Well, I'm glad I don't have to see her again," I said.

And then there was our hero, Roscoe. Kit had reluctantly returned the Downton Abbey-loving doggy back to his real parents. But it was hard on her and Larry, and they'd made immediate arrangements to fly to Texas for a long weekend and visit their human son, Sam.

Meanwhile, I had returned to my little apartment, and after a brief period of adjustment (getting used to how compact everything was), I was back to eating cereal for dinner and enjoying my cozy home.

I stood and headed toward Tom's office door. "Well, Boss, I guess that's about it. I'll now go hit the streets and sell us some property."

He leaned back in his chair, blowing a huge plume of gray smoke toward the ceiling. "So," he said, an amused look on his face, clearly not ready to end our conversation. "Turns out you were saved by a dog—not Culotta."

"Technically, yes. Culotta did show up, but by then we had the situation under control."

"Maybe he can recruit this dog as his new partner. I heard he's been assigned to another precinct."

"Temporarily. He's in New York for six weeks on some kind of training course." I put my hand on the doorknob. I didn't want to discuss Culotta, although it was possible Tom might know more about what he was actually doing than I did.

All I knew I had learned from a hurried voice mail Culotta left me. *Gonna be out of town for a while. I'll be in touch.* I'd made up the part about the training course, and the six weeks, and for that matter, New York. But it was mainly to discourage Tom's gloating expression that was forming on his face. "Gotta go, Boss." I opened the door.

"Hey, Kiddo," Tom said, "do me a favor."

I turned to face him. "What d'ya need?"

"Tell the pooch thanks from me."

Patty and Roz
www.roz-patty.com

About the authors . . .

Now a proud and patriotic US citizen and Texan, Rosalind Burgess grew up in London and currently calls Houston home. She has also lived in Germany, Iowa, and Minnesota. Roz recently retired from the airline industry to devote all her working hours to writing (although it seems more like fun than work).

Patricia Obermeier Neuman spent her childhood and early adulthood moving around the Midwest (Minnesota, South Dakota, Nebraska, Iowa, Wisconsin, Illinois, and Indiana), first as a trailing child and then as a trailing spouse (inspiring her first book, *Moving: The What, When, Where & How of It*). A former reporter and editor, Patty lives with her husband in Door County, Wisconsin. They have three children and twelve grandchildren.

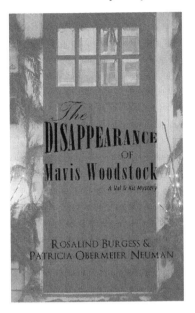

The Disappearance of Mavis Woodstock

Mavis Woodstock (a vaguely familiar name) calls Val and insists she has to sell her house as quickly as possible. Then she fails to keep her scheduled appointment. Kit remembers Mavis from their school days, an unattractive girl who was ignored when she was lucky, ridiculed when she was not. She also remembers Mavis being the only daughter in a large family that was as frugal as it was wealthy. When Val and Kit cannot locate Mavis, they begin an investigation, encountering along the way a little romance, a lot of deception, and more than one unsavory character.

What readers are saying about . . .
The Disappearance of Mavis Woodstock

FIVE STARS! "Best book I've read in a long time; couldn't wait to go to bed at night so I could read this book and then couldn't put it down. TOTAL PAGE-TURNER . . . Cannot wait to read the next book in this series!!!"

FIVE STARS! " . . . well-written mystery . . . first of The Val & Kit Mystery Series. The two amateur sleuths, Val & Kit, are quirky, humorous, and dogged in their pursuit of righting what they felt was a wrongful death of someone they knew from the past. It's full of humorous, cagey, and a few dark personalities that keep you on your toes wondering what or who would turn up next. . . . a fun, fast read that is engaging and will keep your interest . . . A tightly woven mystery with a great twist at the end."

FIVE STARS! "I thoroughly enjoyed this book, laughing out loud many times, often until I cried. I love the authors' style and could so relate to the things the characters were going through."

FIVE STARS! "This was a fun read! The story was well put together. Lots of suspense. Authors tied everything together well. Very satisfying."

FIVE STARS! "Enjoyed this tale of two friends immensely. Was shocked by the ending and sad to find I had finished the book so quickly. Anxious to read the next one . . . keep them coming!"

FIVE STARS! "Mysteries are sometimes too predictable for me—I can guess the ending before I'm halfway through the book. Not this one. The characters are well developed and fun, and the plot kept me guessing until the end."

FIVE STARS! "I highly recommend this novel and I'm looking forward to the next book in this series. I was kept guessing throughout the entire novel. The analogies throughout are priceless and often made me laugh. . . . I found myself on the edge of my seat . . . the ending to this very well-written novel is brilliant!"

FIVE STARS! "I recommend this book if you like characters such as Kinsey Millhone or Stone Barrington . . . or those types. Excellent story with fun characters. Can't wait to read more of these."

FIVE STARS! "A cliff-hanger with an I-did-not-see-that-coming ending. . . . a quick, easy read."

FIVE STARS! " . . . well written, humorous . . . a good plot and a bit of a surprise ending. An easy read that is paced well, with enough twists and turns to keep you reading to the end."

FIVE STARS! "Very enjoyable book and hard to put down. Well-written mystery with a great surprise ending. A must-read."

FIVE STARS! "This is a well-written mystery that reads along at a bright and cheerful pace with a surprisingly dark twist at the end."

FIVE STARS! "I really enjoyed this book: the characters, the story line, everything. It is well written, humorous, engaging."

FIVE STARS! "The perfect combo of sophisticated humor, fun and intriguing twists and turns!"

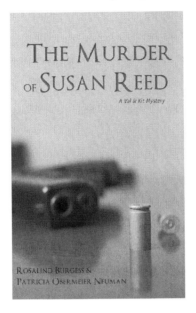

The Murder of Susan Reed

When Kit suspects Larry of having an affair with one of his employees, Susan Reed, she enlists Val's help in uncovering the truth. The morning after a little stalking expedition by the lifelong friends, Val reads in the newspaper that Susan Reed was found shot to death in her apartment the night before, right around the time Kit was so certain Larry and Susan were together. *Were* they having an affair? And did Larry murder her? The police, in the form of dishy Detective Dennis Culotta, conduct the investigation into Susan's murder, hampered at times by Val and Kit's insistent attempts to discover whether Larry is guilty of infidelity and/or murder. As the investigation heats up, so does Val's relationship with Detective Culotta.

FIVE STARS! "I couldn't wait to get this Val & Kit adventure after reading the authors' first book, and I was not disappointed. As a fan of this genre . . . I just have to write a few words praising the incredible talent of Roz and Patty. One thing I specifically want to point out is the character development. You can completely visualize the supporting actors (suspects?) so precisely that you do not waste time trying to recall details about the character. . . . Roz and Patty practically create an imprint in your mind of each character's looks/voice/mannerisms, etc."

FIVE STARS! "Even better than the first! Another page-turner! Take it to the beach or pool. You will love it!!! I did!!!"

FIVE STARS! "Great writing. Great plot."

FIVE STARS! "Once again Val & Kit star in a page-turner mystery!"

FIVE STARS! "I loved this book and these two best friends who tend to get in trouble together. Reminds me of my best friend and myself."

FIVE STARS! "Ms. Burgess and Ms. Neuman are fantastic writers and did a great job with their sophomore effort! I enjoy their writing style and they really capture the genre of cozy mystery well! I highly recommend their books!"

FIVE STARS! "Val and Kit's interactions and Val's thoughts about life in general were probably the best part of the book. I was given enough info to 'suspect' just about every character mentioned."

No. 3 in
The Val & Kit Mystery Series

Death in Door County

Val embarks on a Mother's Day visit to her mom in Door
County, Wisconsin, a peninsula filled with artists,
lighthouses, and natural beauty. Her daughter, Emily, has
arrived from LA to accompany her, and at the last minute
her best friend, Kit, invites herself along. Val and Kit have
barely unpacked their suitcases when trouble and tension
greet them, in the form of death and a disturbing secret they
unwittingly brought with them. As they get to know the
locals, things take a sinister turn. And when they suspect
someone close to them might be involved in blackmail—or
worse—Val and Kit do what they do best: they take matters
into their own hands in their obsessive, often zany, quest to
uncover the truth.

FIVE STARS! "The girls have done it again . . . and by girls, do I mean Val and Kit, or Roz and Patty? The amazingly talented authors, Roz and Patty, of course. Although Val and Kit have landed themselves right smack dab in the middle of yet another mystery. This is their third adventure, but don't feel as though you have to (albeit you SHOULD if you haven't done so already) read *The Disappearance of Mavis Woodstock* and *The Murder of Susan Reed* in order. This book and the other two are wonderful stand-alones, but read all three to enjoy all of the main and supporting characters' quirks . . . I can't seem to express how much I love these books . . . Speaking of characters . . . This is what sets the Val & Kit series apart from the others in this genre. The authors always give us a big cast of suspects, and each is described so incredibly . . . It's like playing a game of Clue, but way more fun . . . the authors make the characters so memorable that you don't waste time trying to 'think back' to whom they are referring. In fact, it's hard to believe that there are only two authors writing such vivid casts for these books. So come on, ladies, confess . . . no, wait, don't. I don't want to know how you do it, just please keep it up."

FIVE STARS! "This third book in the series is my favorite, but I felt the same about the first two as well!"

FIVE STARS! "Just the right mix of a page-turner mystery and humor with a modern edge. I have read all three books and am waiting impatiently for more."

FIVE STARS! "Love, love these two writers! I'm these authors' best fan, and I can't wait for these lovely ladies to write more!"

FIVE STARS! "*Death in Door County* is the third installment in the series, and each book just gets better than the last."

And if you want to read about the mystery of marriage, here's a NON–Val & Kit book for you . . .

Rosalind Burgess & Patricia Obermeier Neuman

Dressing Myself

Meet Jessie Harleman in this contemporary women's novel about love, lust, friends, and family. Jessie and Kevin have been happily married for twenty-eight years. With their two grown kids now out of the house and living their own lives, Jessie and Kevin have reached the point they thought they longed for, yet slightly dreaded. But the house that used to burst at the seams now has too many empty rooms. Still, Jessie is a *glass half-full* kind of woman, eager for this next period of her life to take hold. The problem is, nothing goes the way she planned. This novel explores growth and change and new beginnings.

FIVE STARS! "Love these writers!! So refreshing to have writers who really create such characters you truly understand and relate to. Looking forward to the next one. Definitely my favorites!"

FIVE STARS! "What a fun read *Dressing Myself* was! Although I have to admit I didn't expect the ending. I suppose I was hoping Jessie would have chosen differently. It was hard to put this book down."

FIVE STARS! "Great, easy, captivating read!! The characters seem so real! I don't read a lot, but I was really into this one! Read it for sure!"

31794371R00148

Made in the USA
Charleston, SC
29 July 2014